SLAVE DAY

ROB THOMAS

SIMON & SCHUSTER BOOKS FOR YOUNG READERS

Thanks to Jeff DeMouy, Jenny Ziegler, Michael Conathan, Robert Young, Bob and Diana Thomas, Christine Edwards, Greg McCormack, Loyd Blankenship, Humphrey Brown, Olivier Bourgoin, Kim Ruiz, Anne Moss, Elena Blanco, and Cathy Gruhn. Belated thank-yous to Patty Aitken and John McCartney. Special thanks to David Gale, Jennifer Robinson, and Russell Smith.

SIMON & SCHUSTER BOOKS FOR YOUNG READERS
An imprint of Simon & Schuster Children's Publishing Division
1230 Avenue of the Americas, New York, New York 10020

Book design by Anahid Hamparian
The text for this book is set in 11-point Revival.
Printed and bound in the United States of America
First Edition
10 9 8 7 6 5 4 3 2 1

Library of Congress Cataloging-in-Publication Data

Thomas, Rob.
Slave Day / by Rob Thomas.
p.   cm.
Summary: Relates the events of a southern high school's "Slave Day" auction and
fund-raiser, which leads students, teachers, and even community members to rethink
their approaches to their lives.
ISBN 0-689-80206-4
[1. High schools—Fiction. 2. Schools—fiction. 3. Race relations—Fiction.]
I. Title.
PZ7.T36935S1   1997   [Fic]—dc20   96-24617   CIP   AC

For Doug Chappell—
wish you were here

KEENE DAVENPORT
7:02 A.M.

Laurence is orating. His Highness is careful to pose *just so. Just so* means he's angled in a way that allows him to catch his own natty reflection in the mirror over the china cabinet. He has Terrence and Ally (otherwise known as Dad and Mom) spellbound. They've discontinued their morning rituals: Dad—swearing over the *New York Times* crossword; Mom—laying waste to her sixth graders' math homework. My fifteen-year-old brother is reciting from the Letters to the Editor section of the morning's edition of the *Deerfield Herald*. Specifically, he is reading a letter penned by me. I sit down in my bathrobe and pour a bowl from one of the assorted boxes of healthy, fibrous cereals Terry and Ally insist on. I know it kills *mon frère* that I pay no attention to him. He pauses to welcome me to the breakfast table.

"*As salaam alaikum*, my brother," Laurence says while giving me a raised fist of Black Power. I don't respond, so he returns to his recitation of my fiery screed. With a malicious gleam in his eye, he kicks back his chair, pulls out his shirttails, and adopts the high-volume grunting and braying tones of a Mississippi Delta evangelist.

"'Then it is apparent, if one buys into the logic of local school officials, that this Slave Day, which is obviously and patently offensive in nature, is not perceived as racist simply because it has always existed without comment from those it should chiefly offend—African-American students.'"

Laurence pauses, pretends to mop sweat and tears, and continues.

"'Should we really need to say that the premise of a Slave Day offends us? Should we warn the school board today that we'll object to separate drinking fountains, regulations that banish us to the back of the school bus, lynchings in lieu of suspensions, changing the school mascot to the Sambos?'"

Dad grins at that. Mom stares at Laurence with her mouth open, not like she wants to say something, more like she doesn't believe what she is hearing.

"'If simply knowing what offends us will indeed alter the direction our school officials will take in the future, then let us act now! Rather than betraying our ancestors by mindlessly playing along with this ill-advised charade, simply refuse to be a part of it.

"'I'm calling on all students of color, particularly those eight elected to student council (eight out of sixty in a school fully one-quarter African-American? Hmmm. In the words of Marvin Gaye, "What's goin' on?") and, most importantly, on our first elected black student council president himself to boycott this demeaning ritual. Furthermore, our presence on campus serves as implicit acceptance of the event. Therefore, I say we take a day off. Let's not ride this metaphorical bus of oppression. That should get the attention of those who allow such things to take place.'"

Laurence, then, adds his own paragraph.

"Furthermore, I have a dream that one day the white children and black children of Deerfield will walk hand in hand to Sac-n-Pac and share a Slushee out of the same straw." (Terrence interjects a grinning "Amen, brother" here.)

"'Do the right thing. Fight the power! Keene Davenport, seventeen, A Concerned African-American citizen.'"

My little brother proudly takes his seat at the table to the applause and hallelujahing of my father and the brow furrowing of my mother. I continue shoveling twigs into my mouth.

"So how 'bout it, Tom? You gonna join the boycott?" I say before my next bite.

"Sorry, Malcolm, tempting as it sounds to sit around here in my bathrobe all day watching soaps in the name of Black pride, I've got a quiz in history today. Besides, I'm thinking I might like to get me one of those slaves."

"Mom, Dad. I told you we shouldn't have adopted this . . . ," I begin, but Mom interrupts me.

"Keene, you *are* going to school today."

I recognize the tone. Not once, in my lifetime, have I won a concession from this woman when she speaks like this. Still, there has to be a first.

"No way, Mom. I can't go to school after calling for a walkout. Do you realize how that will make me look?" As I say it, I know it is the wrong approach. I try again. "By going to school, just by being there, I'm saying that Slave Day is acceptable. So next year, the year after, ten years from now, they'll still be having this stupid fund-raiser."

"Well, when my grandchildren ask to skip school, you'll be able to tell them yes, but right now, I'm telling you you're going to school. I'm more concerned with the C on your progress report than I am about a silly school event."

I look to my father for help, but he's just shaking his head. "Metaphorical bus of oppression," he says mirthfully.

BRENDAN YOUNG
7:22 A.M.

As if I didn't have enough stress in my life, my parents named me Brendan.

Brendan Young, to be exact. It's the kind of name that gets you beaten up. With a name like Brendan, at the very least, you can bet on getting wedgicated by some hungus missing-link Billys or Chucks.

Most of the time it's my first name (along with my toothpick limbs, spotty complexion, faint lisp, and ability to long-divide in my head) that solidifies my leperfication. Today is different. Today is Slave Day. My last name's the enemy.

Let me explain.

Robert E. Lee High School, where I'm a sophomore, has 1,481 students. These students are divided up alphabetically into homerooms of twenty-five students each. I'm in Homeroom No. 60. We're the last homeroom—the one with the six leftover students. Each homeroom is supposed to elect one member to the student council. Mr. Zarsky, my homeroom teacher, didn't want to waste cigarette time instilling in us the value of the electoral process, so he scanned the report cards of his class of six and designated me Homeroom No. 60 representative, an honor not unlike being chosen U.S. senator from Rhode Island. I would have considered declination, but the meetings got me out of PE every other week. Whoop, Whoop.

As a rep, even one from Homeroom No. 60, I get auctioned off during Slave Day, the student council's fund-raiser to pay for the following night's homecoming dance. Keep in mind, all the other reps were elected. They're mostly seniors and, without fail, beautiful and popular with one-syllable flight attendant names: Rob, Tish, Chris, Jake. But it's not the prospect of being a slave for the day—carrying books, fetching lunch, escorting my master to class—that has me down. It's the actual auctioning part. I'm going to be the last council member up for sale and, just maybe, the first rep not to merit the five-buck minimum bid. Everyone will get a big laugh out of that. I shouldn't have been shooting my mouth off to Deena about being in student council. If she doesn't already think I'm genetic gubbish, wait until I'm up there on the auction block having an asthma attack.

Then again, maybe Deena will bid on me. Maybe she'll lay down a twenty and say, "Back off, girls. He's mine." Maybe we'll take a blanket down to the river, and she'll make me feed her grapes one by one, and when I place them in her mouth her lips will touch my fingers. . . . Yeah, maybe a DC-9 will crash-land into the gym and kill me before the auction begins.

JENNY ROBINSON
7:25 A.M.

"Whatcha doin' there, Princess?" my father says, wrapping his arm around my shoulder.

"Math homework," I answer.

"Left-handed?"

"Clint's math homework," I say.

"Clint ought to do his own homework," he says, but then he chuckles and pulls the knot of his tie tight. "You two are quite a team. I can see how that boy has enough on his mind already, what with the Liberty Valley game tomorrow night. Mind if I have one of these cookies?" He points to the sugar cookies with the

Hershey's Kisses baked into them that I've been working on for Clint's spirit box.

"Go ahead. He won't miss one." I connect two homely circles into an 8. At first Mrs. Chatfield wrote little notes on Clint's homework saying it needed to be neater, but I've gotten a lot better at printing left-handed. Sometimes I'll miss one or two on my own homework, so Chatfield won't suspect we're cheating. Algebra is one of the three classes Clint and I have together. I wouldn't want Chatfield to snag us and take one of us out of her class. I just wish Clint would do better on the quizzes. She asked Clint how he could do so well on his homework and so poorly on his quizzes. He told her he gets test anxiety. He kind of shuffled his feet and acted like he was really embarrassed. He looked really shy and cute. She asked him if he would like to take his tests untimed after school, when there wouldn't be other students there to make him nervous. He said, "No ma'am. I'll just try harder," and reeled her in.

It reminded me of when he asked me out for the first time. That was thirteen months ago, and we've been together ever since. Well, except for the three weeks we broke up this summer when I found out about Clint messing around with Angie Pear.

It seems Clint, Damien, and Alex (his "posse" he calls them—give me a break) took Clint's parents' boat out waterskiing on Canyon Lake. The Country Estates Posse took all the beer from their parents' houses, and from what I've been told, just "ran into" Angie and a couple of those other senior sluts—Leslie Aitken (the preacher's daughter . . . need I say more) and Trish "Trash" Neuman—and invited them along. This after telling me it was a guys' day out. By the time it got dark, they were all wasted.

Not surprisingly, they started playing Truth or Dare.

Naturally, Clint ended up making out with Angie in the water. Predictably, she already had her bikini top off.

What was almost as bad is that during the truth part of the game, Clint told everyone what we had done together. You know, how far we've gone and all that. It's not *that* far, but it was so humiliating to know he told everyone.

When I found out about it, I put everything Clint had given

me in a big box, wrapped it up like a present, and gave it to him when he tried to take me parking. At first he was so excited.

"You're the best girlfriend a guy could have," he said.

But when he opened the box there was Sammy Panda he won for me at Six Flags. There was the hand-stained jewelry box he made for me. There was the mix cassette he labeled "Romantic Songs." There was the framed picture of Clint in his letter jacket. And finally, there was the gold chain he got me for Christmas.

Anyway, when he saw what was in the box, he started crying. Well, not really crying, but there were tears in his eyes, and he asked me why I was breaking up with him. I told him what I found out about *The Love Boat*. After trying to deny it and getting it put back in his face—I knew too many details for him to get away with that—he went off about how "those bitches" exaggerated everything. Then he blamed it on the alcohol. He swore he would quit drinking. But I didn't budge. I told him to take me home because I never wanted to see him again.

For the next three days I got roses delivered to me. Then he started calling. At first I would let my machine answer, and he would leave these long messages telling me how much he loved me. He even started leaving original love poems on the tape. I've saved those.

Finally I took him back, and he's been so sweet ever since. Well, since football season began he's been pretty distracted, but that's to be expected. He started on the varsity team last year as a sophomore—he was the only sophomore on the team—and this year he's supposed to be an all-district linebacker. He gets so fired up on game days that I can't even talk to him. He goes around punching lockers and doing all this manly stuff that I don't get, but that's fine. I've got so much to do on Fridays. Between student council and pep squad and being junior-class secretary, there's always something going on to keep me busy.

Speaking of which, I'd almost forgotten today was Slave Day. I guess I'm not that concerned. Clint already said that he wouldn't let anyone outbid him.

MR. TWILLEY
7:51 A.M.

Why didn't I just throw the memo away? Why did I let it sit there for weeks? For eighteen years now I've tossed it without so much as a second thought. That's what I should have done this year.

Was it something that Esther said? About having all the life drained out of me? She's been gone a year, and I still hear her voice, and it's still telling me what to do. But what will *this* prove? I tried to tell her, these kids today, they're just not the same as when we first started teaching. She just laughed at me, told me that I was the one changing, not them. But she was wrong, and one day I think she'll see that.

When I first started teaching, students gave me the nickname Mr. History because of how I made the subject come alive for them. I didn't justify the subject with the clichés like coaches in my department used: "Those who forget history are doomed to repeat it." *Pshaw.* No, I made them see history as a grand story, as exciting as any of the novels Esther taught. Students would beg the counselors to get into my class—the bright ones, especially. I've always been challenging. I never bought into that warm fuzzy "new school" of teaching that said dates and names of treaties or significant battles weren't important. "Human history," after all, says Mr. H. G. Wells, "becomes more and more a race between education and catastrophe." Students understood that, and they respected the fact that they *earned* their grades in my class.

I don't grade effort; I grade results.

They still call me Mr. History, though now it's in patronizing reference to how long I've been here. I'll tell them about Washington crossing the Delaware, and some smart aleck will raise his hand and ask, "Mr. Twilley, was the water very cold?" They'll snicker, thinking that I don't catch the drift, but there are no flies on me.

I let the memo sit on my desk for too long . . . thought too much about it. FACULTY, TAKE PART IN SLAVE DAY AND HELP THE STUDENT COUNCIL RAISE FUNDS FOR THE HOMECOMING DANCE.

SIGN AND RETURN TO MR. DENHART IF YOU ARE WILLING TO PAR-
TICIPATE. I signed the memo the day I was served the divorce
papers. When I handed it to Denhart, he nearly fell out of his
chair. He recovered and said something like, "Marcus, you always
seem to surprise me." Denhart—hah. He thinks he's the only
teacher in school who "relates" to the students. They made him
the chair of the English department after Esther left. I felt like
reminding him that it was Esther's recommendation that got him
that position. I still can't believe she suggested him. He's such an
odd bean. He takes his kids outside and lets them have sword
fights when he's teaching *Romeo and Juliet*. They go diddy-wabiddy,
and I have to close the windows to my classroom, thereby anger-
ing my students. He also sponsors the spring break trip to London
each year. He took eighteen kids last year. I don't think the kids
know that he gets free trips for sponsoring them. Get rid of *that*
perk and let's see how many students he takes.

Generally it's just the most popular teachers who volunteer to
be slaves. Or should I say the *easiest* teachers? That's what
shocked Denhart. He knows I run a tight ship. No nonsense. Kids
give me any guff and I ship them right down to the principal's
office. Discipline's *their* job. I'm here to teach. It's the teachers
who let kids get away with murder in the classroom who end up
with their photographs on the sides of coin jars for a "kiss the pig"
contest.

So why am I doing this? It's too late to back out now. They
even announced that I would be up for sale over the PA all week.
The first day they read it, my students all stared up at me, but
they knew better than to cause a disturbance.

CLINT DeFREISZ
8:12 A.M.

I wonder if it's cold enough yet to wear my letter jacket?

Sure, it's colder'n Dracula's dick right now, but it's been
warming up in the afternoons, and I don't want to look like one of

those stupid freshmen swimmers who stand out in the bus circle in the eighty-degree weather pulling a Frosty the Snowman in their easy-as-shit-to-get letter jackets. Anyone who can float can get a letter jacket if they go out for the swim team. Let's see one of them fill a gap, take on Lamar Jones from Liberty Valley or Billy Ramzinsky from New London, put 'em on their backs, stop 'em on third and one. We'll see how many of those skinny Speedo-wearin' breaststrokers would be wearing letter jackets then.

Now, I'm not saying you have to play football to be cool. My homey Damien doesn't play any sport; he's editor of the yearbook. I know it sounds kinda limp-wristed—a guy being yearbook editor—but don't worry. He's not like that. It's just that his eyes are so bad he can hardly play catch. I swear his glasses are bulletproof. Damien's more of a poet. He even helped me write this really romantic stuff that cinched me getting Jenny back when she flaked on me. Jenny's my girlfriend. More on her later. Anyway, my point is just that they shouldn't hand out letter jackets like door prizes. It devalues them for those of us who earned it.

Hell, I'd be willing to give my letter jacket to anyone who would drink one of these each day. It's my own special recipe: two bananas, two eggs, one pint of OJ, three tablespoons of powdered SuperMass, a giant glob of peanut butter, and five ice cubes. Blend into slush. Serve chilled. I call it a Gameface. I drink one a day. Last year I played at 195. This year I'm at 215. The drinks make a difference. I pour my Gameface into the victory mug Jenny made me. Painted on it is my name, number (44), and a picture of General Pissdoff (as those of us on the team refer to our sword-swingin' mascot). It fits into the drink holder in my Jeep. I make myself polish off the mess before I get to school.

Tyke Milton, this all-everything lineman who played a few years before me, moved back to Deerfield after he blew out a knee playing for Texas. He works out down at DAC—that's the Deerfield Athletic Club—where most of us on the team work out during the summer. Anyway, he said he could get me 'roids if I was serious about getting bigger. But Milton has these nasty acne scars and he's balding at twenty, so I told him I'd have to think about it.

I had my Thursday night pregame dream last night, which

sucks, because last night was Wednesday night. I don't want to get fired up too early. No sense in peaking tonight. I don't know why I count on the Dream. It's really more like a bad omen than a motivational sequence. It's just that we're five and one—and the only Thursday night that I didn't have the dream, we lost the next day. So you can see how this could affect my mental preparation.

The dream's bizarro.

In it, the mighty Rebel D is matched up against the Cowboys. Yes, *those* Cowboys. Aikman's calling audibles. I'm staring him down. Blood's dripping down my nose just like in that picture of Dick Butkus you always see in those Time-Life Books. I'm even movin' in slow motion—everyone is—and that guy with the God voice who narrates NFL Films and uses phrases like "frozen tundra" and "battle-hardened warriors" is calling the game. I can hear'm as I'm playin'. We start out holding 'em, but every play we lose one of our players, and the Cowboys keep gaining more yardage. They're pilin' up fifty, sixty yards a clip, but they never reach the end zone. Finally, it's just me against all eleven of 'em. I'm yellin', "Bring it on! Bring it on!" like I don't even know I'm getting my ass kicked up and down the field.

TOMMY PARKS
8:35 A.M.

I can hear the voice. It still sounds a long way off. But I know it'll get closer. I know whose voice it is by the pitch—occupying the range somewhere between the squeal of a Styrofoam ice chest and alley cats doin' the nasty. And the voice is calling my name.

"Tommy! Tommy! Git yo' ass up, boah! You gonna be late fo' school."

I swear to God. When I get married—if I get married—I'm gonna pick me a velvety-voiced woman. I don't care if she's a no-cookin' hog; she's gonna sound like Reba McEntire. The voice is getting closer. I put my head under my pillow, but I yell back at my momma.

"GED" As in *"Let me sleep in. I'll get my . . ."*

The light comes on. I can tell by the glow around the edge of the pillowcase, then I feel my covers start slipping down my back.

"Diploma," she screeches. As in *"Your lazy ass is gonna earn a . . ."*

I am completely uncovered now. "Boah, you din't even take off yer uniform before you went to bayed. Yo' gonna end up with bayed bugs."

I fake sleeping. Miss Amenny taught us how to pretend we're asleep in drama class. I try to remember what she said about taking deep breaths to make it look realistic. I hear Momma leave the room, but I know this is a bad sign. A minute later I start feeling water mist my neck and ears. She's fetched the spray bottle she uses on the ferns.

"Tommy, they oughtta pay you double down at Whataburger. Yo' in that uniform sixteen hours a day. Either that or you oughtn't work so much."

I know it's no use trying to sleep, so I sit up.

"You gonna start paying for my gas? My insurance?" I ask, knowing what her answer's gonna be.

"Shore thang, honey, just as soon as you start chippin' in on the groceries and house payment," she says.

"Trailer payment," I point out. "One-bathroom trailer."

"Well, as soon as you're a famous actor you can buy us a two-bathroom trailer," she says.

"Hell, Momma, I'll spring for somethin' that'd put Graceland t'shame." She heads back into the kitchen. I follow her and pour myself a cup of coffee. I switch to the English accent I used in the one-act play we did in school last year. I played Froggy in *The Foreigner*. "Mumsy, any chance of me gaining entrance to the loo this morning?"

"One day, boah, I'm gonna be on *Oprah* talking about living with my crazy English son, Tommy."

"Thomas, *please*, madam." I say, still in character.

"Anyways, I believe Mandy's already in there," she answers, stuffing a doughnut in my mouth and heading out the door in her Denny's uniform. She's a hostess there. Dan, my stepfather, works the graveyard over at Thermon, the world's leading heat-traced tubing manufacturer and employer of at least four of the Parks clan. That leaves me responsible for my twin half sisters, Mandy and Morgan, for thirty minutes of hell a day. Morgan's not so bad. She still plays Little League baseball. Made the all-star team, as a matter of fact. Takes ten, fifteen minutes in the bathroom, max. Mandy, on the other hand, she's everything bad you can imagine about a seventh-grade girl. She's like Robo-teenybopper. She's got a hot-iron curler in place of one hand and a telephone where the other should be. She's got Momma's voice. So does Morgan, I guess. It's just that Morgan doesn't use it quite so much.

I make my way back to my bedroom. Anytime I bitch about Mandy's bathroom time, she reminds everyone that I get my own room and she has to share with Morgan. Next year she'll get my room. Next year I'll have a place of my own. Thermon pays eight bucks an hour for any warm body with a diploma. (Or a GED, as I've pointed out to Momma more than a few times.) I change into a black T-shirt and fold up my Whataburger uniform. I have to go to work again tonight after play practice. I spray on an extra dose of Right Guard and put on my red King Feed cap. It's easier than busting down the bathroom door to throw Mandy out.

SHAWN GREELEY
8:42 A.M.

Okay, I'll admit it, everything up until now has gone exactly like Priscilla said it would. I mean everything. From the election to the meetings to the duties. I mean, just look at her. Every time she says something, about eight people shit their pants.

"Shawn wants you to get more chairs up on the stage," or "Shawn wants the band to play 'Money for Nothing' when any of the teachers are getting auctioned off." And people just do it.

When I first met her, as a sophomore, I thought she was a bitch. Man, everybody did. I remember I was up at the chalkboard in algebra trying to work this problem with two variables. I can never get the ones with two variables, so I was just sitting up there with my thumb up my ass, and this redheaded transfer student in the front row is laughing. Not even trying to hide it. So the teacher tells her, "Priscilla, if you think it's amusing, maybe you'd like to help Shawn with the problem." Now, most of the time this will shut someone up, but not Priscilla. She goes, "Miss Burnett, you've got to put it in terms a basketball player can understand." Then she turns the equation into this word problem, something like, "Shawn, imagine someone could hold you to twenty-three points."

"Jordan, maybe," I said. *Much* laughter.

"Okay, so Jordan holds you to twenty-three. You check the box score the next day, and you see you made six free throws and you went seven for twelve from the field. How many three-pointers did you make?"

"Three," I said immediately. "That's baby math."

"Well that's all a two-variable problem is. You just deal with the second variable in terms of the first. In this case, X represents the number of two-pointers, and Y equals the number of three-pointers. You know you made seven shots, so to get rid of the second variable, just turn the Y into seven minus X. Voilà . . . one variable."

"Cool, baby," I said. Then I gave her one of my patented Twelves. That's one of my smiles. A Twelve means I show twelve teeth. It's a midlevel grin. I broke out a Twenty at the end of my election speech. It's pretty much my ultimate smile. Does it work? We carried sixty-two percent of the vote.

So I was feeling pretty good about myself. I was sailing out of class, and Keene Davenport was walking out the door in his back-to-Africa threads 'bout the same time. And he said to me (I still can't believe this pudgy brotha had the 'nads), "Think you would've gotten the answer if she would have used watermelons instead of basketballs?"

I shoulda kicked his ass then.

Maybe then I wouldn't be dealing with the Letter to the Editor bullshit today. Seems everyone is anxious to show me the

Herald this morning. See what I'm gonna do. I'll tell you what I'm gonna do—nothing. Maybe flash a Twenty and say, "Keene who?" And you know what? That's all that will come of this junior Spike Lee's big protest . . . nothing.

BRENDAN

9:03 A.M. First period, gymnasium

I could've sworn Mr. Denhart told us to wear our student council shirts today. Now look at me. I'm the only one. Everyone else dressed up sharp, and I'm in this bletcherous red and gray jersey with blue stripes and white stars that would drag the ground if it weren't tucked in. Punt, punt. On the back it says STRONG, PROUD, DEDICATED, which is the student council motto, not just a list of qualities I lack.

I have this moby fine Hawaiian shirt that I'm pretty sure Deena likes. She told me it was ultracolorful. "Like a Fruitopia ad," she said. I only let myself wear it once every two weeks, otherwise people might notice. Today would have been the perfect day.

So I'm sitting here in the last chair in the last row watching the gym fill up, searching for someone who will save me from humilification, when Annabella Guzaldo turns in her seat to face me.

"Hey, Brendan, do you follow *all* the rules?" Annabella's the only other sophomore on the council. We're in all the honors classes together, but the samealities end there.

"No. Do you follow *any* of them?" I'm probably the only boy in school who doesn't call her Madonna. All the football players do. It's because she's Italian, on the dance team, and stars in most of the wet dreams of the class of '97. She's so far out of my league that I'm not even nervous around her. Maybe that's why we're virtual friends. She invited me to a party at her house last year, but I wouldn't have known anyone there, so I didn't show. Pitiful, pitiful.

"So what's with the shirt? Are you hoping for someone with a lot of Rebel pride to bid on you?" she said.

"Mr. Denhart said to wear 'em. I thought everyone would."

"What everyone decided was that it was worth the demerits to not look like a . . ."

She hesitated. So I helped her out.

"What? Geek? Spaz?"

"Confederate flag was what I was going to say. Are we a little sensitive this morning, Bren?"

Annabella is my competition for salutatorian. Neither of us is going to catch Laurence Davenport. My specialties are the hard sciences; hers, the liberal arts.

"I'm not sure how I got into this. I don't think anyone is going to bid on me."

"That's your only worry? Hey, I'm just praying some octopus with too much cash on his hands doesn't decide he wants a love slave."

"I don't think that'll be a problem for me," I say.

KEENE

9:05 A.M. First period, English

"Keene Davenport?"

"Present." I keep my hood up over my head, which is resting on my desk.

Mrs. Paulson peers over her reading glasses, bats her eyelashes condescendingly, and her upper lip curls open as if drawn by a fishing line. "That was quite a letter you wrote to the newspaper, Keene. I really wasn't expecting to see you today."

The class laughs. I hate her. It's her fault I'm at school today. She's the teacher who gave me a C on my progress report, and it's all because of a disagreement we had on an assignment. She wanted us to prepare a book report on any of the selections on our summer reading list. But, lo and behold, every writer on the list was a white European. I asked her if I could do some other book, but she said no.

"These are the authors you'll need to know when you're in

college, Keene. Don't look at everything as a plot against your people."

I did my report on Richard Wright's *Black Boy*, anyway, and she gave me an F on the assignment. There were no grammar problems, no footnoting errors; I didn't use the Cliff Notes like half the class did. On the bottom of the paper, she wrote LEARN TO FOLLOW DIRECTIONS! And get this—she drew a frowning face next to it. Today I'm not going to let her think I chickened out.

"I've just come up with another plan—since it looked like none of the student council members were going to boycott," I say. It's better than admitting that my mom had made me come to school.

"Do you want to share it with the class?"

"You'll see soon enough."

And that's when they come over the intercom and begin dismissing us class by class for the auction.

MR. TWILLEY
9:31 A.M. Assembly period, gymnasium

Look at them. Straggling in here in their White Zombie T-shirts, goatees, nose rings, wearing bandannas to cover their dreadlocks, strutting around in combat boots or tennis shoes that cost as much as my car payment. Half of them carry beepers in case one of their junior-high customers needs a fix. They wear their jeans halfway down their rear ends, but don't worry—they've got their custom boxers with glow-in-the-dark bananas emblazoned on them pulled up six inches higher than their waistbands. Birds of a feather, they are.

And the girls are no better. The ones who aren't pregnant dress like they hope to be soon. Holes in their jeans showing off their total body tans. Halter tops and see-through blouses.

And they tell us we can't enforce a dress code, that we've got other, *bigger* problems to tackle. I tell you, it all starts there. Once students think of school as a professional environment where they're expected to toe the line, the other things—truancy, fighting, drugs—will take care of themselves.

So now I've volunteered to let one of these reprobates boss me around all day. Twilley, which way did you fall off the apple cart?

CLINT

9:32 A.M. Assembly period, gymnasium

"'Sup?"

"Oh, you know, you know."

"Which class you missin'?"

"Twilley."

"Suh-weet!" I say and offer my palm to Alex, who completes the high five and takes a seat in the bleachers next to me.

"Check it out," I say, pointing to the far wall of the gym. All the posters for tomorrow's pep rally are already up but, as usual, Jen's put a special, personalized banner up for her blue-chip boyfriend. It says PUT 'EM IN DEDEEP, DEFREISZ.

"That's one hype lady you got," Alex says.

"Trained her myself," I say.

"Shee-it," he says, but he gives me a high five anyway.

"Where's Damien?"

"I saw him on the way to the gym. He said all his photographers are too stoned to shoot Slave Day this morning, so he has to." Alex laughs, and so do I. It's sort of a joke. You can tell all the photos in the yearbook that Damien took 'cuz they're way out of focus. He's so blind, though; he thinks they're the only shots that look right. "There he is. Down by the podium. See him? He's taking pictures of Jenny."

"Cool," I say. And it *is* cool . . . having your best friend be the yearbook editor. Last year Damien was the sports editor of the book and, natch, there was an action shot on the football spread of me running down this squirrelly assed Crockett High quarterback. I've got two or three shots of Jen taped up on my mirror above my dresser that Damien's printed for me in the journalism darkroom. They're blurry, of course, but it makes 'em look cool. You know, like art.

Damien's pretty lucky he was allowed back on the yearbook staff, let alone chosen editor. After the yearbook came out last year, Mr. Gant, the principal, tried to kick him out of the class. Gant didn't take kindly to one of Damien's headlines. Above a photo of Gant leading school board members on a tour of the new science wing, Damien wrote: PRINCIPAL SHOWS OFF ERECTION. The yearbook staff had only distributed fifty of the books before Gant came storming into the journalism room. He made 'em use razor blades and cut out the headline from every remaining yearbook. The version with the original headline became a collector's item. So guess who's got one? You know it.

I'm groovin' all over Jen in her pep squad uniform. She's wearing this short pleated skirt that shows her legs from her white ankle boots all the way to midthigh. She's got on this tight sleeveless top made out of that heavy fabric you only see in girls' spirit clothing. Her blond hair is pulled into a ponytail and she's wearing this mega-red lipstick that she calls "slut red" that all the pepsquadders are supposed to wear when they're in uniform. I love it, but she refuses to wear it except when she has to, which is just like her. It's that kind of 'tude—and this is only my opinion—that kept her from getting elected cheerleader last year. I'll admit she's no leaper and her voice only carries from here to there, but in the grand scheme of student elections, that's secondary. Votes come from girls who fear you and guys who think they might have a shot at rounding third without marrying you first. Don't get me wrong, I don't want her to come to school dressed like Tiffany Delvoe, but would lipstick really hurt? Sometimes she wears this sweatshirt with a kitten on it. I'm not shittin' you.

Normally the cheerleaders, dance team, and pep squad wouldn't be dressed out until Friday—game day—but, since it's homecoming week and tonight's the bonfire, they are today. I don't usually get to appreciate Jen in her uniform, because on Fridays I go into my zone. People know better than to fuck with me on Fridays. I don't smile on Fridays. On Fridays I start visualizing each play of that night's game. I know the names of the offensive linemen, the quarterback, the running backs I'm going to face. I imagine myself invisible in the other team's locker room. I hear them dissin' me. Sayin' I'm a pussy. Talking about what they're gonna do with Jen after the game. Saying how Deerfield's full of fags.

Last thing I need to do is get my dick hard thinkin' 'bout Jen in her pep squad skirt and slut red lipstick.

TIFFANY DELVOE

9:34 A.M. Assembly period, downtown

This town bites.

I mean, who would put railroad tracks all the way through the middle of a town with no bridges? I've heard Daddy call it, with a straight face, part of our "small-town charm." Boneheaded civic planning is more like it. I'm a half hour late for school, and I've now watched fifty-seven million empty boxcars rattle by at about a centimeter per decade. I should have made a run for it when I saw the guardrail start to come down. Probably would have been the biggest thrill I've ever had in this town. Maybe I wouldn't have made it. Wouldn't that have made for a banner headline in the *Deerfield Herald*? MAYOR'S DAUGHTER SLAIN BY RUNAWAY TRAIN. Who am I kidding? BIRTH CONTROL PILLS FOUND IN DEAD DAUGHTER'S PURSE is how they would have run it. Besides, if I'm gonna get myself killed by a train, I'd rather it kill me because I was speeding *away* from school—not *toward* it. I've got a rep to maintain.

It's not even like I give a shit about a timely arrival at school normally, but this is Slave Day and if I don't use this hundred bucks buying a slave—performing my civic duty—Daddy'll have my ass on a stick. I just couldn't seem to haul my hungover bod out of bed this morning. You know, I never set out to drink on school nights; shit just happens.

Last night, Suzi—she's half Vietnamese, but really cool and

really cute—called and said the Kappas (her sister's sorority) were having a mixer with the Phi Delts (total face jocks). Naturally, there was a keg, and these two guys—Greg and Kip, I think their names were—kept filling our cups. Then this total bitch-hag-from-hell Kappa comes over, all jealous, and asks the guys if, like, they planned on taking us to the Lee High homecoming dance. She even scratched her nose with her middle finger when the guys weren't looking but she knew we were. Anyway, Kip—the cuter one—still looked primed, but Greg dragged him away, so screw 'em. Their loss.

Speaking of boys, all of the don't-make-me-wanna-puke ones at the top of the alphabet are getting snatched up as I sit here watching Union Pacific haul air back and forth across Deerfield. If I'm lucky, I'll still make it in time to get into the bidding for Dan O'Neil. That would be respectable. He's a football player. He's tasty. He doesn't drool or smell his pits. He wouldn't think it meant I liked him. God, you know what would be funny? If I miss Dan, I could bid on Teresa Villejo. That prissy, brown-nosing worm. Suzi and Rainy would laugh their asses off if I made Teresa chauffeur us around at lunch in that Camaro she thinks is, like, ultraflash. Then I'd have her carry *all* my shit to class. I wouldn't even go by my locker; I'd make her carry all of my books. I'd be the master from hell. I wonder if my books are still in my locker. I haven't gotten them out since school started.

If I take advantage of this slave shit, today may not suck.

Oh my god! The train is coming to a complete stop.

JENNY

9:35 A.M. Assembly period, gymnasium

I wave at Clint from the stage as he sits in the bleachers, but he's too busy high-fiving Alex to notice. I probably look pathetic. A flash goes off. I blink and look down and see Damien. He's taking my picture.

"Work with me. Emote. Make love to the camera," he directs.

I try for the distant—yet alluring—look that all the models on the cover of *Vogue* seem to have mastered. I have to hope for "the look," because the cleavage prerequisite is impossible to meet. Damien clicks off a few frames.

"Did that nose come with those glasses?" I ask Damien. It's a running joke. Damien wears these 1950s-style thick black-framed glasses that make him look like Buddy Holly with a grunge haircut—shaved three-inch ring topped with an all-one-length bowl cut. He's working on a goatee, too, which I'm afraid Clint will attempt after the season's over. Damien wore contacts for about three days before deciding it "wasn't him."

"Just for that, I may not bid on you," he says, "and you'll be stuck with that yeti you call a boyfriend."

"Oh, not that! I take it back. They're lovely glasses. The latest in eyewear fashion, I'm sure."

"Too late to apologize now. 'Fraid I'll have to get in the bidding for Madonna, instead. I brought my checkbook from my unnumbered Swiss bank account."

"Oh, you won't need any money. I swear, that girl can't quit talking about you," I say. He knows I'm lying, but he plays along.

"She's red-blooded, ain't she?"

There's something about Damien saying "ain't" that doesn't sound right. It's like hearing your parents describe something as "fab."

Clint has always thought that I found out about the Truth or Dare night on Canyon Lake from the girls, but for the record, I heard about it from Damien. It's not like he called me on the phone to rat on his best friend. I was at a party where Damien was pretty wasted and he just sort of let it slip out. Something like, "I haven't been this drunk since we all went skinny-dipping on the lake." (Long, ugly pause.) "Shit, you weren't there."

Drunk as he was, it wasn't any big trick to get him to spill the details. I've never told Clint, because I know he would major wig. Plus, I'd rather him think that "those bitches" were the ones who stripped and told.

Cool. The crowd's starting the Speller chant.

TOMMY

The legacy of the Speller has been handed down from one gradu-
ating senior to a select junior at Lee High since the dawn of time.
It was David Hamilton, class of '95, who dubbed me his succes-
sor. His decision was based on a number of factors, none of them
the ability to spell. After all, the Speller only has to be able to handle one word: *Rebels*. The trick is . . . the Speller has to form each
of these letters using only his body.

I sit with the Hats. Thirty feet wide by ten rows deep of
feather-pierced Stetsons and oily gimmes from Roscoe's Texaco,
Uncle John's Real Pit BBQ, or King Feed, like mine—the bills
carefully curved into half-moons. If someone could harness the
energy spent on school spirit in this crowd, they could run a Game
Boy for . . . oh, say—two minutes. For most of us, whether it's me
at Whataburger, Rid DeLord at University Exxon, or Mark
Simpson sitting on a tractor till dark, school is a break in the day—
the seven hours we can kick it. Rebel pride? Guys like Rid and
Mark can't afford it. Kick ass or ass-kicked, it's all the same to
them. That's where the Speller comes in.

It starts with a low chant at any school assembly. It doesn't
always come from the Hats. Sometimes the low riders start it.
Sometimes the stoners. The cheerleaders try to ignore it. The
Speller and the cheerleaders have never gotten along. The chant
gets louder and louder, until the Speller must, reluctantly, saunter
down to stem the riot. As soon as the Speller faces the crowd,
there is silence. Then the first letter is formed. While most of my
predecessors used the flared left leg/teapot-handle left arm position for their *R*, I opt for the diving position that functions as the
lower-case version.

"r," whispers the student body.

I form the second letter.

"E." It grows to a stage whisper.

Then "B." A few eager beavers are already screaming it, but
those with any sense of cool grunt the *B*.

"**E.**" Now it's okay to really let it out. Cheerleaders have that lemon-sucking look on their faces by now.

The next part is my . . . what did Miss Amenny call it? . . . my pièce de résistance—the *L*. I'm famous for my *L*. It's the easiest letter, and for years the Speller was content to sit, his butt sideways to the stands, stretch out his legs, and raise his arms. Not I, said the fly. Nope. I do it backward. I lay on my back with my arms above my head, and after hours of practicing in front of the mirror, I can now bring my legs up exactly plumb to the floor. The crowd goes apeshit. "**L.**"

When I make my *S*, no one actually says "S." They hiss. Like a symphony conductor, I use my hands to bring down the volume. Then with two quick punches and a drawn-out lassoing motion followed by another punch, the grand finale: "Rebels! Rebels! Woooooooaaaaaahhhh REBELS!"

Let the cheerleaders follow that.

SHAWN

9:36 A.M. Assembly period, gymnasium

I'm checking out the crowd, trying to figure out if anyone but Reverend Keene himself is going to take part in this so-called boycott. Unlikely. I don't think he even has any friends. Thinks he's too good for everybody. He used to come down to Rickel Park to hoop, but no one would pick 'm up. I'd let 'm run with me every once in a while, but he'd get stripped every time the ball wound up in his hands (which wasn't very often). Pretty soon he'd bring a book, 'cuz he'd have to wait so long to get picked. Then he just quit comin'. Gave up. Now he wants to lead a boycott? Boy couldn't lead a spade.

Top o' that, he knows nothin' 'bout politics. Real-world politics.

Priscilla likes to think she's giving me lessons. Telling me who I should butter up, whose parties I should go to, what promises I can afford to make—and break. But man, I've been a politician ever since I can remember. Who else can hang with the brothas down at Rickel and then tell an O. J. joke so funny that half those Hats'll be sayin', "Go ahead. Date my sister"?

'Sides, who cares 'bout this student council president gig, anyway? Priscilla can run the show. To me, it's just a ticket, an extra line in whatever college's basketball media guide I decide to go to. So, one day, after my illustrious career's over, they'll be looking for the new Ahmad Rashad to host a sports magazine show and do courtside interviews for NBA games. They'll see my degree in communications and minor in speech, but it'll be that student body president thing that'll sew it up.

"He says 'ask' instead of 'axe,' but more than that, he's a people person! Get him a contract!"

Uh-oh, they're calling for the Speller. That means it's time to find something to make myself look busy. I walk up to the microphone, switch it off, and try to say something to the crowd. I look all baffled 'n' shit and try tapping the microphone, but since it's off, it still makes no sound. I kinda shrug my shoulders. By now Trailer Parks is into his routine, but I've gone over to the soundboard, and I'm kinda scratching my head, looking real serious. I turn some knobs about the time the Speller is into the big ending. I hop back up on the stage, switch the microphone back on, and say, "Testing, one . . . two . . . three." My voice goes booming out over the crowd.

I haven't pissed off the misfit Speller fans. I haven't pissed off the cheerleaders. *And*, I've made myself look like some sort of technical sound wizard. Yeah, Priscilla, tell *me* 'bout politics.

Before I start the assembly, I scan the crowd. It looks like the same number of black folk I always see. Then, I spot him. In the very back row, looking like he wants to move back to Africa— Keene Davenport. Now I hafta laugh. Brotha couldn't even convince *himself* to stay home.

Denhart gives me the signal. It's time to start. I clear my voice and lean into the microphone.

"Are you ready for Slave Day!?"

Cheerleaders herky. Drummers in the band pound their snares. The crowd shouts something back that I take as "Yes, Shawn. Please proceed."

"Well, all right then. I know you know how this works, but Mr. Gant wants me to remind you about the rules." (The scattered boos I expected come now.) "First of all, five dollars is the minimum bid, except for the teachers. For them, we'll take whatever we can get." (A few laughs.) "Second, Slave Day lasts from the end of the assembly to the end of the bonfire just before midnight. No taking your slave home with you tonight." (I wag my finger accusingly at the crowd. There's more booing, plus some fool shouts, "I love you, Madonna.") "Slaves will be dismissed five minutes early from class so that they can be waiting for their masters at their masters' classrooms. Slaves will also be allowed five extra minutes to arrive in class. The last rule is that you can't ask your slave to do anything illegal or against school rules." (Assorted boos and aaahs.)

"First we'll auction off the teachers, then all the student council members in alphabetical order. Get those wallets out, 'cuz here we go."

MR. TWILLEY

9:41 A.M. Assembly period, gymnasium

"Marc! It's good to see you up here. We've needed some fresh blood. These students are getting tired of the same ol', same ol'," says Mr. Tristan, the geometry teacher and NHS sponsor.

"Marcus," I say.

"Mmm, that's right." Tristan examines his fingernails, crosses his legs back toward Denhart, and strikes up a new conversation.

Am I really expected to converse with a teacher whom students refer to as the Candy Man? He makes those NHS students sell Skittles for most of the first semester. Now, if students aren't supposed to eat in the classrooms, why do we allow clubs to sell candy at school?

Mrs. White, the typing teacher, leans toward me. "Isn't that Shawn Greeley the sweetest boy? Have you ever had him in class?"

"Last year. Made a seventy-nine." This answer doesn't seem to please her, so I go on. "But he was certainly polite."

"I just think he will go as far as he sets his mind to. He's such a handsome boy, bright, respectful, and so athletic. The other kids seem to really like him too," White says.

"Wit that can creep, and pride that licks the dust," I say, sure she will catch neither the drift nor the theft of Pope's words.

Greeley is explaining the rules of Slave Day, making the most of the spotlight. Maybe this is progress. When I first started teaching at Lee, a black student-body president was unimaginable. I just wish the first one was more of a thinker. Greeley was an adequate student, but he couldn't be accused of intellectualism. Seemed to have a bee in his bonnet. Then again, we've had plenty of white presidents who couldn't even manage to pass my class.

Denhart's the first faculty member up for auction. He sashays to the front of the stage like he's a runway model balancing a book on his head, turning, pivoting, staring off vacantly. The students laugh. Then he flexes and poses in bodybuilder fashion. This almost makes *me* chuckle, as Denhart's an exceptionally slight young man. Greeley opens the bidding, and the students all seem to raise their hands at once. Bidding wanes only after the figure goes above ten dollars. Eventually a senior boy, one of Esther's best students last year, wins out with a twenty-two-dollar bid. Tristan goes for ten to his National Honor Society president.

I'm up next.

TOMMY
9:45 A.M. Assembly period, gymnasium

One thing I'll say about the Hats, they waste little time savoring a moment. When I make my way back into the stands, Rid tells me I didn't point my toes on the *L*. "The Romanian judge gave you a six," he adds. "When you gonna learn that backflip that Delgado used to do?" I see a bunch of bills and brims bobbing at this comment. Delgado was the Speller two years ago, the lowest of the low riders, and something of an acrobat.

"After you learn ta let the sheep out the gate 'stead o' forcin' 'em through the fence."

"Bite me, Trailer."

"Lookin' fer love . . . in all the wrong places," I croon back at him.

By the way. Case I didn't mention it. Some people—all right, most people—call me Trailer instead of Tommy. Trailer Parks. Get it? Pretty funny, huh? Even teachers have slipped up and called me Trailer.

Speaking of teachers, they're starting to auction them off now. I betcha I can guess every teacher who volunteered to be a slave. It's always the same ones. I just can't believe someone is gonna blow twenty bucks buying any of 'em for the day. Shit, that's a full tank of gas. Plus, I doubt those kiss-asses even make the most of it. Make 'em sing the alma mater, maybe. Call 'em by their first name. Oooh, not *that*!

Wait a minute. Is that Mr. Twilley up there? What's that rat bastard thinking? That someone here likes him? Not likely since his wife left. Apparently she didn't think much more of 'm than the rest of us. That sumbitch failed me for the year with a sixty-eight, and I busted my ass in there. All right, I busted my ass for the last six weeks, but most teachers let you slide if they see you working hard. Not Mr. History. He probably beats off, thinking about turning in failing grades.

All right, Twilley's up. This oughtta be rich.

MR. TWILLEY
9:47 A.M. Assembly period, gymnasium

Dead silence.

Dead silence turning into uncomfortable dead silence. I hear tittering and realize it's coming from behind me. From the teacher section. *Et tu, Brute.*

Greeley makes a new pitch.

"Come on, let's see some hands. This is probably your only chance to get your way with Mr. Twilley. Remember, there's no minimum bid on teachers."

Now the students start laughing. I try to think of students who might bid on me. They would have to be A students. Students who understood that all the hard work serves a purpose. Every year I get a letter or two from former students saying, "Mr. Twilley, I didn't realize at the time why you were so tough on us, but now that I'm in college . . ." So where are those students now? Surely one or two see the logic behind the pop quizzes, all the reading, the research papers.

Greeley visits Denhart, unsure of what he should do in this situation. The crowd is in hysterics, but somehow I'm detached, analytical. It was never my aim to be a popular teacher, just respected. Like Churchill, I offer my blood, toil, tears, and sweat. Is that not enough? Is that not worth a dollar or two?

I wouldn't have thought it was possible, but the noise level just got perceptibly louder. I look down and see Thomas Parks—sixty-eight last year, though he almost saved the day—striding toward the stage. I have no earthly idea what he's up to.

TOMMY

9:48 A.M. Assembly period, gymnasium

It's moments like this that keep me comin' to school. I mean, I don't know what the geezer was thinkin' when he volunteered for Slave Day, but he sure's gonna get more 'n he bargained for.

"Make way! Clear a path!" I say as I work my way down to the floor again. Now, someone really should stop me from what I'm about to do, but if it's one thing I've learned: If you look like you know what you're doin', no one messes with you. The further I get out onto the gym floor, the louder the carryin'-on gets. I hop up on the stage and move toward Twilley. For a second, I catch his eye. I expect to see confusion, but what I see instead makes me want to laugh. He's scared.

I stroll around him, stroking my chin, sizin' him up like he's a used car. I kick one of Twilley's shoes like it's a tire. Mr. Tristan's laughin' so hard, I think he's gonna have a coronary. Twilley's got this crooked expression on his face. I think he's tryin' to play along, so what the hell. I reach up to his jaw, and before he figures out what I'm doin', spread his lips apart and check his teeth. The crowd roars, but I see Denhart start walking toward me. My time's about up, so quicker'n you can spit, I dig a handful of change out of my pocket, lean into the microphone, and bid.

"A dollar fourteen," I shout.

"Sold!" shouts that black dude who's always on the microphone.

Twilley just stands there starin' out at the crowd. I'd swear he was vibrating. I know it sounds weird, but he looked like one of those players in old-timey electric football 'cept he wasn't moving anywhere. I figure that—since he's my property—I oughtta deal with it.

"You can sit now," I tell 'm.

BRENDAN

9:49 A.M. Assembly period, gymnasium

I'm in trepidation mode. Total, moby trepidation mode. That's going to be me, but with a five-dollar minimum bid, nobody's gonna want to bid on me—even as a joke. I thought about giving Lloyd five dollars so he could make an offer, just in case no one else would. Now, I wish I'd followed up on that.

KEENE

9:49 A.M. Assembly period, gymnasium

See now, that just proves my point. They try to tell us that Slave Day has nothing to do with race, that it's not a parody of that "ugly chapter" in American history. What they're really doing is glossing over it, making it funny. Just like *Hogan's Heroes* made yucking it up in a Nazi prisoner camp look like a frat party—Slave Day does the same thing with a few hundred years' worth of suffering. Trailer Parks checks Mr. Twilley's teeth, and everyone here thinks it's the funniest thing they ever saw. But that's what they *really* used to do. That was real life!

It doesn't look like my letter had any kind of effect. Every black face present and accounted for. There's Laurence sitting down there with the debate team, laughing like he doesn't have a care in the world. His life is right on schedule: valedictorian, then Ivy League, med school, house in a prestigious suburb, summers at the Inkwell.

And I sit up in the audience like some old plantation-house nigger, my silence looking like acceptance of the status quo.

But what can I do? They've started auctioning off the student council members now. Shawn Greeley has the crowd eating out of his hand. Laughing at his jokes. Settling down when he gives 'em a stern look. They look up there, see a brother running the show, and suddenly everything's hunky-dory. Wanna play "Dixie" as the school song? Bully. Of course, it's dandy to wave all these Confederate flags around. Sure, let's name the school for a general who tried to keep an entire race in chains. Why not? This is the South, y'all. Shawn Greeley doesn't seem to mind, and isn't he popular? Don't we all love to watch him play basketball? Don't we all love to watch him? . . . wait a minute.

SHAWN

9:52 A.M. Assembly period, gymnasium

Some ugly shit goes down on Slave Day. It's entertaining in the same way as those blood films in drivers ed are—just watching who bids on who. All the dark, hidden secrets bubble their way up to the surface. Rumors, crushes, jealousies—they all emerge from the depths. Now, most of the bidding is done by girlfriends for boyfriends and vice versa, or friend for friend, but lots of times, folks just be biddin' to dis each other. Ex-girlfriends bid on boys to piss off current girlfriends. Or worse: Current girlfriends bid on ex-girlfriends just so's they can demean 'em all day.

Eventually it's my turn, so Priscilla takes over the auctioning part. I stand up at the front of the stage, but I don't do any of that wacky posin' stuff that Denhart and some of the goofier council guys try. I'm Mr. Laid-Back.

This light-skinned sophomore girl gets in that all-important opening bid—not that I was worried, ya understand. She's cute, but I'm hoping for somethin' major-league. Then bids start coming from everywhere. Couple teachers even stay in through the ten-buck range. Coach Preppernau stays in through fifteen. Finally it gets down to three major players: Humphrey Brown, LaTisha Caldwell, and Carla Strahan.

Humphrey's probably my best friend 'cept it seems like we hardly see each other anymore. In junior high we were like the biggest rivals. He was still playing basketball and I still played football. Now he QBs the Rebs, and he's always gone on weekends on recruiting trips. Last weekend they flew him up to Penn State. The week before it was Michigan. Says he's gonna get outta the South no matter what.

LaTisha and I hung out off 'n' on last year. She's fine 'n' all that, but she kept asking for more from me. "More what?" I'd say, but she'd shake her head and come back with "You just don't get it." But I get it, all right. I just ain't willin' to part with it. Then one day she tells me she's late.

I say, "Late for what?"

She just says "Late."

. . . *hello.* "Late late, you mean?"

"Yeah," she says.

So for four days I've got the mornin' sickness. I'm throwin' up. I can't eat. I keep picturin' the sentence in the media guide. "Shawn's two-year-old, Shawn Jr., lives with the child's grandmother in Deerfield." Then they'd run a quote sayin' how much bein' a father has matured me. Damn if that ain't a tired story. Day LaTisha got her period I went down to Roscoe's and got, like, two pounds o' brisket. I hadn't noticed how hungry I was. We didn't see each other much after that. I heard she was seein' some Kappa

Alpha Psi up at Central. Guess that's through.

Now Carla, she's the toughest chick I know. You know how most white girls will get drunk and pull you into some closet at a party or somethin'? Then act like it never happened? Carla ain't like that. She's a player. Or a liberal. Same thing in my book. Anyway, she doesn't even care that 'bout half the white guys in school won't touch her 'cuz she's dated a couple brothas.

Man, any o' the three of 'em, and I'd be set. I'm pretty sure Humphrey'll drop out o' the biddin', and shore 'nuff, at eighteen bucks, he's through. So LaTisha and Carla are going back 'n' forth a dollar at a time. I don't know why some of the fine girls say getting auctioned makes 'em feel cheap. To me, it's a rush. I decide to flash a few teeth while they up the pot.

"Twenty-one dollars."

"Twenty-two."

"Twenty-three."

Then I hear it, and I know 'zactly who said it. My day has just been shot to hell.

"Thirty!"

Keene Davenport wants me to be his slave.

KEENE

9:53 A.M. Assembly period, gymnasium

I wait to see if either of those girls are gonna go any higher, but I don't hear another bid. Oh man, this is sheer genius. The fact that I'm keepin' Shawn from spending the day with one of Lee's loveliest just frosts the cake. The vice president girl is taking a long time waiting for higher bids. She keeps lookin' over her shoulder at Shawn, but he's holding firm to that "nothing fazes me" face o' his. At least he's lost the lawn-jockey grin. Finally she closes the deal. "Thirty dollars is the bid. Going once. Going twice. Sold!"

Question is, Where am I gettin' this hypothetical thirty dollars?

I know. I spot Laurence's moon face turned around gawking

at me. I raise my eyebrows, and he knows immediately what's up. He shakes his head no, but I'm sure he's got the cash on him. I make my way down the bleachers to where he's sitting with the master debaters.

"Guess if you can't beat 'em . . . ," he says when I reach his row.

"How much cash you got on you?"

"None. You're not gonna catch me ridin' this metaphorical bus of oppression," he says. His geeky friends squeal and giggle.

"You're gonna be ridin' my foot up your butt if you don't open up that wallet of yours."

"Ghandi, King, Davenport—our esteemed leaders in nonviolent resistance."

"I'm gonna count to three," I say. "One . . . two . . ."

"Tell you what," Laurence says. "I'll give you the cash if you stay away from me for the rest of the day. Better yet, until you graduate. People are starting to think we're related."

"That's it?" I say. Like I really want to hang with Laurence, anyway.

"Yeah. Besides, I'm tired of watching Shawn scam his way onto the honor roll. It devalues it for those of us who really belong there."

"Whatever."

"Be careful," he says as he takes the money out of his wallet. "He may forget how friendly he's supposed to be after you snake a day with Salt 'N' Pepa away from him."

CLINT

10:10 A.M. Assembly period, gymnasium

"Can you believe Trim? I mean, I gotsta give it up to 'm. Man's got his priorities straight," Alex says.

Timm Trimble, our GQ split end, has just spent forty-three dollars purchasing the Madonna Territory.

"If you ask me, it's a bargain. I mean, look at her," I say.

Alex stares across at the stage, licks his lips, and speaks, "The good thing 'bout Trim gettin' her is that, if he gets anything offa her, we'll get to hear about it."

"Yeah, and if anyone's up to the job, it's Trim."

High fiveage.

"So when're you gonna have Jenny stories to tell?"

I take a second or two deciding whether to answer the question or frog the shit outta Alex's arm. I go ahead and answer. "Oh, prob'ly not 'til 'bout six or seven hours after the wedding ceremony."

"You're not throwin' in the towel, are you?"

"Naw, man, I'm givin' it a hundred and ten percent. She just thinks we should wait. I don't know what for, though. I mean, she told me she loved me 'n' all that."

"Have you told her 'bout what you got waitin' in the wings? Man, there's plenty o' girls here who'd dribble off those Bobbie Brooks," Alex says. "There's Tracy Wilcynski. Tina MacQuarie's always rubbin' on you in art. Plus, you already know Angie'd do you."

"Yeah, but would you wanna hold hands with Angie? Walk class to class with her? She's got a mouth on her worse than yours. Plus, she'd be willing to 'do' 'bout half the junior class."

"Yeah, but who says you gotta make her your girlfriend? You don't see Trim tyin' himself down. He's like a bee movin' from flower to flower," Alex says, grinning at his own poetic nature.

"Dude, I like havin' a girlfriend. If you could ever con a girl into datin' you, you might understand it—someone's always waiting for you after the game, little notes and presents in your locker, ready-made plans on Saturday night. Doesn't that sound good to you?"

"I guess," Alex says, sounding unconvinced.

"So why ain't you plowin' through this infinite supply of available poontang?"

"'Cuz it ain't necessarily available to a backup JV lineman driving a Nova. I have to live vicariously through you. And, real frankly, if you keep datin' Jenny, I'm gonna have to see if Timm Trimble is interested in having a sidekick."

ROB THOMAS

"Give me at least one more day. Maybe I'll be able to make some use of this slave thing," I say casually, though I've been thinkin' 'long the same lines. I mean, there's plenty o' girls here who'd be willing to go the extra mile to keep their boyfriend happy. I sure don't want to wind up being the only virgin on the planet.

JENNY

10:17 A.M. Assembly period, gymnasium

I feel so sorry for Annabella Guzaldo. Timm Trimble is like a walking IQ test for girls. Fail it and you find yourself in the backseat of his Mustang out at the end of some deserted road—or so I've heard. Sure, he's beautiful, and he's not stupid, but can you trust someone who always has a line ready?

"Jen, you sure must be in good shape."

"Why's that, Timm?"

"'Cuz of all that running through my dreams you been doin'."

Lame, lame, lame, lame, lame. And you know he's sayin' the same thing to everyone on the dance team.

I'll say this for him, though, he's observant. Last week, after I got my hair cut, Clint doesn't notice all day, but the first time Timm sees me after Chem II, he's like, "Sweet 'do, Jen. Let me know when you're a single woman." I'm halfway tempted to tell Clint—not because I can't take care of myself—but because I think the posse thinks of "Trim" as some kind of legend.

Then again, maybe I should say something to Clint, like, "Imagine having Timm Trimble pay forty-three dollars for you." And then kind of swoon. Nothing keeps Clint in line like a small dose of jealousy.

Jen, stop it. You're sounding like all those girls you can't stand.

So it's finally my turn to be sold. Why are my palms sticky? They shouldn't be. One of the best things about having a boyfriend is that you don't have to sweat things like this. Before I had a boyfriend, I was always nervous. Worried that maybe the phone wouldn't ring. Worried that I was acting too obvious or too shy in front of cute guys. Worried that I'd have nothing to do on weekends when all my friends were going out.

I try to smile as I walk toward the front of the stage. I wish this stupid skirt had pockets; I don't know what to do with my hands. A flash goes off. Damien has captured me looking like a complete doofus.

"Time is running out to get yourself a slave!" Shawn announces. "Do I have an opening bid?"

Everyone in the crowd just chatters away with their friends. I don't think anyone is even facing the stage, which is fine. I feel like intermission. Clint shouts his bid.

"Five dollars!"

"Five dollars is the bid," Shawn says indifferently. Clint is standing up, scanning the crowd. He's wearing this tight black T-shirt. The sleeves bunch up above his biceps, and you can see the outline of his chest even from here. His hair is still wet and sticking up at all these weird angles, because he drives to school with his Jeep top off. Still, he looks good. He looks scary. One of the things I like about Clint is that he doesn't try too hard. Half the guys here use hair spray and spend more time in front of the mirror than I do. No one else bids, and I'm about to be sold for the absolute minimum. Of course no one's going to bid against Clint. He should have known that and at least started at ten dollars. A lot of people have gone for ten. Not Jenny Robinson, you can get her cheap.

"Ten dollars!" The voice comes from right below me. It's Damien.

CLINT

10:19 A.M. Assembly period, gymnasium

"Oooh, burn," says Alex.

"What the hell's he doing?" I ask out loud, though I'm really talking to myself.

Alex answers anyway. "Looks like he's makin' a play for Jen."

"Naw, he's just dickin' me . . . bein' funny," I say. I kinda laugh, then I shout.

"Eleven dollars."

And Damien bids fifteen. Now my homie ain't so funny. Now he's makin' me look bad, and I can't understand what he's out to prove. People round me have started payin' attention, and I can hear 'em whisperin'. I can only imagine what they're sayin'. If Damien's not careful he's gonna make people think we've got some weird love triangle goin'. Peculiar thing is, Damien's not even lookin' up here. If he was fuckin' with me, he oughtta be laughin' and pointin' at me.

Mom gave me an extra twenty this mornin' for Slave Day, but I didn't think I was gonna have to spend it all. I didn't 'spect anyone'd be biddin' against me. What the hell. I'll put an end to this now.

"Twenty dollars!"

JENNY

10:20 A.M. Assembly period, gymnasium

I look down at Damien. He's staring at me, and I can tell he's looking for some kind of sign. It's just like one of those cartoons where you see the dollar signs in the character's eyes—except with Damien, they're question marks. I want to disappear. I close my eyes and try to shake my head no as inconspicuously as possible. What is Damien thinking?

"Twenty dollars going once," I hear.

When Damien bid ten dollars, I was honestly thankful. I figured he was doing it so that Clint would have to bid higher, so I would sell for more than the minimum bid. Damien's just that considerate. Besides, I've always been closer to Damien than most girls are with their boyfriend's best friend. We've never fought for Clint's attention or anything like that.

"Twenty dollars going twice."

But when he bid fifteen, everything got freaky. You could hear the crowd start murmuring. Clint must be hyperventilating. I stare out at the bleachers and let my eyes lose their focus. I don't want to look directly at anyone. I've got the feeling that I've still got this smile frozen on my face. What a ditz.

"Sold!" Shawn finally says.

TIFFANY

10:24 A.M. Assembly period, parking lot

Here it is, just where I left it: the pride of the hill country—Robert E. Lee High School, built in 1947, renovated in '51, '69, '83 and, of course, last year. It's not like I'm an architecture groupie. *Everyone* here knows the history of the school. It's almost impossible not to because they haven't torn anything down. The original building is now the English wing. There's no air-conditioning, and the classrooms have got these giant paned windows and flash antique-looking radiators. In the new science wing, there're no windows—just skylights that you can't see out, lab tables you can't write on, and central air that keeps the rooms at a perpetual nipple hard-on frigidity. Daddy opposed the bond election last year that would have paid for a whole new school. "Fiscal responsibility," he said, but come on. He just wanted his alma mater preserved like a fucking shrine.

When they built the new science wing, they also purged a slew of parking spaces. Consequently, I'm parking the Probe (Why couldn't Daddy've been a Lexus dealer instead of Ford) out here in BFE by all the lowriders who don't like anyone parking on either side of them. I've got the only horn on the row that doesn't play "La Cucaracha." I'm running pretty half past for the auction, but handcuff me to the headboard if you think I'm gonna sprint up to the school like some eager freshman. I pull down the sun visor and check my lipstick in the mirror. It's a bit chilly this A.M. for the halter top I'm wearing. I can feel my stomach bumping, but I paid hard-begged lucre for this tan. I'm gonna get some mileage out of it. All I've got with me is a tiny purse containing real ID, fake ID, dinero, pharmaceuticals, car keys. You should check out some of these librarian chicks walking around here with

Hefty bags. What the hell do they keep in there? It can't always be that time of the month. Sure, I've got one big purse, but it's for sneaking bottles into football games and movies.

So I've got the stroll working. Suzi says it's artistry, walking with as much attitude as I do.

I figure, if you got it . . .

As I'm walking, I just imagine I'm the tide and each hip is a wave slapping against the shore. Don't try this at home without first consulting a chiropractor, a priest, and the local obscenity laws.

I roll into the gym and my first thought is that someone died—not a creature is stirring. Everyone has these real glazed-over looks on their faces. I see Suzi and Rainy looking as comatose as everyone else. I go sit by them anyway.

"Where's the beef?" I ask, noticing the scrawnster occupying center stage.

"Done been sold off," answers Rainy. "You missed all the prime cuts. That scrap's all that's left."

"What!?" I say, horrified.

"He's the last one," Rainy says.

BRENDAN

10:27 A.M. Assembly period, gymnasium

I'm up, and all I can think of is Kyle Gallon, my best friend through eighth grade. His family moved to Dallas the summer before our freshman year, and I've only seen him twice since then. Kyle was smarter than anyone I know, even outwhizzed Laurence Davenport. He wasn't great-looking or a jock, but he was cool and everyone knew it. He always knew the right thing to say. In sixth grade he started going with Shanie Fauver, *the* Shanie Fauver. I'm not sure if they ever kissed, but they played handsy-holdsy between classes in front of *everybody*. Anyway, when Kyle was around I never felt stupid. I never felt this uncool.

So, anyway, in seventh grade Kyle's face breaks out really bad. I mean *really* bad. Some of the guys—even some of the girls—

started calling him "Helen" because of his sameality with Mount Saint Helens. But here's the thing: Kyle didn't change at all. He didn't lose an epsilon of confidence—even after Shanie zeroed him. Right before Christmas, our homeroom had a gag-gift exchange and some Hat gave Kyle a bottle of Oxy 10. Everyone cracked up when he opened the package. Kyle didn't get embarrassed at all. He opened the bottle and sniffed the cap as if it was the cork to a wine bottle, then pretended to take a sip, delicately smacking his pursed lips like he was savoring some primo vintage Chardonnay.

"Mmm . . . a rather thin and herbaceous nose, but enchanting notes of pear and melon on the finish. *This* is a revelation!" he gushed in this cheesy French accent. Our classmates either laughed with the joke or shut up because they didn't get it. The next day, Kyle put a bottle of that lice-killing shampoo on the Hat's desk with a big bow on top of it. Our homeroom thought that was even more hilarious. The Hat went ballistic, started threatening Kyle. To this day people still call him *Rid*.

See, if Kyle were here, I wouldn't have any frettage.

But he's not. So I do. Chiefly: Which exit do I flee through when no one bids on me?

"And now for our last slave. This is your final chance to be a slave owner for the day," Shawn Greeley tells the crowd. You can hear the student body collectively sigh. They're bored with the auction by now—not a good sign. "Who will open the bidding for" (Shawn checks his clipboard) "Brendan Young?"

I spot Deena. She's digging through her purse! She's probably seeing if she's got enough money! Have enough . . . have enough . . . have enough . . . Wait, what's that she's taking out? A comb? She turns and says something to that owl-eyed friend of hers. She's laughing about something, but it's not me. She's not even paying attention, which is good because . . .

"One hundred dollars!"

I'm sure it's a joke, but no one's laughing. They're staring at a spot over by the gym doors. I know it's where the voice came from, but something's not right. Tiffany Delvoe is standing in that spot. Tiffany Delvoe, who I've never spoken to before in my life.

Tiffany Delvoe, the girl—no, the woman—who Lloyd's got a picture of taped up in his locker. Five feet eleven inches of tan skin, straight butt-length brunet hair, gravity-defying breastal appendages, and a walk that Lloyd calls the Sexual Preference Checker.

"If you don't get a bit stiff watching that," Lloyd has said on more than one occasion, "you can pretty much bet on being a charter member of the RuPaul fan club."

"Did you say a *hundred* dollars, Tiffany?" Shawn says into the microphone.

She shouts back, "Yeah." Shawn looks back at me, but I'm spying on Deena. She and Owl Eyes are pointing over at Tiffany, their mouths wide open. Virtual cool. Then, in what I think is the funniest part of the day, Shawn reopens the bidding.

"Do I hear a hundred and five?"

I turn and face Annabella Guzaldo. "You only brought in forty-three dollars?"

KEENE

10:32 A.M. Passing period, gymnasium

So what do I do now? A couple people from Mrs. Paulson's class walk up to me and say, "Good plan," after the assembly breaks up, but to call this a plan really stretches the definition of the word. If I *had* a plan, it's over now. I guess that's the reason I hesitate before I walk over to the line where we're supposed to pay for our slaves. I wonder if I've already made my point. Maybe Shawn understands now that slaves didn't get to walk around all day bagging on some superfly master—slaves had to go with whoever bought them.

Playing this out . . . maybe it's a bad idea.

The student council members have gathered in a little cluster near the auctioning podium on the stage. I look for Shawn, but it takes me a minute to find him because he's off to the side. As usual, he's laughing. The two ladies he's talking to are laughing as well, and they keep glancing over here. Must be laughing at me.

"Who's your slave?"

I look down and find that I'm at the front of the line.

"What?"

"Who's your slave?" repeats the councilhead holding a clipboard. "Who did you buy?"

I feel for the wad of bills in my pocket, knowing I haven't proven a thing except that I'm able to throw away Laurence's money.

"Uh, Shawn Greeley."

The collector scans his clipboard and says it'll be thirty dollars. Reluctantly I pull the cash from my pocket and hand it to him.

"All right," he says, "he's all yours."

"Joy."

MR. TWILLEY

10:34 A.M. Passing period, gymnasium

The remaining tedium of the assembly allowed me plenty of time to collect my thoughts and plot a course of action. I must have been three sheets to the wind when I agreed to participate in this event. Well, I've certainly learned my lesson and, as Melville says, "woe to that pilot of the living God who slights it."

I remove a five-dollar bill and approach Denhart once the assembly has run its course. A knot of students are gathered around him, awaiting instructions. I hesitate in hopes that they will disperse, but none do, so I edge my way in.

"Denhart, may I have a word with you?"

"Certainly, Marcus."

I glance about. The students have paused, but their attention is now focused on me.

"I was thinking it might be better for all concerned if I just make a donation—one substantially larger than the bid for me"—I hold up the bill—"rather than play this out over the course of the day. It was obvious to all those who attended that I wasn't in high demand as a slave, anyway."

The students switch their attention to Denhart, who fidgets a bit. I don't understand his reluctance. My solution would bring in more money.

"Marcus, I suppose it would be fine with me," he says, looking around at the assembled children, "if Tommy Parks will agree to it as well."

"Surely you're not saying that I have to get permission from Mr. Parks. You may not realize this, but," I whisper this next part to Denhart, "he failed my class last year." I speak out loud again. "This is simply his way of getting even."

"Well, that's supposed to be part of the fun for the students," Denhart says. "Look, if Tommy doesn't mind, I don't either."

It's at this juncture that Mr. Parks makes his presence known, demanding from the jump-ball circle my immediate service.

"Yo, Mr. T! These books ain't getting any lighter."

And I know that I have no chance of spending the day in peace.

TIFFANY

10:37 A.M. Passing period, gymnasium

I tell Rainy and Suzi to wait while I hand over the C-bill to this council plebe who stuffs it in a big interoffice mail envelope.

"Make sure you put that down under Delvoe Ford," I tell him.

The *Herald* always lists the top Slave Day contributors in its homecoming edition. Daddy's got his campaign ad. My job here is done. The scrawnster I bought pussyfoots over to where I'm standing. He's got his hands stuffed deep in his pockets and he's staring down at my Manolo Blahniks.

"Solids or stripes?" I ask him.

"What?"

"Oh, I'm sorry. Thought you were playing pocket pool."

His left hand comes flying out of his jeans pocket, but his right hand gets stuck for a second. When he manages to get it loose, the white lining of his jeans pocket comes out with it. He looks up at me, takes a breath, and then tucks the pocket back inside his jeans.

I look over to Suz and Rainy and make sure they're catching this. They are. Suz has her eyes covered; Rain's shaking her head. The scrawnster says his name is Brian and offers up his hand.

"You must be stark raving, Brian," I tell him, "if you think I'm shaking that thing. I know where it's been."

He stutters. I leave him there and head to the gym doors. As Suz, Rainy, and I head toward the math building, I quiz Suz on what happened after I bailed last night. She radiates insta-guilt.

"Oh, that Greg came back over and started talking to me."

"Uh-huh . . ."

"And we ended up going for a ride."

"Did you, now?" says Rainy with that fake drama voice she uses all the time. I swear, one day she's gonna talk to me like that, and I'm going to uncork my Mace on her.

I skip right down to the vital info. "What did he drive?"

"Tiffany, it's questions like that that give women a bad name," Rainy spews.

"A Trooper," says Suz.

"New or used?" I ask.

"New."

I think for a second. "There's a nuclear family in his future. He buys his clothes out of the J. Crew catalog. Some day he'll get a golden retriever if he doesn't have one already. Athletic, but not a jock. He's close with his parents. Might get a tattoo, but that'll be his *big* rebellious statement. Overall, I'd say a solid guy. He's not gonna drum for Pearl Jam, but he won't leave you for Courtney Love, either."

"This is sick," quacks Rainy.

"It's their game," I say. "I didn't write the rules. I just learned 'em early."

"But it's so shallow . . . choosing guys because of what they drive."

"Oh, and I've seen you riding shotgun in so many Escorts and Civics," I say. "Besides, I'm not saying you should choose the guy with the hottest car. I'm just saying you can tell a lot about a guy from the car he drives. Women today, we're not left with much to worry about."

"How so?" says Rainy.

"Look. Back in caveman days, our prehistoric sisters had to find the guy who was going to keep the saber-toothed tiger out of the cave, bring home the woolly-mammoth steaks. We went for big and dumb."

"So not a lot's changed," says Suz.

"Some girls will tell you that, nowadays, it's not the biggest club or biggest biceps, necessarily; it's the three C's—cars, clothes, castle. It's the promise of a better future. Me? I say get your own damn stuff, then you can take home the tan windsurfer in the Gremlin."

"I still think that, no matter what car a guy drives, a great personality is . . . ," Rainy starts.

"Color me nauseated," I say. "So, Suz, tell us everything that the boys at the Phi Delt house already know. What sights did you and ol' Greg take in on your little ride?"

SHAWN

10:38 A.M. Passing period, gymnasium

"I don't know, girl," I say, "I just don't think I'd look good in that baby blue. Sure, Jordan went there 'n' all, but he was a country boy at heart. Chapel Hill seemed like a big city to him. Me, I like the sound of UCLA, USC, maybe even St. John's. L.A., the Big Apple—that's where you make a name for yourself."

Cynthia Brown twists another strand of her hair around her finger. Every time she sees some college play on TV she's gotta come up to me and tell me that's where I should play next year. I give her the time of day 'cuz I hear her friend's a freak. So, even though I'm talkin' to Cynthia, I'm playin' her amazon partner.

"What about you, Denise?" I say, smiling and letting my eyes stare all the way into hers. "Where would you like to see me get off?"

Laughter. Much laughter. They think this is even funnier than what I told 'em 'bout Keene Davenport waitin' to play ball, readin' *The Autobiography of Malcolm X* on the sidelines. In the middle of these good times I feel a tap on my shoulder. I turn and—lo and behold—there's the devil I've been speaking of. He's holding out one of his books.

"Let's go," he says.

I turn back to Cynthia and Denise. "Sorry, ladies. Massa here wants his books toted to class."

"Well, you bes' run along, then," says Cynthia. Denise tee-hees some more.

I take Fat Boy's book and make my way to the gym doors where a mob of football players have spontaneously huddled. Meaty-ass hands fly up for automatic high fives as I cut through the group. I look back and notice Keene dodging 'em as he tries to slip out the doors behind me. I take a deep breath and survey the courtyard outside the gym entrance. I let the morning air fill my lungs. The chill means one thing to me: Basketball season is almost here. That's when real life begins, and everything else—school, ladies, recruiting trips, student council—gets put on autopilot. Standing here, I can't help thinking about how the Lee High gym needs a real name. All the Austin schools name their gyms for past coaches and players. You know, Greeley Square Garden has a nice ring to it.

"I've got trig with Coach Preppernau next," says Keene when he finally makes it outside.

"Well, let's move it, then," I say as I head off in the direction of my basketball coach's class.

As I make my way across campus, I work the usuals. I rub Bald Dennis's head for luck. I tell Hat king "Stump" Milton that I'll try to make it out to his deerblind for poker Saturday afternoon. Andy Thistlewaite, our power forward, lets me know these two cheerleaders from Liberty Valley want us to meet 'em at Dairy Queen after tomorrow night's football game. I see *our* head cheerleader, Trinni Rea, leaving the girls gym, so I go on and on about how hype the gym looked for the assembly. I slide by the back door of the cafeteria, where Miss Killarney slips me a hot-out-of-the-oven frosted strawberry surprise cake. As I pass by the office, Mr. Gant lowers his walkie-talkie and yells at me.

"Hey, Shawn! How's that shooting arm feeling? Is it too early to order us a championship banner?"

"Might as well, G.," I answer.

Before he returns to the office, Mr. Gant shoots an imaginary basketball toward me in that old-timey, Bob Cousy–looking, from-the-chest-era way.

"All net, G.," I shout before the door closes behind him.

The Pillsbury Doughboy speaks for the first time during the trip across campus.

"I'm gonna throw up."

By now the tardy bell's rung—not that that's going to be a problem with Coach P.—but we have been pretty much left alone. My first thought is that I should put any thoughts of trying to show me up out of the boy's head. I close in on him and bend down, getting my nose six inches from his.

"You got somethin' to say?"

"Yeah, back off, slave."

I know it looks tough on paper, but the squeaky-voice way it comes outta his mouth, it mights as well have been, *"Please don't hit me, sir."* I try to think what I could do to the Reverend here with one pop, but then I decide it wouldn't be worth it. Bad pub, without a doubt. Naw, I think a better plan is to let the boy hang hisself. It should teach him a lesson: Laughin' gets you farther than whinin'. What's more important—maybe he'll learn that whatever else happens today, when all is said and done, I'll still be me, and he'll still be him.

CLINT

10:38 A.M. Passing period, outside the gym

"What the hell was that all about in there?" I ask Jenny as I hand her my backpack after the assembly.

"What?" she says, like she thinks I'm stupid.

"What was up with Damien?"

"He's *your* friend. Why don't you ask *him*?"

I can tell it's in my best interest to chill; Jen looks pissed.

"Look, Shug," (She knows I'm kiddin' if I call her "Shug") "as my slave for the day, you're gonna have to lose some of that attitude. I don't wanna hafta get out the whip . . . just yet." I kiss the top of her ear.

"Were you really only going to bid five dollars for me?" Jen asks without looking up at me.

I bend down to her eye level and take her chin between my thumb and index finger. I raise her face until her eyes meet mine.

"I thought we could use the extra money to go somewhere special for lunch. Maybe skip the Golden Arches for once and go to Bennigan's or The Olive Garden."

"Clint, I would have sold for less than anyone else up there."

"Seriously, I didn't think that sorta thing was important to you."

"For future reference, it is."

"So now I know."

We look at each other for a few seconds. Jen takes my hands, stands on her tiptoes, and kisses me. Then she wipes her lipstick off my mouth.

"You got my algebra homework?" I ask.

"Yes, master," she says.

BRENDAN

10:44 A.M. Second period, computer science

I just spent ten minutes in the lobby of the inner circle—where cuspy-fine girls say anything right in front of me. It's just like that dream I have where all the lockers are taken in the boys dressing room, so they make me dress out with the girls and nobody notices I'm not one. The whole dance team is stripping down right in front of me, and they're talking about everything that's never made sense to me before: how come they can dance so much better than guys, what they really mean when they say you're cute, why the most assholish guys get the best girls. In my dream it all makes sense. I understand them. But then I realize I'm dreaming, so I tell myself I've got to concentrate, try to remember. That way

I'll still know the secret when I wake up. But it never works.

As soon as Mr. Ramsay is through lecturing, I log onto one of the LONS. The LONS are the terminals that are part of the Lee Online Network System. Every classroom in the building has at least one terminal, but in computer science there are enough computers for everybody. Lee got some huge grant two years ago to install the system, so now we're part of this national pilot program. The mainframe—everyone calls it the Overlord—is in the administration office. From any terminal on campus, you can log on to the Overlord and send mail to anyone at Lee, check your transcript, access any local Internet sites, write and save your own papers, see if a book you need is in the library. You can print out anything you want, because every classroom has its own Laser-Writer. All the clubs set up bulletin boards where they post their agendas, minutes, meeting places, and times. Teachers have home pages where they list homework. Some of them even upload their handouts, so you can print them out whenever you're ready to work on them. You can even access the system from a home computer.

My computer screen name is PPARKER, which is short for Peter Parker, Spiderman's secret identity. I don't tell my password to anyone. Security reasons. After I log on, I see I've got mail from everyone I know. As expected. Even a few people I don't know. This is the one place on campus where I'm right at home. I open up the first piece of mail, the one from Lloyd, aka MENTOR.

BREN,

I'VE ALWAYS WANTED TO KNOW SOME-THING. ★ DO ★ FRIES COME WITH THAT SHAKE?

FROM GANDALF . . .

I'M WRITING "THE BALLAD OF BRENDAN." IS THIS THE CORRECT SPELLING OF ★ COMMONER ★ ?

From the falcon . . .

IS IT TRUE GODDESS DELVOE HAS A TATTOO ON HER BUTT THAT SAYS "BRENDAN FOREVER"?

From r2d2 . . .

TRY NOT TO BREAK HER HEART.

From q . . .

DETAILS! DETAILS! DETAILS!

HAS SHE MADE YOU LICK HER BOOTS CLEAN YET?

Since it would take forever to try to answer everyone separately, I just do a "reply to all" command that instructs everyone to check in at the Dark Side of the Moon—our own hacker bulletin board. I post this message there:

I OUGHT TO PRINT OUT YOUR JUVENILE MAIL AND HAND IT TO TIFF. SHAME, SHAME. IT WOULD PROBABLY CONVINCE HER THAT EVERYTHING SHE BELIEVED ABOUT THE COMPUTER SAVVY (PERPETUALLY HORNY/GEEKY TO THE NTH) WAS TRUE. I WILL KEEP YOU POSTED HERE CONCERNING THE STATE OF THE WORLD. IT'S BETTER THAN LISTENING TO YOU FLAME ALL DAY. AS FOR THE EVENTS OF THIS MORNING, I THINK IT'S OBVIOUS THAT OUR MAYOR'S DAUGHTER RECOGNIZES QUALITY WHEN SHE SEES IT—AND IS WILLING TO PAY FOR IT. ON THE WAY TO CLASS, WE HAD A PLEASANT CONVERSATION CONCERNING THE IMPORTANCE OF AUTOMOBILES IN TEEN CULTURE. HER FRIENDS HAD SOME INTRIGUING INSIGHTS AS WELL.

PPARKER

I go ahead and call up Tiffany's schedule, so I'll know where I'm supposed to go for the rest of the day. We're not supposed to be able to access schedules, grades, discipline reports, and all that, but I cracked that password—CHAMPS78—day one. It's what the only banner we have hanging in the gym says. Do they think they're dealing with pinheads here? You know, it's funny, but Tiffany didn't make me *do* anything on the way to her last class. She didn't have any books to carry. She acted like I was just one of the gang, like it really didn't matter what she said around me.

JENNY

10:46 A.M. Second period, algebra

I think I might die.

I sit right behind Clint in algebra, which makes it convenient in case I need to whisper answers or want to scratch his neck, but sometimes he'll turn all the way around and just face me. Which is what he was doing a minute ago, telling me about the posse's plans to drive down to Mexico for spring break. Then, without so much as a warning, Mrs. Chatfield calls Clint up to the board to work one of last night's homework problems that she's just been explaining. It's the first time all year she's made Clint go to the board, so if he's not prepared, I swear, it's her own fault. These teachers treat football players like the jocks sign their paychecks.

I'm freaking out because we've already turned in today's homework and "Clint" got this one right. What's she going to think when he can't do the first step? I don't think "chalkboard anxiety" is going to play with Chatfield. She's none too happy; I guess she's finally decided she's seen enough of the back of Clint's head.

As Clint walks to the front of the class I notice his fingers crossed behind him. Mrs. Chatfield starts explaining the next problem, but I'm more interested in Clint's progress. It's tough to see how he's doing, though, because his body blocks out his work. Why is it that some of the biggest guys have the tiniest handwriting? He's scratching out something, which I guess is a good sign.

He finishes and sets the chalk back on Chatfield's desk and returns to his desk in front of me. I'm almost afraid to check out his answer, but I take a quick peek.

It's right.

He leans up and whispers in my ear. "Cake."

"That's very good, Clint," Chatfield says. "Would you mind explaining your steps."

"No, ma'am," Clint says. Then he goes through the problem, explaining how he came up with the answer. He even throws in a shortcut that I hadn't thought of. "Oh, and ma'am?"

"Yes, Clint?"

"Sorry about not paying attention."

Gross. Mrs. Chatfield's prison-guard face melts and the corners of her mouth turn up ever so slightly.

There've been a couple of other times where Clint's told me, "You're so much smarter than me" and it's seemed like bull. He does fine in the classes we're not in together. Once he explained to me how much more money I would make by putting my college money in CDs rather than a savings account. He was figuring the rates in his head, just spitting out numbers like a calculator. He was on the honor roll way before we started dating. So why have I been doing his math homework for him every day?

MR. TWILLEY

10:46 A.M. Second period, world history

"Clear your desks and take out a sheet of paper."

Without comment, my students put my instructions into action. Despite my tardiness, every student was in his seat and quiet when I arrived. Never set rules you're afraid to enforce—General Patton said that. Contrary to what students may say, my rules aren't any more severe than most teachers' here. I'm just not afraid to enforce them.

"This pop quiz will cover the reading you were assigned last night. Please use your blank piece of paper as a cover sheet."

My classroom is arranged with five rows of six desks. It's been that way since I began my career here. I place the quizzes on the front desks of each row. The sheets are handed back quietly.

"You have fifteen minutes to complete the quiz."

I stand in the back of the classroom during quizzes. This way, students don't know where I am, and they're more apt to do their own work. Within thirty seconds, the usual suspects have turned over their quizzes and lain their heads down on their desks, accepting with little fight their zeros.

Someone knocks on my door. This is a rare occurrence. I take care of all my clerical duties—roll sheets, excuse notes, field trip forms—promptly. I've even gone so far as to hang a DO NOT DISTURB sign on the door handle. If you're not steadfast, you end up with reporters from the school newspaper knocking on your door to interview students, mothers asking you to give Junior his lunch money, even peers strolling in hoping to borrow chalk. It's a wonder some teachers get anything done. Maybe they don't.

I open the door prepared to give whoever's on the other side a piece of my mind, but it turns out to be William Gant, our principal. I taught him back in '62. He's been my boss for the last eight years.

"Mr. Twilley, I'm sorry to interrupt your class."

"Yes?" I say, hoping this will be quick.

"I thought I ought to tell you that one of the hall monitors just discovered your car's been vandalized out in the faculty lot."

"Did you catch the kids who did it?"

"No," Gant says. "I was hoping you might have some ideas."

This is the fourth time this has happened since the beginning of last year, so I can't say I'm surprised. I'm just hoping that one day they might actually catch one of the little hooligans and hang him.

"I'll give you a list of the students who failed the first six weeks, and I'll highlight the names of the students who I think it might be." I pause, then look at Gant. "It won't do much good, will it?"

"Probably not—not without a witness."

"What did they do to the car?"

"Eggs, shoe polish. They slashed one of the tires." Gant's

walkie-talkie crackles. Someone needs him in the office. "Look, Mr. Twilley, why don't you give me the keys, and I'll have the auto shop kids clean it, detail it, and change out that spare. If you want, we can even trade parking spaces. My spot is right up by the office. No one will mess with your car there."

I hand him the keys to my car. "You can have them clean it, but you keep your own parking space. I won't let them intimidate me, William."

Gant takes the key from my hand, shrugs, and heads back toward the office. I step back toward my door, but I glance in its window before entering, and plain as the nose on my face, Trevor Wilson is leaning over the back of Tamika Jackson, copying off her quiz.

I enter the room purposefully, walk right up to the desk of Tamika, then Trevor. From each I confiscate the quiz. Realizing that I now have the attention of the entire class, I return to my desk, withdraw my red pen, and make a grand sweeping motion that can only mean a zero.

Tamika stands unsteadily, holding on to her desk. "Mr. Twilley," she says, "what are you doing?"

Her voice is shaky, and she has begun tearing up.

"The penalty for cheating is a zero and documentation of the incident that goes in your permanent record," I say evenly.

"But I wasn't cheating!" She begins sobbing.

"Collusion is a type of cheating. You were letting Trevor copy your work."

"No I wasn't. He was just whispering something to me."

"Since when is talking allowed during tests? Also, why weren't you using your cover sheet? Either of these, on their own, could be construed as cheating."

At this point, Tamika covers her face with her hands and somehow makes it to the door. I consider stopping her but decide it's probably best if she visits the lavatory and freshens up, collects her wits. I really am shocked by her behavior this morning. She's normally one of my best students. As the door bangs closed, a few of the students surrounding Trevor begin giggling. No doubt reacting to some comment from the young scholar. It doesn't matter. As Dr. Samuel Johnson has said, "I hope I shall never be deterred from detecting what I think a cheat, by the menaces of a ruffian."

"Pass your quizzes to the front of the room and take out your text. Let's begin."

KEENE

10:51 A.M. Second period, trigonometry

The thing about Coach Preppernau is even though he's a coach, he's the smartest, toughest math teacher in the school. I mean you've gotta have it together to even think about taking one of his classes, but Shawn's reduced him to his minion, sitting at the podium drawing up plays with King Dunk. The man who won't let us turn in homework in anything other than #2 pencil, but he'll let Shawn hotdog on the court like he's a Harlem Globetrotter. Coach looks up from his play diagramming and tells us to work on the odd-numbered problems—the ones with the answers in the back of the book—for the remainder of class. Busywork. Hell with that, I start on the evens. I'll just tell him I got confused. Least this way he'll have to be the one who grades them.

Good thing I'm able to stand up to guys like Shawn Greeley. Like when he got in my face before class. I had to back him down, show him he wasn't going to push me around like one of his usual butt-kissing hangers-on.

It was the only battle I won, though. I wasn't making much of a point by having him carry my book to class. It was tough to tell who was leading whom. I felt like I was in one of those stupid "Family Circus" cartoons where a dotted line shows how come it takes Billy thirty minutes to get home from across the street. Face it. *Shawn* led *me*. I was the one getting an education—Greeley's ABCs of running a campus with nothing but buttery charm and a sweet J. I should consider myself lucky he didn't take us down by the home-ec wing to kiss the babies in the Family Planning Center. If I don't do something about it, Shawn's going to make Slave Day look as harmless as the NAACP.

Whatever else I care to say about Mom, she knows me better

than I know myself sometimes. She knew I would have been happy to write my letter, sit at home all day, then blame everyone who didn't join the boycott for not changing the system. She probably just thought I was being lazy, copping out. Dad may talk the talk in the family, but it was Mom who came down to my junior high and "had words" with the teacher who tried to tell us Malcolm X was a black supremacist who believed in killing white people.

Speaking of Malcolm, what would he do in my position? I have this poster hanging above my bed of Stokely Carmichael and Bobby Seale and these other Black Panthers holding assault rifles. The caption underneath comes from something Malcolm X once said, BY ANY MEANS NECESSARY.

And there it is. My answer. *By Any Means Necessary.*

I finish the last of my even-numbered problems and take the piece of notebook paper up to the front of the classroom, where Coach and Star powwow in X&O bliss. (Apparently, they don't make Shawn go to class anymore.) I ask permission to go to the nurse's office. I take the grunt I receive in response as a yes.

TOMMY

10:52 A.M. Second period, drama

Twilley's gonna need some serious training. Vocal training first. Needs to learn to speak from his diaphragm. That head voice of his was hardly heard when he heralded my arrival to drama class. He's probably used to speaking in his classroom, where he never has to raise his voice, but in this zoo, volume's key. He'll get more chances to introduce me, though. To keep him on his toes, I'm gonna change my title each time. Here at the door he announced me as "His most royal person, the Prince of Tides, the Count of Monte Cristo, Lord Thomas Orin Parks." Miss Amenny is the only one who really paid any attention, though.

"Orin?" she said.

"Top o' the line," I answered, but I don't think she caught it.

See, my initials spell *TOP*. Momma said she did that on purpose, sorta for luck. I've always hoped someone would pick up on it. It'd be a better nickname than Trailer, but what kiss-ass lets you pick your own nickname?

Most of the students in the class are working crew for our fall production of *Tom Jones*. It's my first time to have the lead, and as reward, I don't have to build sets. I usually help anyway. Need to. After all, you know how many thespians it takes to nail two two-by-fours together? The answer's six. No shit. Folks in this class—guys and girls—are handier putting on eyeliner than swinging a hammer.

Way I got into drama in the first place is pretty funny. My sophomore year in English class, we were sent down to the auditorium to watch them do *To Kill a Mockingbird*. The bozo they had playing Atticus kept forgetting his lines, so I would shout out suggestions every time his brain locked up. Suggestions like "Scout, pull my finger" or "Let's go toilet-paper that weirdo neighbor's house." The play sucked, but I was getting big laughs, at least until Miss Amenny had me removed from the auditorium. She met me down at the VP's office and gave me her lecture on theater etiquette. I told her I'd pay better attention if her actors could remember their lines.

"You think you could do better?" she asked.

So here I am.

Not everyone's so happy about it. Rainy Anderson threatened to quit the show if I got the lead. She's been in drama since her freshman year, and she's been getting the female lead since she was a sophomore. Rainy wanted Gil Peyton to get the Tom Jones role. She says it's because I don't have any respect for the theater, but I know it's really because she has to kiss me, and we don't exactly run in the same social circles. I've already plotted my revenge. On closing night she's gonna get my tongue about halfway down to her lungs.

We don't really do any rehearsing during the class period—too many cast members have different drama periods—so the only stuff that gets done is set work. Since I don't have to do any of it, I borrow Miss A.'s keys and open up the costume shop. I love this place.

The room is supposedly organized chronologically, starting with animal skins and ending with these butt-ugly tinfoil spaceman getups. In *Tom Jones* I get to wear some of the flashest shit in here—black capes, black leather riding boots, white gloves—but best of all, a stovepipe hat. I'd just as soon dress in costume every day. You would too if your personal wardrobe was limited to three or four pairs of Wranglers and a dozen promotional T-shirts in assorted sizes. (I got three Marlboro shirts from when they offered them for sending in ten proofs of purchase. Marlboro's Momma's brand.)

I'm browsing the aisles, picking out costumes with potential, when Miss Amenny walks in.

"What are those for, Tommy?" she asks.

"Do you know where I can get a ricksha?"

"A what?"

I try to explain. "A ricksha—one of those gook taxis. You know, they're pulled by a peasant instead of a horse."

"Gook is an offensive word, *Trailer*." She's so subtle.

"Chinese, Japanese, dirty knees, look at these—it's all gook to me."

"Tommy!"

"Sorry, Miss A. Too many afternoon John Wayne movies during my latch-key years. *Sands of Iwo Jima, Operation Pacific*—that's where I learned history."

"I think I see why you failed Mr. Twilley's class, now," Miss Amenny says.

The worst part about failing the class—even worse than having to repeat it this year—was that it kept me out of *Much Ado About Nothing*. I only had a small role, Dogberry, but it was the best role in the play.

"I failed the class because the man's a psychopath."

Miss Amenny gets this sly look on her face. "So he expected you to study, huh?"

". . . *and* do book reports . . . *and* read about a quarter million pages a night, and then, just for good measure, do a fifteen-page research paper. If that isn't enough, the man's an A-hole. He cuts you no slack."

"Tommy!"

"Well, he is."

"I won't let you talk that way. I started teaching the same year as Marcus, and he was the sweetest, most professional colleague you could ask for."

"You've been here as long as Mr. History?"

She nods. I can't believe it. The man's a fossil. Miss Amenny still shows up at the high school dances, and, from what I hear, brings her boogie shoes. She does all these old-fashioned dances to whatever the latest hits are, dragging the male teachers—especially the young coaches—out on the floor with her. Sure, Miss A.'s got some wrinkles, and she always calls herself "that white-haired old lady," but I never would've guessed she's anywhere near Twilley's age.

"He's not even sixty, Tommy."

"And you?"

"I'm twenty-nine." Miss A. flutters her eyelashes and pats the back of her hair. She makes me laugh. I pick up an Indian headdress and pull a toga off a hanger.

"Do we still have that crown, the one with the gold leaves that we used in *Julius Caesar?*" I ask. She digs through a box at the end of the aisle and pulls it out. She flings it at me like a Frisbee. I place it on my head. It's good to be the king.

TIFFANY

11:02 A.M. Passing period, social studies hallway

Brian's waiting for me after class. He looks like a puppy dog. It'd be funny to wing a ball down the hallway and see if he'd fetch it. God, last period I didn't even notice that he followed us all the way to class.

"Hey, Brian," I say.

He mumbles something into his chest, or with this specimen, whatever you'd call the space between his neck and belly.

"What?"

"It's Brendan," he says.

"What's Brendan?"

"I'm Brendan. That's my name. Not Brian."

"Yeah, well, Brendan. Why don't you go ahead and take the day off. Now that I think about it, I don't really need a slave. It was sort of an impulse buy."

Brendan looks crushed. He just stands there while the herd thunders by. Behind him I notice Shawn Greeley picking cotton balls off the floor. He's singing something, but I can't quite make it out.

"Why don't you have me do something? There's no sense in having a slave if you're not gonna make him do anything," Brendan pleads.

I take a look at the boy. My first instinct is to take him shopping. He's wearing Keds, for chrissakes, Wal-Mart jeans, and a digital watch that I'd bet tells him the time on Planet Vulcan. I don't even want to talk about the student council jersey that poofs out and overlaps six inches below his beltline. Funny. His hair isn't bad. All bangs. He could play keyboards for one of those Manchester acid-house bands. Average sophomore complexion, though his pimple cream is starting to flake on him. All things considered, it could be worse. I take out a pen and tell Brendan to hand me his textbook. I jot down my locker number. The only reason I can remember it is that it's 666. No shit. I see that cheerleader Trinni Rea raise her eyebrows at me from across the hall, like she thinks I'm handing out my phone number to this youngster. Fuck it. I grab both Brendan's shoulders, pull him next to me, and whisper my combination to him. I put my lips right next to his ears and exhale heavily as I do it. I wink at Trinni at the same time, like, "Bitch, we'll see if you can steal my man."

"Get my government book and meet me . . ."

"I know where your next class is," Brendan says, his eyes glazed, his smile dreamy.

"Creepy," I tell him.

SHAWN

The way Keene looked at me when he ordered me to do this, you'd've thought he was gonna explode with pride, like he was Christopher Columbus and somebody had just shouted "Land, ho!" I know what Fat Boy was hopin'—that I'd back down in some way, or that I wouldn't do what he said. That I'd suddenly start talkin' like Dikembe Mutombo and say, "My ebony brother, thank you for showing me that what I was taking was the path of darkness." Or some shit like that.

Ain't happening, though.

"De camptown ladies sing dis song," I chirp. The song is my own idea. I smile right up at Keene like I'm a happy child at work. Try all he like, the boy can't manipulate me. He drops cotton balls every few feet down the social studies wing hallway, and I shuffle up behind him and pick 'em off the ground and toss 'em into the paper bag he handed me.

"Doodah. Doodah."

I think he wanted this to be his own little exhibition. He was hopin' to draw a crowd and deliver some message about the suffering of our ancestors, but I've stolen the show. I'm getting the big laughs, not the massa. I got an old Negro trudge goin', and whenever Keene says, "Mind your work," I make my eyes big and white, like black folks' in those old movies where everything seemed to scare the shit out of 'em. Stump Milton and his Hat buddy Carl are laughin' like a couple Ed McMahons.

As we're makin' our way down the hall, people back up against the lockers and howl. Whites, blacks—makes no difference. What's Keene thinkin' now? Maybe it'll cross his mind that the civil rights movement ended twenty years ago. When we make it to the intersection where the social studies and art wings meet—probably the most crowded hallway in the school—Keene starts dropping a bundle of the cotton balls.

"Swing low, sweet chariot, comin' for to carry me home."

And my constituency? They laugh. Slave Day—it's good clean fun.

BRENDAN

No one saw. I'd be legendary right now if one single person I know had been there to see Tiffany Delvoe practically lick my ear. I try not to jog as I make my way to her locker. I've been imagining what I might find in there: desperate-sounding letters from Chris O'Donnell, modeling requests from Italian fashion magazines, uncashed inheritance checks, a dead body. Who knows? I may never forget her combination. Her tongue was like a branding iron searing the numbers directly onto my cerebral cortex. I'm nervous—Pant, pant—as I reach her locker and spin the dial of the combination lock.

I'm dismalated by the actual contents. All her textbooks. None of them covered like they're supposed to be. I pick up the government book Tiffany asked for. As I slide it out, I notice a photo taped to the inside of the door. In other students' lockers this is normal. I mean I can count at least three sophomores I know of who have Tiffany's yearbook photo hanging next to their Cindy Crawfords. You just wouldn't expect it in Tiffany's. But this isn't a teen mag pinup of some superhunk. It's an actual photograph. The shot is blurrified with that fuzzy 1970s color, but you can see an older man with a little girl. They're both bundled up, and the girl is wearing a hood. I guess it must be Tiffany. Maybe her grandfather there with her. The little girl is holding a big gift-wrapped box, and she's got this hungus smile on her face. The kind of smile that it's easier to make when you're little and you don't know about death camps in Bosnia or what really goes on at the dog pound. I guess I've been standing there for a little bit when the warning bell goes off. I take off for the government wing.

TOMMY

Twilley's late to walk me to my next class. He'll pay.

I'm sitting on the steps of the drama room. I've changed into a toga, and I've got the crown of leaves—"laurels," Miss A. says—resting on my head. I'm testing myself. I'm standing just like the statue of *David*, while everyone walks by during the passing period. Rid DeLord hawks up a loogie and launches it at my feet as he passes, but I ignore his ass. I'm in character.

Finally Twilley shows. I see him approaching. I'd like to see a little more hustle out of the man, he's a good five minutes late, but this is going to make our arrival in English all the more worthwhile. He seems puzzled by my posture and costume, but he says nothing. I relax my pose, shadowbox for a moment to just keep Twilley on his toes, blow a snot rocket, then wag my finger at the old coot.

"Time passes. Will you?" I say. Twilley's got a hand-lettered poster hanging by his room clock that says that. I've never understood the connection. I tap my wrist where a Rolex might be, in a parallel universe where Whataburger drive-through tellers are the shit.

"Excuse me?" Twilley says.

"Likely story," I say. "So why are you late?"

The muscles in Twilley's jaw tighten, then release before he answers. "I had to take care of a discipline problem in the office."

"You got a note?"

He picks my books up off the theater steps. "Let's go," he says.

"Are you forgetting something?" I say.

"Such as?"

"*Such as*, who's in charge."

Twilley's jaw muscles threaten to break through his cheek skin this time, but he manages a polite, if sarcastic, tone when he says, "Whenever you're ready, *Your Highness*."

"Saucy," I say. I pantomime a whipping motion. "Hyaaah."

And we're off for English. At first I stay a good ten feet ahead of the man, like he's my gook—sorry, Chinese—wife, but that gets boring. I let him catch up and take a good long look at Twilley, maybe for the first time. Man's bald—or nearly so. He's got that Captain Picard ring of gray. His eyes are wrinkled up, but I guess not any more than Miss A.'s. He wears bifocals. Cheap ones. I'm sure the frames came free with the prescription. Maybe they were flash in '69 or whenever it was he got them. His eyes are a bit on the small side, which gives him his famous weasel look, plus he's got this broom of gray hair shooting out his nose, which any sane single man would yank out. Twilley needs to take a Weed Eater to his. Now that I'm thinking about it, I notice Twilley's taller than I'd imagined. Definitely over six feet. He's got me by a couple inches, but he walks all hunchbacky. I decide that's the part that makes him look so ancient. That and his clothes. He's got on this clownish brown corduroy jacket, a green button-down, and a wide orange and white barbershop-pole striped tie.

The tardy bell rings as we enter the English building. The hallways are nearly empty, so there's no sense in making Twilley perform. Good thing is, Mrs. Paulson'll have the class simmered by the time we get there. Twilley heralding my presence should go over big.

"Remember," I say, "it's 'Lords and ladies—I present to you the Godfather of Soul, the King of Pop, the Legend of Rock and Roll, his Royal Badness, the artist formerly known as Thomas Orin Parks.'"

Twilley stares at me.

"Got it?"

"Got it," he says, flatter than my seventh-grade sisters.

"And try to say it *out loud* this time."

But when we get to the room, no one's there, and I remember that we're supposed to meet in the library today to start working on our research papers. I tell Twilley this, but he starts doing his Igor impression back toward his own classroom rather than the library.

"Hey! Slave! Library's this way." I point to the north entrance.

Twilley stops, rotates, and speaks so quietly that I have to strain to hear him.

"I'm required to be in my class five minutes after the bell. I don't have time to make it to the library. Had you known your class was meeting in the library, I would have been happy to escort you there. Blame this on your inability to pay attention in class. A trait that I see wasn't limited to your study of history." Then he heads back toward his classroom.

"Hey, old man, you were the one who was late!" I shout down the hall, but by the time it's out of my mouth, the giant double doors are swinging shut. "Hope you have a stroke!" I add.

CLINT

11:11 A.M. Third period, field house

"Come in here, boy. Want you to take a look at what you'll be up against tomorrow night." Coach Rossy, our defensive coordinator, calls to me from the Coaches Den. The lights are off, so I know they're lookin' at game film. I drop the load of practice jersey laundry I'm doing—my one and only duty as coach's aide during third period—take my last pure gulp o' fresh air and duck into the room. Secondary coach Coach Lamme and Coach Rossy are both, as usual, smokin' these fat Cubans. I guess they haven't seen the NO SMOKING ANYWHERE ON SCHOOL GROUNDS—STATE LAW sign hangin' in the gym lobby.

"Pull up a chair," Coach Rossy says. "This here just illustrates my point."

"Yes, sir." I try to say it without losing any air.

"Rewind that last play, Lammy," Rossy says, then he zeroes in on me. "You know who that is, don't you?"

Of course I do, dickhead. It's Lamar Jones, 157 yards on sixteen carries against us last year, all–Central Texas as a junior, currently leading the district in total yardage.

"Yes, sir," I answer. On the screen I watch as Jones busts through the Martindale defensive line, hurdles a linebacker who stupidly tries to leg tackle him, jukes the free safety, then starts on a footrace with a cornerback toward the end zone.

Coach Lamme gives the play-by-play. "He . . . could . . . go

". . . all . . . the . . . way." Jones has put five yards between himself and the defensive back by the time he crosses the goal line.

"Now go to the other play we were watching, Lamme," Rossy says. The assistant coach fast-forwards through the next set of downs, then lets the tape run at super slow. "Watch this!" Rossy says, totally stoked.

This time Jones accelerates through a hole that's opened up between the guard and tackle, but just as it looks like there's daylight, the Martindale strong safety closes and about decapitates Jones.

"Hoooooo, doggie!" Rossy says as he slams his fist down on the table. "That's puttin' some leather on 'm. Now, DeFreisz, watch what happens next."

I wanna watch, but Rossy's fist made this Styrofoam cup on the table tip over, and I can feel somethin drippin' down my jeans leg. Shit! It's someone's spittoon. I've got coach saliva runnin' down my leg.

"Pay attention, DeFreisz, this here just proves my point."

"Uh, Coach, can I . . ."

"Righ'cheer. Watch Jones on the next play."

I try to pay attention. This time there's a gapin' hole in the line, but Jones kinda dances around, makes a couple useless jukes in the backfield. By the time he gets to the hole it's closed up. Jones is runnin' straight up.

"My four-year-old girl could tackle 'm the way he's runnin' now," Rossy says.

I can feel the grainy drool hit my sock. I look around for a box of Kleenex and spot Humphrey Brown in the doorway. He's checkin' out the game film, but he's smart enough to stay out in the fresh air. Since he's a senior and the quarterback, his coach's aide duties are even more cush than mine—all he has to do is put away the rubber basketballs that the coaches roll out for all those PE All-Americans.

"Now this just proves mah point, DeFreisz. DeFreisz! Pay attention!"

"Yes, sir."

"You hit one of these brothers hard enough, they just fold.

Like a deck of cards." Rossy makes a church steeple with his fingers and has it crumble to demonstrate his point. I check out Humphrey to see if he's pissed off by Coach's theory, but he's moved outta the doorway. "You gonna do some stickin' tomorrow night?"

"Yes, sir!"

"Gonna put some boys in comas?"

"YES, SIR!"

"Well, then," Rossy says, lookin' pleased and running his thumbs inside the elastic bands of his shorts. "We ain't got nothin' to worry 'bout."

TIFFANY

11:14 A.M. Third period, government

I'm trying to picture Mr. Warren naked.

Word has it that he used to be a high-dollar entertainment lawyer in L.A. Daddy heard out at the club that Mr. Warren was cruising home from a party at Jack Nicholson's the night that big earthquake hit. The car right in front of him plunged into an abyss where there used to be an I-10 overpass. Mr. Warren took the incident as a sign from God and hightailed his ass back to his hometown. Now he's both the most overqualified teacher and most eligible bachelor at Lee.

I haven't figured out yet if I want him, but I've sure been trying to make him uncomfortable while I'm deciding. Since I'm eighteen and can write my own excuse notes, I'll skip, then bring him a letter saying I was seeing my shrink about my nymphomania, or one from my doctor noting that, after extended testing, I was certifiably disease free. Warren gets red-faced and flustered and says, "Tiffany, *please.*"

I aim to.

Still, he hasn't done anything that could get him fired yet. Maybe he's gay. That would serve me right.

Mr. Warren—I call him Bobby when there's no one else

around—has asked me to ask Daddy if he'll come in and speak when we get to the local government chapters. I can just hear ol' Martin now, "I came to Deerfield with nothing but a ten-dollar bill and a truckload of ambition." Your standard rags-to-riches story. (He doesn't mention that he was sixteen at the time and the ten bucks was his allowance.) Do you think he'll include the part about knocking up the richest girl in town? From what I gather, that's the most important step in a quick rise to power. I shouldn't rag on the guy. He took over Grampa's Ford dealership, and within a few years doubled its profits. The only reason he ran for mayor was because the doofus in office blocked a zoning request Daddy made that would have allowed Delvoe Ford to expand its used-car lot into some environmentally protected area of Rio Vista Park.

During that first election, Martin was a man possessed. He outspent the incumbent something like eight to one. There was a DELVOE FOR MAYOR sign driven into every welcome-mat-size patch of grass in town. Now, *there's* an important lesson for the class— money is power. My classmates better learn it now. God knows I have.

I didn't think Daddy was gonna have much to do as mayor once he got the zoning fixed, but he certainly warmed up to the job. Somewhere down the line he decided he liked cutting ribbons at new factory outlet stores. He liked golfing and drinking on the tabs of the Deerfield gentry. He liked being interviewed about local tax problems. He liked it so much that he sold half of the Ford dealership to his friend Mr. Milligan, who he now calls "that Yankee sumbitch." Daddy made a killing, though. Now he only has to make appearances down at the dealership. That Yankee sumbitch sells the cars. Daddy just counts the money.

I tell you one thing. I'm not having Marty come down here in the mood he's been in these last few days. He comes home and just sits out on the porch sipping Wild Turkey. He yelled at me last night for coming home late. Since when did I have a curfew? Most of the time we get along. He was the oldest of four boys, and I've got two older brothers. They're both at Princeton ("Why? Because we can afford it. That's why!"), so I'm, like, the first *girl* he's ever had to deal with. Gotta hand it to him. Marty didn't change. He just treats me like I *am* a boy. Always has. Maybe that's why most girls tend to piss me off—all that silly, fake, giggly bullshit. I can just see through it. The only thing that pisses me off more are the stupid boys here who can't.

TOMMY
11:19 A.M. Third period, library

What kind of library is this, anyway? Nothing about Quentin Tarantino—possibly the greatest artist of his time? *Pulp Fiction, Reservoir Dogs, True Romance?* Man, I'd give up a nut to be in one of his pictures. I could see me now.

T. O. Parks IS Slim Travis—one tough-talking Texan. They took his Lincoln. They took his woman. They took his pool cue. This summer, he's heading to the City of Angels to get his pool cue back!

I had to beg Mrs. Paulson to let me do my paper on Tarantino. She wanted me to do Neil Simon. I pretended I'd never heard of him, just to watch her tear up.

"You won't be able to find anything on Tarantino, Tommy," she warned. But I said I wanted to do it anyway. So far, though, it's looking like she was right. I find one dusty book on filmmaking that talks about the latest technical advancements of *Superman.* The only magazines we get here are *Time* and *Newsweek.* I find an article on violence in films, but it just barely mentions Tarantino. I give up and go ask Mrs. Carlson, the librarian, where I can find anything else. She gets on one of the LONS, punches a few keys, and comes back with a printout of articles.

"They're all available up at the Central library. They won't let you check them out if you're not a student, but you can photocopy them."

"Thanks," I say. Great. When the hell am I going to have time to go up to Central and spend the day in the library? While I'm standing up at the counter I have an idea. "Mrs. Carlson, do you keep all the old *Stars & Bars* somewhere?"

"In the back," she says.

"Can I see them?"

She walks out from behind the counter and motions for me to follow her. She leads me to a door at the back library, unlocks it, and lets me inside what looks like a little meeting room. On shelves along the back wall are all the old copies of the Lee yearbook. I'm dying to see what Father Time and Miss A. looked like all those years ago.

I pick up the first yearbook on the shelf—*Stars & Bars 1922*. It's thin and bound in leather. Flipping through the pages, I check out all these pictures of humans who are supposed to be students. They all look thirty, though, in their coats and bow ties, the girls in their Southern-belle dresses. There are no action photos of anything, just group shots and these huge individual portraits. I check out the faculty pictures. No Twilley, no Miss Amenny. I stop to think. Miss A. said she started teaching when she was twenty-one. To be in *this* book, she'd have to be about a hundred today.

I add forty and pick up the 1962 *S&B*. This one has an index at the back of the book. I'm stunned. There's, like, a million pictures of Twilley listed. I start looking up the pages. There he is in the group shot of the Quiz Bowl team. Here's another of him in a T-shirt. The caption underneath reads EVEN TEACHERS GOT THEIR HANDS DIRTY DURING THE HOMECOMING WEEK HALL-DECORATING CONTEST. MR. TWILLEY, SPONSOR OF THE SOPHOMORE CLASS, PUTS THE FINISHING TOUCHES ON A CLASS OF '64 POSTER. HEY, MR. HISTORY, LOOKS LIKE YOU SPELLED A WORD WRONG!

They called him Mr. History then? Why? He doesn't look much older than the students in these pictures, all of them in their buzz haircuts. Twilley, with a full head of hair, has a paint brush in his hand and paint running down his arms. I find another shot of him with a leg of chicken in his mouth at the faculty/student picnic. Sitting across from him is Miss A. Wow, not too shabby. All the other women teachers I've seen have their hair up in these Super Glue hairdos, but Miss A. looks like Nancy Sinatra from that video they show all the time. The one about boots. Her hair is long, full, and straight. Miss A. looks, well . . . groovy.

I start going through the books one by one. I can't believe it's the same guy in these pictures that wouldn't allow the Spanish Club to collect canned foods in his room at Christmas last year, because he said it wasted class time. In the 1965 book I find a shot of him wearing a Stetson and a fake mustache. He's untying Miss A., who's in a petticoat and a bonnet. The caption says IN THE PRODUCTION *DIRK SNIDELY MEETS THE PECOS KID*, THE FACULTY SHOWED OFF A WIDE RANGE OF ACTING TALENT. HERE THE PECOS KID, MR. TWILLEY, RESCUES ZELDA PETTICOATS, MISS AMENNY, FROM THE CLUTCHES OF DIRK SNIDELY, MR. HAWTHORNE. MISS AMENNY SAID SHE WANTS THE FACULTY PLAY TO BECOME AN ANNUAL EVENT.

In the 1966 book there's a shot of Mr. Twilley giving a student a piggyback ride during—get this—Slave Day. In the 1968 book I start seeing shots of black students. I hadn't even noticed that there hadn't been any before that. In 1971 Twilley wins the favorite teacher award, and I'm positive that I have been sucked into the Twilight Zone.

In the 1972 book, there's a photograph of Twilley—he's got huge sideburns—standing next to Mrs. Twilley, except her name in the caption is Esther Harris. The caption says MISS HARRIS COVERS THE ROMANTIC PERIOD OF WORLD LITERATURE FOR MR. TWILLEY. In the 1974 book, Miss Harris has become Mrs. Twilley. Twilley wins the favorite teacher award again that year.

In the 1976 book I discover it.

You know there are certain things you believe in that make you who you are. Take me. I believe in things I can see. Rivers flow downhill. Fries take three minutes to deep fry. Rid DeLord has three nipples. But what I see here could change my whole philosophy. You see, I'm not sure I can believe this, even though it's right in front of me, in living color. The caption says MR. TWILLEY RELENTS TO PRESSURE FROM THE STUDENT BODY TO PERFORM AT THE NOPE TO DOPE ASSEMBLY. HE SAYS HE LEARNED HIS ACT AS A YELL LEADER AT OL' MISS. And in the photo, plain as day, Twilley's forming an *R* with his body.

Martians killed Elvis. Santa Claus lands on the roof of our trailer every Christmas. Yale Drama School is going to offer me a full scholarship. And Mr. History . . . he was the first Speller.

BRENDAN

Almost as soon as I sit down at one of the LONS to start writing captions for my school carnival photos, Deena comes strolling over. Win, Win.

"Is it true that you're cousins with Tiffany Delvoe?" she asks.

"No," I say, shifting into industrious mode. "We're just friends. That's all."

"A hundred dollars—that sure is a lot of money," Deena says. I shrug.

Lloyd laughed at me for signing up for yearbook. He said I was a major socialite wanna-be. Not true. I just knew that Deena had signed up for the class. I waited until she turned in her choice sheet last spring, then I hacked into the schedule bank. Deena keeps standing next to me. She's so perfectly pretty. Now, I don't mean perfect like Tiffany or Annabella are perfect. I mean perfect like "exactly right." For me, that is. She's short—real short. Barely five feet. She has dark, shoulder-length hair, and her face is made up of all these small elf parts: thin lips, tiny nose, penny-size green eyes. I know the way I'm describing her she might not sound pretty, but she is. Best of all, she's got a flaw. Just like a Shakespearean hero. See, one of her two front teeth is dead, so it's gray. Grosses out some guys—including Lloyd—but I don't mind.

Damien Collier, our editor, approaches us. I know he's been uptight about deadline, but today he's Mr. Perpetual Motion.

"So what are y'all working on?" he says, knowing full well that we're just talking.

"Deena's helping me with my captions," I say. Deena expresses thanks with her tiny eyes.

"Cool," says Damien. Then, unexpectedly, he sits down at the LONS next to me. I look at Deena.

"I guess I can take it from here," I say.

"Okay," she says. "Let me know if you need any more help." Then she returns to her seat.

Damien starts typing insanishly. I'm thinking Deena and I

might've pulled off the deceptification when Damien mutters, "Women." Guess not. I look down at the first carnival photo and see it's of Blimp Stimmons throwing a paper airplane through a hula hoop. At most schools you could just write a caption that says SOPHOMORE RANDY STIMMONS THROWS A PAPER AIRPLANE THROUGH A HULA HOOP and be done with it. Not if you work for the *Stars & Bars*. Damien has lectured on caption writing a zillion times.

"Anyone can look at a photo and see what's going on. Your job is to tell the reader the story behind the picture. Tell them something they can't see for themselves!" he says.

Okay. How 'bout . . .

IN JUNIOR HIGH, BLIMP STIMMONS WAS YOUR GENERIC, PUDDING-GUTTED, INVISIBLE, PIMPLE-FACED LEPER. HE WAS A BUDDY, THOUGH. A COUPLE YEARS WITH A WEIGHT SET AND AN EXPENSIVE DERMATOLOGIST TURNED HIM INTO THE VARSITY-FOOTBALL-PLAYING BLOCKHEAD WE ALL KNOW AND DESPISE TODAY. HERE HE TOSSES PAPER AIRPLANES THROUGH A HULA HOOP OBLIVIOUS TO THE FACT THAT HIS GIRLFRIEND IS OUT COPULATING WITH TIMM TRIMBLE.

I'm pretty sure that won't make it in the book, but Damien might get a good laugh out of it. I look next to me, and I'm surprised to see he's already gone. What the hey. I call up the Dark Side of the Moon. Let's see what the intelligentsia have to say.

Ah, yes. I should have known they wouldn't let me down.

First of all, Lloyd has begun a list of Possible Reasons Tiffany Delvoe spent $100 on Brendan Young. My favorites . . .

⋆ *SHE MISUNDERSTOOD SOMEONE MARVELING OVER THE SIZE OF BRENDAN'S HARD "DISK"—THE FALCON*

⋆ *NO ONE'S TOLD HER THE REAL REASON WE CALL BRENDAN "MICROSOFT"—Q*

I also discover that my so-called friends have set up a betting board revolving around my performance for the day. I'm getting even money on "sitting on her bed." Everything else goes rapidly downhill. My "making it" with Tiffany is paying out at a thousand to one (minimum bet—one dollar), kissing her (above the ankle) pays ten to one, her kissing me (anywhere) goes up to twenty to one. Other milestones: holding hands at school (twenty to one), second date (thirty to one), Tiffany sitting in Brendan's lap (ten to one), Brendan sitting in Tiffany's lap (two to one).

I post a new memo:

LAMOIDS,

F.Y.I. TIFFANY HAS ALREADY KISSED ME. I CAN STILL FEEL THE HOT TRAIL OF HER SALIVA RUNNING FROM MY JAWBONE TO EARLOBE. SHE CAN BARELY KEEP HER HANDS TO HERSELF. CAN YOU BLAME THE POOR GIRL? SHE'S ONLY HUMAN.

KEENE

11:29 A.M. Third period, typing

"I almost didn't come to school today."

I look up from my typing workbook. Speaking to me is Sleepy Roberts. This is shocking for any number of reasons: First, Sleepy is rarely awake during the school day; second, this is the third class I've had with him, but it's the first time I've heard him talk. Even though Sleepy's tall and bony, his voice comes out sounding like Barry White's.

"Why?" I ask, wondering why he ever comes at all.

"I read your letter. I dug it."

"So what made you decide to show up?"

"I knew it wouldn't work," he says.

"Why not?" I ask, way too defensively for a person who didn't participate in his own boycott.

"Because no letter's gonna get a bunch of redneck administrators and retired-Klan school board members to change their racist traditions."

The most common rumor about Sleepy is that he's a twenty-something-year-old who's failed three or four times, but I've heard other stories: One, that he got kicked out of private school because someone caught him making a bomb in his dorm room; and another, that he's the illegitimate child of an African monarch sent away for an education in America. He doesn't have an accent, Texan or foreign, but he is darker than anyone here. He makes me look Swedish. I think he's going to say more, but he just stands there staring at me like he's never laid eyes on me before.

Eventually, Sleepy pulls up a chair from the empty desk next to mine and continues to enlighten me about Southern politics.

"If you want to get them to get rid of Slave Day, you're going to have to hit them with something they care about. Now, do you think they really give a shit whether a bunch of colored nobodies no-show for a day?"

"Well it makes a statement . . ."

"Twenty-four hours later that statement wouldn't mean dick to anyone who could actually change anything."

"So we just live with it? Laugh it off each year?"

I wouldn't have thought it possible, but Sleepy's voice gets even lower. "No," he says, "we figure out something they do care about, and we aim there." I'm trying to figure out what he means by that, when Sleepy leans closer to me. "You know, you got some people on your side out there before class."

"You think?"

At first I was sure my cotton plan had backfired on me. I thought Shawn had put on such a minstrel show that everyone was too entertained to get the point. But then, right at the end, I had a feeling he pushed it too far. By the time we reached the foyer not everyone was laughing. I was watching the eyes of some of our brothers and sisters who didn't think much of Shawn's act. Maybe some of them had started out laughing, but if they watched it too long, their expressions began to change. Now that I think about it, I can remember Sleepy—Kool & The Gang Afro and all—glaring at Shawn.

Shawn gloated afterward and offered to "get me some lemonade from the big house." It was clear that he thought he'd had the last word.

I look at Sleepy, and I know Shawn was wrong.

JENNY

11:32 A.M. Third period, yearbook

You know how, if you watch one of those *National Geographic* shows where they show you some animal you've never heard of, and they talk about how this animal thrives in the desert because that's the only place where this certain beetle that the animal eats lives? Well, that's Damien in the yearbook room. This is where Damien thrives.

I want to talk to him, but he's cruising around, making sure everyone's doing something constructive. Our first deadline is a week from tomorrow. The way he handles people—it's amazing. It needs to be, because you know Mr. McCartney isn't gonna crack the whip. McCartney even gave Damien a key to the room, so that he could come up here and work anytime. So there goes Damien: helping Roberto with his French Club story, showing Everly and Kim for the eighth time how to number the mugshots, telling Eric which photos he needed printed yesterday. If I told Eric I needed something ASAP, he'd say, "Blow me," and I'd get the shots a week later. But with Damien, it's like, "No problem, boss."

When he's here, in this room, he's got everybody's respect and he knows how to use it. It's when he's out with Clint, or worse, Clint and Alex, that he crashes and burns. He tries too hard. Clint and Alex listen to all that rap stuff and end up talking like the Beastie Boys. Damien just ends up sounding dumb . . . well, dumber. On top of that, Damien's not a big guy, but he tries to keep up when those two start drinking. It seems like Damien's always the guy they end up having to drive home and put to bed. He's been drinking a lot lately, even though those other two quit: Clint because of his promise to me, and Alex out of respect for football season.

Last year in Mrs. Sessom's English class, I made the mistake of saying out loud that it was ironic that Damien Collier, Alex Clayton, and Clint DeFreisz all ended up sitting next to one another. (She puts everyone in alphabetical rows.) Mrs. Sessom heard me. She says, "Honey, there's nothing ironic about that. It's just coincidence. Irony is when words convey the opposite of their intended meaning."

"Oh," I said.

"It's like when you call a huge man Tiny," she explained further.

"Or like when we call Damien the Beast," Clint added, high-fiving Alex.

So that's how I remember what irony is—Damien being the Beast. He got the name because of all those *Omen* movies where the devil was supposedly named Damien, and they kept referring to him as "the beast." But our Damien is the furthest thing from a beast. He's always polite. He looks at you when you're talking to him. You can tell he's really listening to every word and thinking about what you say.

The three of them have been friends since Boy Scouts. There's a picture of their troop hanging up at Clint's. They've never grown apart. That's amazing in some ways, because they all have completely different life plans. Alex is going to go to Central and get a degree in whatever will make him enough money to raise a family and play golf every weekend. He may never leave Deerfield. Clint wants a scholarship offer to a major college, "One where ESPN gives the highlights *every* week." There he plans to study sports medicine. When he was a freshman he snapped a tendon playing ball. *"It sounded like a cork popping out of a champagne bottle."*—he's said that a hundred times. He had arthroscopic surgery and was back in the lineup four weeks later. Anyway, it was this miracle of science that gave Clint his calling as a healer.

Damien says all he wants is to see the world.

"Not like a tourist, though," he says. "I want to work and live overseas. Argue politics on the Champs-Elysées. Have affairs in Barcelona with women named Isabella and Carmen. Swill Guinness in a Dublin pub."

Like he has enough guts to skip college. We'll see.

I'll hand it to Clint; he's never deserted his friends. Even after he became a big-time jock. Last year, when he was the only sophomore on the team, he kept getting invited to senior parties, plus a couple of the older guys really wanted to take him under their wings, but Clint just shrugged off all the attention, kept hanging with his buds, didn't go anywhere that Alex and Damien weren't welcome.

So then, what was Damien thinking when he was bidding on me today? That's what I need to talk to him about.

But Damien's in his editor zone. Now he's working on the computers. Maybe if I sit here looking confused about this layout he'll rush over to see what's wrong. Normally Damien and I either hang out or work together (I'm the Student Life section editor) all period, but today he hasn't said one word to me. I watch him as he grabs something out of the printer, reads it to himself, folds it, writes something on it, and puts it in his pocket. He tells Mr. McCartney he's leaving to do interviews (for what?). It looks like I won't talk to him all period. He grabs his Goodwill-special sports jacket and pushes his glasses back up his nose, but before he walks out the door, he fishes the paper out of his pocket and sets it in front of me. I read what he's written on the outside.

READ THIS, THEN DESTROY IT.

KEENE

11:39 A.M. Third period, library

I got permission to come to the library after Sleepy helped me come up with a plan. We decided my job for the day was to use Shawn to raise grassroots consciousness. We had to think for a while to come up with something as showy as we wanted. When we finally had an idea, I asked Sleepy if he thought we were going too far.

"How could we?" he said.

But I'm wondering again as I search the index of one of the Robert E. Lee biographies I've found.

"See, what you don't understand," Sleepy explained earlier, "is that Shawn's the kind of guy who wants it both ways. He's even more afraid of upsetting white people than his own kind."

Still . . .

Everyone knows Robert E. Lee, the guy with his picture up all over the school, was a general for the Confederacy and that he was a slave owner, but what's less known is that he made a number of speeches about slavery as well. Speeches that compared blacks to livestock. At least that's what Sleepy says. That's the sort of thing I'm looking for now, but I'm not having any luck. I'm not surprised, since all three biographies the library has available were written before 1959. Every one of them talks about what a great man and patriot Robert E. Lee was. How was he a patriot? More people died in the Civil War—lots of them because of what he did—than in any other U.S. war. And what for? So a bunch of rich Southerners could keep getting their tobacco harvested for free. Not exactly my definition of a patriot. John Brown tries to arm the slaves, and we're taught he was a madman.

I'm waiting in line to get help finding some newer articles, but Miss Carlson's spending all her time with that cowboy Speller. Behind the counter I notice Tamika Jackson with her head in a book. The pin on her shirt says LIBRARY AIDE, so I'm tempted to ask her for help, but she's got this glassy look in her eyes that makes me afraid of interrupting her reading. I was in the same AP English class as Tamika last year. I hardly ever talked to her, but I feel like I know her through her essays. Mr. Sullivan had Tamika stand up and read everything she wrote.

When she would finish reading, Mr. Sullivan would give the class a lecture about how if we put more time, effort, "and most importantly . . . heart" into our work, we would one day deserve to breathe the same air as Tamika Jackson. You'd think that after all that, people would tend to hate the sister, but no one did. I think everyone looked forward to hearing her stories. She *did* write with more heart than any of the rest of us.

I remember this story she wrote about a popular boy she fell in love with in seventh grade who didn't know she was alive. Every day she goes to school and figures out random, funny ways of making him notice her. Everyone laughed when she read it, but when she finished, a few of the girls were crying and I was trying hard not to. It was just so sad. It's the kind of story that probably everyone, especially me, has lived out, but she was able to make everyone experience it again in their heads.

I used to think a lot about her last year, when we were in the same class. I mean, she really seemed to have it together. Plus—and I'm not just saying this—she's one of the finest girls in school. She's got these Chinese eyes that make her look exotic. Half the time her hair's in cornrows, like today, and she dresses like a Gypsy with all these scarves and earrings that go all the way around one of her ears.

I usually make it a practice to not think too much about high school girls. It seems like most of the sisters here won't even talk to you unless you're on some sports team. College is going to be different. In college, girls start looking for different things: a good mind, values, someone who doesn't want to play the whole planet. At least that's what Mom told me. Dad said I ought to go out for the basketball team. For a while I went to the park and played some, but it wasn't really working, so I would tell him I was going to play, but I'd take a book with me and read instead. Somewhere along the line we came to an understanding.

I guess one of the best things about Tamika is that I always got the feeling that she was more interested in what was going on inside a person than what they could do with a ball in their hands. A couple times in English we had to peer-edit each other's papers, and I'd scan her whole essay looking for a place I could underline a linking verb or suggest a comma. Usually without any luck. She'd bring me my paper back after she'd read it, and she'd ask me what I wanted the reader to learn from the story. Then she'd tell me what she took away from it, and if the two didn't match, she'd suggest ways of getting my point across. Now, I'm a capable writer, but I promise you, the best papers I turned in to Mr. Sullivan all year were the ones Tamika helped me with.

She looks up and catches me staring at her.

"Hi, Keene," she says, wiping her eyes. "Can I help you find something?"

First off—she knows my name. I wasn't sure.

"Uh, yeah, uh, I'm looking, uh, for, uh, something by Robert E. Lee. Or, uh, I mean, uh, *about* Robert E. Lee." I hold up the biographies I've found. "These are pretty old."

Tamika takes the books from my hands and checks the copyright dates. "We've got some newer stuff in the back," she says, walking out from behind the counter. I follow her to the far wall of the library. She pulls out the encyclopedia of biographies and starts to look up Lee, but before she can find him, tears start streaming out of her eyes and she has to cover her face with her hand.

"What's wrong?" I say. "Look, it's not that important. I could do my report on someone else."

"It's not that," she says, trying to stop sobbing. "They're going to kick me out of National Honor Society."

That takes a second to sink in. What does it have to do, after all, with Robert E. Lee? And how could Tamika Jackson be getting kicked out of National Honor Society? She's probably the best English student in the school, *and* she gets good grades in everything.

"Why?" I ask.

"They said I was cheating."

"Who said that?" I ask.

"Mr. Twilley," she says. That, at least, makes sense. The man is a good teacher, but, Lord, is he paranoid about cheating. "This ruins everything," Tamika adds. I step forward and put a hand on her shoulder and she just sort of melts into my arms. Cool.

Tamika sniffles, and I wish I had a handkerchief that I could pull out of my pocket, but naturally I don't. I rub her shoulders in a reassuring way, not like I'm operating. The Speller guy walks back past the bookshelf that shields us from the rest of the library, and I kind of jump back from Tamika. That probably makes me look like I'm doing something I shouldn't be doing. I can be such a spaz sometimes.

It occurs to me that the only reason I've shown up for NHS meetings for the past year is because Tamika was always there. Maybe I'll quit in protest. *Good thinking, Keene, that would leave three black students in the group.*

You know, now that I think about it, Tamika is the only *female* of color in all of the honor society. What's up with that? Maybe if we had some multicultural education around this place, we'd be represented properly. Every year the number of black students in the honors program seems to get cut in half. When I was a freshman, we had a good mix, but now it's, like, a sea of white faces. And what about our *faculty* representation here? Three black teachers and one teaches drivers ed, one coaches JV basketball, and one monitors the in-school suspension program. Most of the black faces we see on campus belong to the custodial staff and the lunchroom ladies.

By any means necessary.

I tell Tamika I don't need the Robert E. Lee books.

I don't need to know the facts for the speech I'm going to write. More than two hundred years of white American history has shown me one thing. The ends *do* justify the means.

CLINT

11:47 A.M. Third period, field house

I'm sitting in my drawers, just starin' at the dryer spinning round 'n' round waitin' on forty practice jerseys and my Skoal-stained 501s, when Humphrey walks in the laundry room. He sits there for a minute without sayin' anything, but that's pretty standard behavior. He's what they call a "quiet leader." He doesn't hop up 'n' down or slap butts like some guys. He leads the team in touchdowns, but when he scores, he doesn't high-step or dance or rip his helmet off and pose in front of the crowd.

Trim, on the other hand, kneels and crosses himself in the end zone, like God himself chose to award his devout follower a chance to get more boo-tay. Boy ain't seen the inside of a church since he went out with Leslie Aitken, daughter of Pastor Aitken, long enough to "teach her how to drive standard." That's what Trim calls it. You figure it out.

(A word here about end zone celebrations: I won't tolerate them. If you're lucky enough to score on the mighty Rebel D., just hand the ball to the ref, and get back to your huddle. Once, a Pflugerville tight end made the mistake of pointing at me as he danced across the goal line. The next time he came across the middle I got a flipper up under his face mask. Cost us fifteen yards, but they had to bring a stretcher out. There was no more dancin'.)

Anyway, we're sittin' there, me and H. B., and I know somethin's on his mind. He's pickin' at a sticker on the side of his helmet. On the back of his "hat"—that's what the coaches call 'em—he's got about a million little Confederate flags that we get for amazing plays. I got a bunch myself, but not nearly as many as Humphrey. Finally, he speaks.

"What do you s'pose Coach meant in there?"

"'Bout what?"

"That part about, 'if you hit a brother hard enough, he just folds'?"

I sit there perplexed. Coach talks like that to the defense all the time. I've just never thought too much about it. Now that I'm thinkin', it's making me uncomfortable.

"Naw, you don't have to answer that," Humphrey says. "I know what he meant by it." He peels off one of his Confederate flag stickers and begins working on another.

"Coach didn't mean nothin'," I say. "He's just talkin' 'bout any team's runnin' backs. It just so happens that most of 'em are brothers. I wouldn't take it personal."

Humphrey doesn't say anything. He just peels off another one of his Confederate flags, sticks it on the side of the dryer, and walks out of the room.

JENNY

11:49 A.M. Third period, yearbook

I wait until Damien has been gone a few minutes before I even think about unfolding the note. I check to make sure no one is reading over my shoulder. That's just what I'd need. Yearbook attracts all the major socialites at Lee. Gossip would be all over campus within seconds. Confident I can read in peace, I begin unfolding.

JEN,

I'D LIKE TO BEGIN BY APOLOGIZING IF I EMBAR-RASSED YOU DURING TODAY'S ASSEMBLY. MY ORIGI-NAL GOAL WAS TO KEEP YOU FROM BEING EMBAR-RASSED. I DIDN'T WANT TO SEE YOU SOLD FOR THE ABSOLUTE MINIMUM. SO WHY DID I KEEP BIDDING PAST TEN DOLLARS? THAT'S WHAT I'LL TRY TO ANSWER HERE.

DID YOU EVER READ CYRANO DE BERGERAC? IT'S A FRENCH NOVEL ABOUT THIS BADASS SWORD FIGHTER WHO'S GOT A COLOSSAL NOSE. HE'S IN LOVE WITH A GIRL NAMED ROXANE, BUT HE KNOWS SHE'LL NEVER LOVE HIM. AT FIRST, ALL CYRANO WANTS TO DO IS MAKE ROXANE HAPPY, SO HE HELPS OUT THIS GUY WHO HE'S SURE ROXANE DIGS. SEE, CYRANO CAN-NOT ONLY WHIP SOME ASS, HE'S A SERIOUS POET. HE GIVES THIS GUY THE WORDS HE'LL NEED TO SEDUCE ROXANE, EVEN THOUGH IT BREAKS HIS HEART. EVENTUALLY HE FIGURES OUT HE SHOULD HAVE MADE HIS OWN PLAY FOR ROXANE, BUT BY THEN IT'S TOO LATE. HE DIES MISERABLE AND ALONE.

I'M HOPING TO AVOID THAT, SO I GUESS IT'S CON-FESSION TIME . . .

THOSE POEMS THAT CLINT LEFT ON YOUR ANSWER-ING MACHINE—I WROTE THEM. AND IT WASN'T LIKE I TRIED TO PUT MYSELF IN CLINT'S 14EEEES. THEY CAME FROM THE HEART. THEY WERE MY THOUGHTS, MY FEELINGS.

AND ANOTHER THING. I WASN'T REALLY AS DRUNK AS I WAS PRETENDING TO BE THE NIGHT I LET THE CAT OUT OF THE BAG ABOUT THE TRIP OUT TO CANYON LAKE. I GUESS I HELPED CLINT GET YOU BACK—AT LEAST PARTLY—BECAUSE I FELT SO GUILTY. THAT WAS,

UNTIL NOW, THE WORST THING I'VE EVER DONE.

I'M NOT GOING TO LIE TO YOU ANYMORE. FIRST OF ALL, CLINT IS A GREAT GUY. HE'S THE BEST FRIEND I'VE GOT, AND I KNOW IF THE SITUATION WAS REVERSED, HE WOULD NEVER BE DOING WHAT I'M DOING NOW. HE'S LOYAL TO HIS FRIENDS, THAT'S A GIVEN. CLINT'S PROTECTED ME WHEN GUYS HAVE WANTED TO KICK MY ASS, TAKEN CARE OF ME WHEN I'VE BEEN DRUNK, ENCOURAGED ME WHEN I START TALKING ABOUT BEING SOME GREAT WORLD TRAVELER. BUT THAT'S WHAT HE'S DONE FOR ME. MY QUESTION IS, WHAT DOES HE DO FOR YOU?

I KNOW THAT BEFORE THE END OF THE DAY I'M GOING TO RUN INTO CLINT. IF YOU'VE SHOWN HIM THIS LETTER, I WON'T HAVE TIME TO EXPLAIN. HE'LL CUT ME OUT OF HIS LIFE WITHOUT A SECOND THOUGHT. EVEN IF YOU DON'T TELL HIM ABOUT THIS, I'LL PROBABLY HAVE TO LIE TO HIM ABOUT THE ASSEMBLY, SAY I WAS JUST GOOFING OFF.

IF YOU DON'T HAVE THE SAME FEELINGS FOR ME THAT I DO FOR YOU, TRY TO PRETEND THIS NEVER HAPPENED. AT LEAST I'LL SLEEP BETTER KNOWING I TRIED. IF, HOWEVER, YOU DO HAVE FEELINGS FOR ME, MEET ME HERE IN THE YEARBOOK ROOM AFTER THE BONFIRE.

DAMIEN

I know I should destroy the note right now. Destroy the note and tell Damien that I'm in love with my boyfriend. But I don't. I fold the note back up and stick it in my purse.

Five minutes left in class—time to meet Clint.

TIFFANY

11:55 A.M. Third period, government

My pager starts vibrating at the same time the bell rings. I check the number. Stellar. It's this guy—Ian's his name—that I met up in Austin at a party last weekend. Eighth call in five days. I've been letting him dangle. He's a film student. He says he wants to put me in his movie.

I get up to leave and notice my eager peon waiting for me at the door. He pulls along beside me as we head for the double doors. When we get outside the building, I stop.

"Shit! Hey, Brian, I left my government book on my desk. Would you mind going back for it?"

"Uh-uh," he says, and he bounds back to Mr. Warren's classroom. I take a detour toward the pay phones in the courtyard. Both phones are busy, but I hover over some freshman girl who's yammering to her junior high boyfriend. She gets the point soon enough and tells "Baby" she'll see him after school at the bowling alley. Young love. It makes me misty.

I dig through my purse, but all I come up with is thirty-five cents. Not enough for a call to Austin. I never have change. I always put it in those jars for "Jerry's Kids" or leukemia victims or starving Guatemalans—whatever. I'm a saint.

I notice that sleuthdog Brian's tracked me. He's standing there watching me scavenge my purse. "You got any change, Brian?" I ask.

"It's Brendan," he says.

Right.

"Dial this number," he says. Then he starts spouting digits while I punch the matching buttons. After the tenth or eleventh, he says, "All right, now. You should have a dial tone."

Sure enough, it's there.

"Is that your calling-card number?" I ask.

"It's *a* calling-card number," he answers cryptically.

After seven rings, Scorsese Jr. answers. "Yello," he says.

"It's Tiffany. You paged?"

Ian says he wants to have a business lunch with me. Discuss a shooting schedule. Get me a script. "Are you free?" he asks.

"Tell me about the part again."

"Oh, Lou Ann? She's got a big heart."

"That's it—a big heart?"

"And a drawl. Think of Laura Dern in *Wild at Heart*. Lou Ann's simple yet complex. She stands by her man, but she's her own woman."

Sounds familiar. But I don't really want to go to trig anyway, so I agree to meet E. T. at Mad Dog's, a hamburger palace on the Drag.

I head toward the parking lot. Brian hesitates.

"Isn't your class this way?"

"Yeah, but Austin is this way," I say, pointing north. I keep walking. I don't hear any footsteps behind me, so I assume my boy is staying on the plantation. Momentarily I catch the distinctive sound of Keds slapping concrete. Brian's sprinting to catch up.

CLINT

11:56 A.M. Passing period, near field house

What'd I do wrong this time? Jen's walkin' me to class, but she's givin' me the silent treatment.

"I order you to speak," I say.

She barks a couple times, then hangs out her tongue and starts panting. Now this may sound like it was playful, but she wasn't smilin' or lookin' at me. Then, talk about piss-poor timing, Angie walks by and winks. What a bitch!

Jen lets go of my hand and puts three or four feet between us.

"What're you doin'?" I ask. This time *I'm* pretendin' I'm stupid.

"I saw that," she says.

"You didn't see me do anything. I can't control what she does."

"You must not have made it very clear to her that you've

got a girlfriend," Jenny says, lookin' dead ahead.

"Believe me, it's clear to everyone in this school that I've got a girlfriend."

"I can think of two people it wasn't very clear to this summer."

I am so sick of this jealous-girlfriend act. I take Jenny's shoulders in my hands and try not to sound pissed—just frustrated. "How many times am I gonna hafta say I'm sorry for that? I'll tell you what. I'll say it one more time, but that's it. Okay, are you ready?" Jen blinks. That'll hafta do for a yes. "I'm sorry. Now, that's it. You can't keep makin' me pay for that. It happened months ago."

"Every time I see her I can't help thinking about it," Jen says. "You two've gone as far as we ever have. And I know she knows that!"

"First of all, there's no such thing as 'us two.' Second of all, there's a simple way we can change the situation."

"Clint, we've talked about this. I just don't think I'm ready . . ."

"Fuck it," I say. "I know this speech by heart."

SHAWN

11:56 A.M. Passing period, flagpole

Fat Boy's handed me these index cards. I read through 'em real quick. Where'd he get this shit?

"What am I supposed to do with these?" I ask, though I've got a pretty good hunch.

"You're going to do something you're good at," he says. "Give a speech."

"You want me to read this?"

He nods and tells me to read it loud. I stand by the flagpole and wait for the bell to ring. Hopefully nobody'll notice and I can just get this out of the way. I consider not doing it, but Priscilla told me that a lot of the council members are bitching about the stuff their masters were making them do. "It's important," she said, "that we act like we're willing to do everything everyone else is doing." Easy for her to say. She doesn't have to read this.

The bell goes off and pretty soon the courtyard is full of people. Before anyone notices, I start the speech.

"I am Robert E. Lee," I begin. All the racket goin' on round me continues. So far so good. "I am Robert E. Lee, and I believe that the Negro is livestock—livestock that can be bartered in the same manner as any dairy cow, studhorse, or pig for slaughter."

"Hey, Shawn! Speak up, man. We can't hear you."

It's Sleepy Roberts. Where did that no-talking brotha find a voice? Then a circle starts to form around me, and a couple more young bucks yell at me to talk louder.

"Start over, Slave," says Keene. "Nobody can hear you."

So it looks like my plan to stay anonymous is doomed. I go to the reliable backup. I can make this funny.

"I AM ROBERT E. LEE," I shout. I don't want that part misunderstood.

Then I switch to my white-guy-with-something-up-his-butt voice. "I believe the Negro is livestock." (I put my fists on my hips and give an "I mean it!" nod for impact.) "Livestock that can be bartered in the same manner as any dairy cow" (I point at some big-tittied girl up front and get a few laughs), "any stud" (I wink—more laughs) "horse, or pig for slaughter." (I point at my master, and presto, it's like an evening at the *Def Comedy Jam*.)

I shouldn't have worried about this. More people have crowded around the circle. This is fun. I glance down at the card and keep going.

"I AM ROBERT E. LEE," I shout again. "In 1862, I spoke to the Confederate Congress, and I told them that the Negro was incapable of reading or writing." (I look up and scratch my chin. Then I flip the index card upside down, look confused, then flip it back the right way. I stutter through the next line like I'm on *Sesame Street* and I'm just learning to read.) "Th . . . that only mul . . . mulattoes could master those skills. I recommended that those of mixed blood who learn to read or write should be destroyed before they incite their fellow slaves to turn against their masters.

"I AM ROBERT E. LEE, and you've named your school after me."

A couple of the same brothas who told me to speak up start booing. Boys better be booin' the speech and not the speaker. Some people got no sense of humor.

Stump Milton yells, "Somebody shut him up."

Right, Stump. You tell fag jokes all day, last period Dr Pepper was spewin' out your nose when you were watchin' me pick up cotton balls, but *this* pisses you off. I look down at the next line of the speech. Ain't no way I'm readin' *this*. The warning bell rings, keeping me from havin' to flat out refuse.

I am Robert E. Lee, and if you were a slave, I slept with your mothers, daughters, sisters, and wives. You named your school after me.

I wonder if that's true.

JENNY
11:58 A.M. Passing period, flagpole

It always comes down to this—put out or shut up. It seems like half our dates these days end in the same fight. We start kissing, but he doesn't know when to stop. I can't just say, "That's enough," I have to actually take his hands off me.

He wants to know, "Don't you ever get turned on? Is it ever hard for you to stop?"

Even the question makes me feel dirty. Don't ask me why. But, yeah, I get turned on, but if I told him that, he would just press the issue harder. One time I said, "Clint, of course I'm having fun. I just know how to keep my head," and he says, "I'm sure you know how to keep your head. I'm hopin' you'll learn how to give it."

It was so gross, but we both started laughing. That was one of the nights we didn't fight.

So things are ugly as Clint and I head for our locker. Well, my locker. Clint's is in the foreign language wing. We keep most of our stuff in mine, because his is so far out of the way. When we get close, though, we find our way is blocked.

"What the . . . ?" Clint says.

Students have blocked the sidewalk by the flagpole, and they're laughing. I'm too short, though, to see what they're laughing at. Clint's not in the mood to wait for the mob to clear out. He grabs my hand.

"Come on," he says.

He starts pushing people to the side, clearing out a path for me to follow. When I clear the final line of people, I can see what everyone's enjoying so much. Shawn Greeley is making some kind of speech. I sort of want to stay and listen—Shawn is *so* funny— but Clint doesn't even slow down.

"Where do you want to go for lunch?" Clint asks as he pulls out our English books and hands them both to me. "Keeping in mind that I'm pretty much tapped, that is."

"I don't care," I say because I know it's a trick question. We're going to Bonanza. It's Thursday—All You Can Eat Chicken-Fried Steak Day.

We begin the walk to our English class. "How 'bout Bonanza?"

"Fine."

Then this thought pops into my mind. If I were dating Damien, where would I be eating lunch today? Would I have a say in it? A real say? Antonio's at the Falls, maybe? That Chinese place he always goes to—Hunan Beings? Or maybe he'd make a picnic. That would be so him. When he was dating that freshman on year-book staff last year, Elaine Something, he was always doing little things for her: leaving flowers in her locker, giving her rides every-where. Then she goes and dumps him. D.'s always getting dumped. Just once I wish he'd do the dumping. He's always asking me for advice about girls. "What do y'all like?" he wants to know, like I'm the ideal person to ask. I don't think girls or, for that matter, any-one really knows what they want. Look at me. I'm evil! Check the evidence: I dropped Peter Blackstock, one of the nicest, smartest guys in school, because I heard rumors that Clint liked me; I'm thinking about picnicking with Damien while I'm walking with Clint to class; I didn't even destroy Damien's note like he asked . . .

". . . is that what you want?"

I'm snagged. "Huh?"

"I said, Is *that* what you want?"

"What was the question?"

Clint takes his seat as we enter our English class. "Forget it," he says.

MR. TWILLEY

12:02 P.M. Fourth period, teacher's lounge

I'm afraid Thomas Parks might be on drugs. After gleefully harassing me all morning, he barely spoke to me between classes this hour. He wasn't in costume, either. He just walked beside me and kept staring at me. It was all so unnerving. It's not until his cohorts in auto shop started hooting that he felt a need to make me perform. Just as well. You know what they say, "Idle hands, devil's workshop."

I pour myself a cup of coffee and take a seat at the conference table in the middle of the faculty lounge. Virginia Mills is knitting on one of the couches and Lucy Berry is running answer sheets through the Scantron machine. I take out my red pen and the quizzes from my previous two classes.

"Marcus, Marcus, Marcus," Mrs. Berry says, "get with the program. You spend way too much time grading papers. I tell you. This machine here—it's saved my life. I don't know how I ever taught without one."

The machine clacks and spits out another graded test.

"I just can't figure out how to get one to grade an essay question," I say.

"You are too much," Mrs. Berry says. "Such the masochist."

Mrs. Mills joins the conversation without looking up from her knitting.

"He sure *must* be a masochist to volunteer for Slave Day. Marcus, what were you thinking?" She continues without waiting for an answer. "And you see what happens, you get sold to Trailer Parks."

Mrs. Berry picks up where Mrs. Mills leaves off.

"The entire year I had Parks in class I had nightmares. I dreamed I was lecturing during my teacher evaluation—Gant sitting in the back of the room—and Tommy kept interrupting. Asking if we could fingerpaint 'like we usually do.' Breaking into a coughing fit every time I said the word 'objective.' Asking me, 'Is this going to be on the test?' after everything I said. Worst of all, he kept calling me 'Loose.' And I would say, 'That's Lucy! I mean . . . uh . . . Mrs. Berry.'

"The day I actually got evaluated, Tommy was absent, but I was so nervous that I botched my lesson plan anyway."

Mrs. Mills takes the baton.

"It's an outrage that administrators even have the nerve to evaluate us. Who do they think they are? They sit over in their ivory tower, thinking of new ways to make a mess of the schedule, new ways to make school easier for our poor deprived children, new ways to put the burden on us instead of them. I'll tell you what. If I've said it once, I've said it a thousand times, if they think they can . . ."

But I have heard her a thousand times, so I tune her out. I remember when I never had the time to visit the teachers lounge. Very little, after all, gets accomplished here. A lot of fist shaking, primarily. About our lousy administration. About our lousy kids. Esther always refused to come in here. "I got into teaching to work with kids, not to talk bad about them behind their backs," she'd say.

"Oh, Marcus, has Leonardo Tristan found you yet? He's looking for you," Mrs. Berry says, interrupting Mrs. Mills's tirade.

"Whatever for?"

"It seems you caught one of his kids cheating this morning. You know they get kicked out of the honor society if they're caught cheating?"

"Yes, well . . ."

"Well, Tamika Jackson showed up in his classroom during third period bawling, claiming that she wasn't cheating and that you hate her."

"I don't hate Tamika. She's one of my better students. I admit I'm disappointed that . . ."

"She's one of the few minority students in the NHS. Tristan is worried that she'll . . . "

"It just goes to show you," Mrs. Mills interjects, "that the quality of kids is declining. Honor society used to mean something. These kids today." She throws up her arms rather than risk describing youth in the '90s.

"Anyway," Berry says, "he wants to ask you if she can get off with a warning, since she's never been in trouble and since she wasn't really the one doing the cheating."

"Allowing a student to cheat is the same as cheating," I begin.

"I know. I know. You don't have to convince me. I'm just saying Tristan wants to talk to you."

"Put your foot down on this one, Marcus," Mills adds. "We can't keep lowering our expectations."

"I'm aware of that, Virginia."

Berry shuffles her graded quizzes and exits. Mills returns to her knitting. Finally I can continue grading.

SHAWN

12:07 P.M. Fourth period, art

I'm Coach Preppernau's aide this period. Mostly means I walk around or shoot in the gym. I'm headin' in that direction as I walk by the door to the art class. Humphrey waves me in. Spread out in front of him is a watercolor painting of his Rottweiler, Biscuit. The man can paint. Gonna major in art in college.

"We gotta talk," says Hump.

When we were in junior high I used to get Humphrey his girl-friends for him. He'd have half the good-lookin' ladies in school dyin' to be with him (the half who didn't want me), but he'd never ask 'em out. Could never get the words outta his mouth. So Humphrey would tell me who he liked and I'd get 'em together. He's gotten a little better since, but not much. Good thing is, he doesn't *have* to talk much. Call plays, 'bout it. Thing about Hump, when he does talk, he's usually got something to say. Nobody's got less bullshit than my man; whereas I talk so much shit on the court *I* don't even know what I'm sayin' half the time.

So when Humphrey sets down his brush, I got my ears on.

"I'm thinkin' 'bout quittin' the football team," he says.

I crack up. "Fuck you, boy. I thought you had something serious to tell me." I punch his shoulder. (His non-throwing arm.)

"I'm serious," he says. And from the look on his face—and because I know that Humphrey Brown has never told a joke in his life—I'm sure he is.

BRENDAN

12:14 P.M. Fourth period, Tiffany's Probe

Brendan, what are you thinking?

You're *not* thinking—that's what Mom and Dad would say. Dr. and Dr. Young. They're both professors up at Central: Mom in physics, Dad in math. They're big into rational thought. I don't think they'd quite understand skipping a history quiz to motor up to Austin in the middle of a school day. *Maybe* Dad would understand if he saw my company. Then again, probably not. And what was I thinking, giving Tiffany that access code? Showing off? That's the sort of thing that gets the Secret Service on your butt. It was a pretty safe number. It's the one phone repairmen use to check lines, but if Tiffany remembers it and starts using it all the time, I could be woefully bustified.

Deerfield is hurtling by my window. The road to the highway takes us right through the heart of Little Matamoros, Deerfield's barrio. Rows of old pastel pink- and teal-colored houses fly by. Skinny mongrel dogs pace their tiny fenced-in dirt patches, and multitudinous hanging plants turn front porches into virtual gardens of Babylon. As we speed along, I think I can imagine how Russian serfs felt when they watched the royal family's carriage pass through their fields. I understand now why they picked up their hammers and sickles. Tiffany rolls down all the windows electronically. I get a mouthful of her hair. I'm not complaining; it smells . . . I don't know . . . expensive.

"Hey, Scraps, what sort of car do you drive?" says Tiffany.

Scraps? What does she mean, Scraps? I think of my mom's '89 Tempo in the driveway at home. My parents say I can drive it when I turn sixteen next year.

"Uh, I don't drive yet."

Tiffany makes a fake disappointed face and snaps her fingers. "Shucks," she says.

Tiffany accelerates as she enters the highway. I lean over and check the speedometer as she merges. She's doing seventy-five with all indications pointing to greater speeds to come. I notice that I'm the only one in the car buckled up. What the heck. I'm a wildman. I click the release.

TOMMY

12:21 P.M. Fourth period, auto shop

Okay, before you start thinking I'm some slacker grease monkey, *this* is how I ended up in auto shop: I forgot to turn in my elective choice sheet, and when the deadline passed, Mr. McCormack, my counselor, just took the matter into his own hands and chose for me. Auto shop was no shocker. After all, he keeps calling me into his office to give me pamphlets from trade schools and junior colleges. Last time it was for a refrigeration school in Tulsa.

"How's the fine arts doctoral program there?" I asked him.

"Ha-ha," he said, and I don't mean that he laughed. I mean he *said* "Ha-ha."

"You are one funny kid," he said. Then he looked me over. Maybe expecting another "joke" before tacking on, ". . . but it's time you get serious about your continuing education."

"I don't know," I said. "I'm on the managerial fast track at Whataburger. Next month they're going to train me on the shake machine."

McCormack didn't get *this* joke.

"Well, congratulations, Tommy! Maybe a career in the service industry *would* suit you."

But auto shop isn't all that bad. I don't have to study for it.

Just change the oil in the principal's Beemer every blue moon. I'm making an A, and if you've seen my grades, you know how rare that is.

Anyway, I wasn't making Twilley perform as we were walking out to the shop building, but I noticed all the guys looking at me like, "So, funny man, make us laugh." All I could think of were those yearbook photos, so I told Twilley he had to carry me piggy-back.

He stared at me for a few seconds, then turned around and crouched. I hopped aboard. Now, I ain't no huge dude. Like I said, I ain't even as big as Twilley, but that didn't stop the old man from creaking with every step he took. Sounded like a bowl of Rice Krispies. Plus, he was breathing hard after a few steps. Ain't hard to please the auto shop boys, though. They yee-hawed and high-fived. He dropped me as we passed under the garage doors; I whispered my new titles to him. He put his hands on his knees and tried to catch his breath.

"Ladies and gentlemen," he panted.

Ladies?

"The man who put the spark in plugs, the over in drive, Mr. Goodwrench himself, Tommy Parks."

One or two people clapped. The others stopped paying attention the second Twilley set me down. After Twilley left, the class jacked around for a while before Mr. Radakovich slammed his eighteen-inch "board of education" down on one of the work-benches—his usual way of getting our attention.

"All right, you wastes of sperm, I wanna see elbows and ass-holes rest o' this period. I need this car washed and detailed, plus the flat changed out. Pronto. *Capisce?*"

Wow. Trilingual. Radakovich was in charge of a motor pool in the army, and his leadership style didn't change much when he started molding the minds of America's next generation of grease monkeys. Works, though. We've been elbows and ass-holes since the minute he issued the command. I notice right off that the Buick in question is Twilley's. Guess it's the TWILLEY IS A DICK shoe-polished across the back windshield. The antenna's been busted, but when I check it out closer, I see it's rusted.

Someone did that a long time ago. Twilley's just never bothered to fix it. There's bits of eggshell starting to stick to the paint job. I can't believe that I'm having to clean this up on a day where Twilley's my slave. I get out the Shop-Vac. I'm the only one in class who's mastered this piece of high-tech equipment. I open the ashtray, secretly hoping that I'll find the remnants of a roach. Hot damn, I'd have fun with that! No such luck. His ashtray looks like it's never even been opened. Not even gum wrappers or loose change. Man, I don't smoke, but my ashtray in the pickup is like a black hole. Losing lottery tickets, bottle caps, two-year-old french fries. I keep every worthless thing in the world in that ashtray.

Some student papers are stuck in a history book on the front seat. I thumb though the first few: C, F, C, D–. So this guy was the students' favorite teacher twenty years ago. How did *that* happen? Is there something about getting old that makes you mean? I wonder what I'll be like when I'm his age. Still stuck in Deerfield. Still working the drive-through.

"Whataburger. Whaddya want? Turn that crap you call music down so I can hear ya! Speak up! SPEAK UP! No, you can't get guacamole on that. Why? 'Cuz I just told you you can't. That's why! When I was your age, we didn't even have guacamole. You didn't hear us complaining."

Can't imagine it. That ain't happening to me. To hell with Twilley. I don't care what he won twenty years ago. I bought myself a slave. This kid's gloves are coming off.

KEENE

12:24 P.M. Fourth period, government

Today's lesson in Mr. Warren's class—how politics affect us personally. He asks the class if anyone has any examples from their own lives, but he's met with a wave of anti-intellectualism.

"I can't even vote," hyucks a Skoal-dipping pundit.

Then Eron Davis, who had a brother killed by friendly

fire during the Gulf War, says, "Politics don't mean jack to me. Don't never change nothing."

This gets me to wondering about two things: Does a triple negative retain the statement's original intent; and, if Eron is willing to let his government send his brother halfway around the globe to die, what hope do I have of getting people to care about Slave Day?

"I know a lot of you can't vote yet," Mr. Warren says, "but that doesn't mean you're not affected by politics." He tells us how, when he was in high school, the government decided that if you didn't register for the draft, you couldn't receive any financial aid for college. "That put me in a tough position. I didn't believe the draft was constitutional, but I needed that money to go to school."

Charity Mathews raises her hand and asks, "What did you do?" The rest of us were quite willing to go to our graves without thinking twice about it.

"I sold out," says Mr. Warren. "I registered. I'm not real proud of that, but I justified it at the time by saying I would become a lawyer and help people fight their way around it."

Charity speaks up again. "But I thought you were an entertainment lawyer."

Mr. Warren grins sheepishly. "Things worked out a little differently than I planned them."

Still unable to get the class to chime in with their own brushes with politics, Mr. Warren asks us what we think the legal drinking age should be. Students start shouting numbers ranging from four to sixteen.

"But who gets the final decision what the drinking age is going to be?" Mr. Warren asks.

The class decides the state legislature is responsible for that. "Well, then," Mr. Warren says, "politics *do* affect your lives."

After that, everyone decides some political blunder has ruined their lives. Trinni Rea tells us the tragic tale about her brother not being able to get into UT law school because he's white and male. "Now how's that fair?" she says. Poor baby.

Next, some surfer wanna-be complains about the re-zoning at Rio Vista Park. "I lost my lifeguarding job when they closed the pool."

I consider how these tragedies would play at a high school in South Central Los Angeles. Mr. Warren humors them, anyway, then he calls on me. I ignore the groans.

"Keene, what's your example?"

"You know, I didn't want to believe this at first, but it's hard not to now," I begin. "I've heard that Mr. Twilley's trying to get Tamika Jackson kicked out of NHS. Supposedly for cheating. Now she's already the only black girl in the whole group. It doesn't take a genius to figure out what's going on there."

"Keene, you're not saying that Mr. Twilley is kicking her out because she's black—," says Mr. Warren.

"Look, all I know is that every honors teacher here is white, and each year they decide who can stay in the program. Every year there's fewer and fewer—"

Then Charity interrupts me.

"Mr. Twilley said Tamika was cheating? Who's smart enough that Tamika would want to cheat off him? That doesn't make sense."

"They're saying she cheated off Trevor Wilson," I announce.

I know that it was really the other way around, but telling it like this causes a bunch of murmuring around the classroom. No one believes for a second that Tamika would cheat off Trevor. As I look around, I can almost see doubt creep across the faces of the white students. Eron speaks for the blacks in class.

"That's messed up," he says.

Mr. Warren looks at me and kind of tilts his head like he's trying to figure me out. I wonder if he remembers teaching us about spin doctors, about how they're able to make slices of truth work for their cause. I remember the lesson pretty well.

JENNY

12:33 P.M. Fourth period, English

I sit across the room from Clint. Mrs. Carney splits up couples as soon as she figures out who's together. She waits for the first time the two of you so much as look at each other, then boom, you're six rows apart. She's one of those teachers who you can tell never had a boyfriend when she was in school, so she doesn't want anyone else to have one. Mrs. Carney doesn't seem to mind that Tina MacQuarie sits right behind me and yaks up a storm. Tina's a bud, but she's been going with a guy from the county's "other" school, Hays(eed) High—where ag is the only elective—for two years now, so English is the only time we speak anymore. I know exactly what she's going to ask about today. Tina never lets me down.

"What was up with Damien Collier this morning?!" she says so loud I'm afraid Clint will hear her.

"Oh, you know how guys are." I'm not sure this makes any sense, but it's the sort of answer that will intimidate most girls. I mean, who wants to admit they don't know "how guys are"?

"Yeah," she says.

See?

"But think about it," Tina continues. "What if Clint wouldn't have had the cash on hand to outbid Damien? You would have been stuck all day with that freak." She looks a bit embarrassed, but she picks right back up. "I'm sorry. I know he's, like, Clint's best bud and all, but he wears *used* clothes. He's got one of those Moe haircuts, and have you seen his car?" (I have. It's a 1970s station wagon with fake wood paneling on the doors.) "I would let my parents drive me to school before I showed up in that. Look at you, girl, you've got it made. Clint's one of the sweetest guys in school—and believe me, there aren't many of those here. The boy is hot. Plus, that's one tough-looking Jeep he drives."

Do I ever sound this shallow? I don't ever say things like this out loud, but is this the way I think? You know, at football games, when I'm sitting with the dance team and they call out Clint's name for making a tackle, I get some sort of weird sense of pride out of it. And I know in my heart of hearts that it's not me being proud of him—it's me being proud of me. I want all the girls around me to notice. Isn't that demented?

"Damien's a sweet guy. He just didn't want Clint to get away with bidding only five dollars on me," I say.

"Aaah," Tina purrs. "That *is* sweet."

TIFFANY

Sixty thousand students crammed onto a forty-acre campus—no wonder there's no parking. Thank God for handicapped spots, or we might still be orbiting.

We walk along the Drag—the coffee shop, book, and record store–lined street that runs beside the UT campus. Some guys in UT physical plant jumpsuits are using a water blaster to try to get rid of graffiti on the sidewalks. Brendan stops walking and stares at the huge water compressor. Yep, he's got a Y chromosome.

"Brian, I'll buy you the *Big Machines and Monster Trucks* video if you'll keep up."

"Brendan," he stammers.

Mad Dog's is packed, but Ian's not hard to spot. He's the one with the palest skin, the grimiest clothes, the stringiest hair, and the *Film Threat* promotional baseball cap. Funny, at the party he looked a lot more like Ethan Hawke. It must have been *really* dark—that, or I was *really* smashed. He waves to me. God . . .

There's only one chair, so I send Brian to get me some onion rings.

"Is that a friend of yours?" Ian asks, his eyes following my servant. I recognize the unspoken question. Men—transparent at any age.

"My lover. I'm a dominatrix," I say.

Ian laughs, but it sounds forced. One to nothing, Tiffany. Ian hands me a script and says to take a look at it. I start flipping pages. He's tells me how he guinea-pigged at a drug testing center for the "tidy sum" it took to bankroll the project. I nod and say uh-huh every twenty seconds or so, but I'm more interested in the script than in what he's saying. It has its good points: Lou Ann gets lots of lines, she packs heat, her clothes stay on. And its bad points: Most of her lines have exclamation points after them (AAAAAAAHHHHHGGGGG!); she doesn't blow *any-one* away; and she dresses like some inbred moonshiner's wet dream—butt-revealing cutoffs and tablecloth-strip halters.

Brian returns with the rings, then stands behind me. If only he had a palm frond to fan me.

"So why me?" I ask.

Ian sips his cappuccino reflectively before responding. "You have the right, uhm, uh, the right . . ." His eyes venture from my eyes to my mouth. They inspect my chin, canvass my neck, contemplate my chest. If he doesn't answer soon, he'll be performing a gynecological examination. "The right look," he finishes. Has this "So you want to be in movies" routine *ever* worked for Mr. Director, here? I swear, sometimes it seems like the only thing college guys have over high school guys is that they don't expect you to wear their letter jacket.

"That good-hearted look?" I say, my eyes wide with naïveté.

"Yeah," says Ian. "Good-hearted but worldly wise. Hey, maybe you could come up to my flat . . ." (Flat? My God! He lives in England.) ". . . and we could rehearse?"

Why doesn't he just ask whether I'm interested in seeing his ceiling? "Oh I'm sorry, Babe"—I reach over and pinch his pasty cheek just below the carefully cultivated black bags under his eyes— "but Brian here has to get back to boot camp. He's AWOL right now. Gotta bolt."

This confuses my wanna-be director. Again he forces a laugh, but he gets up and walks us out of Mad Dog's. I wonder if he's got another appointment set with some other "good-hearted" leading lady. Better luck next time, pal.

Ian squints at the sun once we move outside. Maybe it's the first time he's seen it.

"You've got my number. Give me a call. We can talk more about the part," he says.

"What are these?" Brian asks, picking the perfect time to interrupt. I look down to where he's pointing. I realize I'm standing on the graffiti the UT workers are trying to water-blast out of existence. Disturbingly, I'm camped out over the outline of a body, the kind that you see in television crime scenes. Ian looks put out, but he answers.

"Thirty years ago, this psychopath—Whitman, I think his

name was—took a bunch of rifles up to the top of the tower"—he points up to the twenty-two-story UT tower, which looms over the campus—"and he just started blowing people away. He killed twenty-something people before they took him out."

"And these are left over from then?" Brian asks. Doubtfully, thank God.

Ian laughs this superior laugh. Maybe I ought to set him up with Rainy.

"No, no, no. There was a big controversy over whether the UT board of regents should put up a memorial for the victims in conjunction with the anniversary and all. They decided against it, so someone decided to spray-paint their own memorial. All of these are supposedly painted exactly where the people were killed."

Brian reaches down and touches the outline. What a freak.

"Personally, I wouldn't have used neon colors for the job," blathers Ian. "I think the starkness of black on white would have provided a more chilling image."

"Deep," I say.

MR. TWILLEY

12:57 P.M. Lunch, auto shop

When I arrive in auto shop to pick up young Mr. Parks, I find him in the backseat of my car. I suppose that means he's expecting a ride to lunch. I'm not even buckled up before he barks an order.

"Follow that car!" he says.

"What car?" I say.

"They're getting away with the diamonds!"

That's when I realize he's pulling my leg. I start the car and pull out of the garage.

"Go through the student parking lot," says Parks.

"The faculty parking lot is the more direct route," I say.

"Well, la-di-da," he says, so I obey his request and take the long way.

"What is our destination?" I ask.

"Lotta Taco, Smithers. And make it snappy."

Parks rolls down both back windows, and as we slowly make our way out of the lot, he waves to passing students with such an air of dignity that I feel as if I am a Secret Service agent charged with guarding the president. It's evident that this is the effect for which Mr. Parks is hoping as well.

"If they get too close—shoot them," he tells me.

I exit through the gates in front of the school and head toward the highway. While the upscale Mexican food restaurants are near the central campus, Lotta Taco sits on the I-35 frontage road. It's a converted Tastee-Freeze that has been catering to the locals for the past decade. Back when it was still Tastee-Freeze, I would bring the Quiz Bowl team here for cones. As I exit the highway, I realize that I haven't heard a sound from the backseat. I adjust my rearview mirror so that I can see Parks's face. I discover he's dozed off. How can one go from full speed to out cold in a matter of seconds? As I stop the car, Parks awakens and hands me two crumpled dollar bills from his pocket.

"Five bean-and-cheeses," he says, "and a water. Can you float me three cents?"

"Of course," I say, amazed that $2.03 can purchase five tacos. "We're not going in?"

"Can't. Got to rehearse," he says, shutting his eyes and resting his head back against my seat. I'm reminded of the seemingly infinite number of times I was forced to drop books next to Thomas's desk in order to wake him up. When I return to the car, I see Parks has spread out across the length of my backseat, but he pops up as soon as I open the door. I hand him the weighty bag of food.

"*Gracias, señor,*" he says more ethnically than any of the members of *Los Reyes del Camino,* the local low-riding club. Then he proceeds to insert half of the fat, soft taco in his mouth. Refried beans bleed out at the corners. There has been some discussion among the teachers in the lounge concerning Mr. Parks's personal hygiene, and I'm vaguely aware of a strange odor. I had originally written it off as the after-stench of industrial cleansers, but on second thought, it smells more like a can of deodorant has been used to fog the car.

"You got kids?" Parks says.

"Excuse me?"

"Little Twilleys."

"No."

"Why not?"

"That's a personal question, Thomas."

"If you say so." He wolfs down another taco, then forces out words. "Just seems funny. That's all."

"Why is that?"

"Being a teacher and all. Most teachers have kids." Then he resumes the inhalation of his food. I'm left to consider my lack of posterity. Esther and I tried. Well into my forties, we tried. In 1975 a doctor told us that we could be one of the first couples to give birth to a baby fertilized in a laboratory, a test-tube baby, but I decided against it. It just didn't seem right to me, a baby conceived in a vial. Plus, we were getting up there in years. The doctor said Esther was healthy enough, but who knows with that sort of thing?

If we had gone ahead with it, I'd be a father now. And maybe I'd still be a husband.

CLINT

1:06 P.M. Lunch, Bonanza

Taped to the glass of the front door, right as you walk into the restaurant, there's an eight-by-ten glossy of Humphrey Brown on Bonanza's WE SUPPORT THE REBS! poster. Forty-two guys on the team, and we all have our own posters. They're hung up at all the local businesses in town that buy ads in the football program. 'Course, most of the merchants who buy ads suited up in the Red, Blue, and Gray at one time or 'nother. I know, 'cuz every time I walk in one of these places, the owner wants to tell me 'bout some pass he caught or some tackle he made.

Now, some people will try to tell you—and you shouldn't believe these people for a second—that the posters are distributed randomly to the businesses. That's a loada BS. The coolest places get the best players. Bonanza is where most of the team eats during the week. On Thursdays it's packed with guys eating two or three chicken-fried steaks. Jody Anderson set the team record with seven at one sitting last year. Over the years Bonanza has had the Tyke Milton, Warren Stewart, Fred McCabe, and DeWayne Haynes posters. All of 'em went on to play major college ball. Last year my poster was up at Margaret's Unisex Salon. I caught so much hell, but sophomores are always in the shit places. This year I'm at Whataburger, which is pretty cool. It's open twenty-four hours and everyone goes there after Taco Cabaña and Dairy Queen close. Next year, though, I better see me when I'm comin' in here for my Thursday meal.

I guess Jen's over whatever was buggin' her. She actually stuck her hand in my back pocket on the way out to my Jeep. Then, once we got here, she jumped up on me. Right now she's ridin' piggyback.

"Duck," I say as we pass through the doorway.

"Pig," she says. Then she jabs a finger in my ribs and tickles me.

"Oh, you are *sooo* funny."

Everybody's here. The dining room's already filling up with football players. Jenny's still on my back as I cruise around, lookin' for a table. It doesn't look like we're gonna get one of our own. I'm hopin' to spot Alex, but before I can find him, Annabella Guzaldo calls me. This is weird; I've never met the girl in real life.

"Why don't y'all sit with us?" she says.

Now that I'm payin' attention, I can tell she was really talkin' to Jen. They're both Rebelettes, but I didn't know they were friends.

"Yeah, let's sit with them," Jen says.

I give Trim "Is this cool?" eyebrows. He shrugs, so what the hell.

I let Jenny down, and we both step t'ward Madonna's side o' the booth. She wants me to sit next to Trim? I'd look queer. I mean, it's one thing if there are four guys at a booth. Then it's fine to sit next to another guy, but when there are two guys and two girls? Get conscious. Sometimes girls just don't think. I sit next to

Madonna, and Jen sits across from me. Right then a waitress is at our booth. Trim and I order the chicken-fried steak special with iced tea, the girls order the salad bar. Jen gets a Diet Coke. Madonna gets a regular Coke.

"So how're things workin' out with your slave? She treatin' you all right?" Trim says.

Honestly, I keep forgettin' it's Slave Day. Guess that's what happens when you buy your own girlfriend. An answer like that sounds lame, though.

"She's been a bit uppity. Too much spirit. You know how it goes."

"Those are the worst kind," Trim says. "You gotta get 'em trained right off the bat." Trim takes a gulp of his water. "Annabella?"

"Your Highness?"

"I've got some water on my lip."

So Madonna pulls a napkin out of the dispenser, leans across the table, and wipes Trim's mouth off. As she leans forward I fight my desire to stare at her body.

"Cool," I say. Then I have a thought. "Say, Jen, get me the lemon from that table for my tea." I point to a table where Bonanza owner Walter Braintree is sittin'.

Jenny reaches across our table, picks up the bowl of sliced lemons, and sets 'em in front o' me.

"I don't want *these* lemons," I say. "I want *those* lemons."

Trim sticks up his hand. High fiveage.

JENNY

1:12 P.M. Lunch, Bonanza

There was something in the way Annabella asked us to sit with them that made me say yes, even if it did mean sharing a table with Timm Trimble. She was practically begging for company. Now I wish we hadn't joined them. First of all Clint makes me sit right next to Timm, and now he's showing off, trying to be King Stud.

I look over my shoulder at the table where Clint wants me to get the lemons. There's just one man there, and it doesn't look like he's eating. He's just reading a newspaper. I recognize him. He's at all the football games and booster club meetings. This shouldn't be too bad. Sighing, I get up from the booth and walk over to the man's table.

"Excuse me. Sir?" I say while I stare at the man's tie clip, which is in the shape of a little football. "Would you mind if I borrowed your lemons?"

"You don't have any lemons on your table?"

He sounds concerned about the lemons, which strikes me as really funky.

"We have lemons, all right. It's just that these lemons are better than our lemons." I know I'm still staring at his tie clip, but I try smiling.

He looks over at our table, grins, then glances up. "So who am I talking to?" he asks. And it dawns on me who this guy is. He owns this place. He's maybe the biggest Rebel-backer in town.

"I'm Clint DeFreisz's girlfriend," I say, motioning with my head back toward our table.

"Do you have a name of your own?"

"Uh, yeah. It's Jenny . . . Jenny Robinson." Then there's this silence that makes me fidget. "My dad's Tanner Robinson. He's the athletic director up at Central."

"Of course. I know Tanner. I didn't know he had a daughter in high school, though. Do you have any brothers?"

"One. He's in seventh grade."

"He an athlete?"

"Plays quarterback."

"Good for him!" the man practically shouts as he picks up the bowl of sliced lemons and hands them to me. "That boyfriend of yours is quite a player."

"That's what I hear."

The man laughs. "Now, you know better than to bother him on game days, don't you?"

"No one gets near him on game days."

"Women—bad for the legs." He laughs some more. Gross.

TOMMY

1:25 P.M. Lunch, theater

I want to be off book before anyone else in the play. Off book means you don't have to look at your script during rehearsal; you've got your lines memorized. I've never had so many lines before. It's tougher than I thought it would be. That's why I've been trying to spend my lunch hours in here. Twilley, who's followed me into the theater, takes a seat in the front row.

"No you don't. Up here. Chop-chop," I say.

He takes his time climbing the stairs to the stage. I hand him my script and tell him to go downstage right. This is a test. He moves to the front of the stage, the right side if you're facing the audience. He hasn't forgotten his old faculty play days. He passes.

"Act three. The scene with Tom and Partridge. You're Partridge."

"I didn't know you were in drama, Thomas."

"Only when I'm eligible," I say.

"And you've got the lead in *Tom Jones*, I see. What a funny, funny play."

I used to think so. Now I'll have to reevaluate.

Twilley continues, "Did you see the movie? Albert Finney played Tom. It won best picture, you know."

"I saw it on the *Late Late Show* after one of my Whataburger shifts. I thought it was an episode of *Benny Hill* at first." Twilley grimaces, but I ignore him. "Okay, give me my cue," I say, and we begin rehearsing the scene.

At first the ancient one does little more than read the words off the page, sort of like those gomers who sign up for drama because they think it's an easy A, then sit in the back of the room, refusing to act like anything other than the dumb stumps they are. Even though I'm mostly trying to learn my cues, I need a little more energy from my partner.

Twilley, as Partridge, gives me my cue, ". . . that's very serious from a woman of her reputation."

"Partridge, what illness has befallen you, my good man?" I

grab Twilley/Partridge by both shoulders. "Open up. Say aaaah. You sound close to death. Clap got your tongue?"

"No, no, no," Twilley says, "your line is . . ."

"I *know* what my line is, but it's tough to say it when I'm performing with someone who couldn't get cast as a corpse."

Twilley drops his chin and peers at me over the top of his glasses. He makes his eyebrows connect above his nose. He opens his script and this time delivers the line in someone else's voice. Someone else's booming, clear voice. ". . . that's *very* serious from a woman of *her* reputation." Twilley stresses the same words Miss A. told our regular Partridge to stress.

I do my best Henry Higgins from *My Fair Lady*. "By jove, I think he's got it."

"Then say your line," Twilley says. "I don't believe you know it."

But he's wrong. The next line's one of my favorites in the play. "Why won't women leave me alone?" I clutch my heart. "Oh, Partridge, beauty like mine is a curse."

"I pity you, sir," says Twilley/Partridge with just the right amount of sarcasm.

"I dare not be . . . I dare not be . . . uh . . ."

"Uncivil," Twilley prods.

". . . to Lady Bellaston, for then she would deny me . . . uh . . ."

"Entry to her house."

We work on the scene for the next fifteen minutes. After the first few times through it, Twilley isn't using the script anymore. Partridge doesn't have as many lines as Tom, but I'm still impressed. He's even getting into it a bit. At one point he takes a few steps toward me—and dress me in silk and call me Princess if he don't lose his hunchbacky lurch. When we finally make it all the way through without Twilley having to help me with a line, I hear clapping from the seats. The stage lights keep me from seeing who it is.

"Bravo! Bravo!" says Miss A. as she walks down in front of stage.

"Thanks," I say. "Do you think I ought to . . ."

"No, no, no, no, no, no. Not you, Tommy. It's Mr. Twilley who I'm applauding. I haven't seen you on a stage for a long time, Marcus."

Mr. Twilley mumbles something, but I can't really hear it. His eyes drop back into the script. He blushes. Swear to God. Then he does his monster walk into the wings.

"What was that?" I ask Miss A.

"Oh, Tommy, don't worry about it."

CLINT

1:26 P.M. Lunch, Bonanza

While the girls are off at the salad bar, I'm tryin' to tell Trim 'bout Humphrey overhearin' Coach Rossy, but I don't think he's catchin' the drift o' my story.

"You had coach spit runnin' down your leg?" he says. "And you just sat there? Man, I'da busted outta there inna heartbeat. Screw the game film."

So I think, never mind, I'll change the topic. Somethin' Trim is more concerned with.

"So has the investment been worth it?" I say, nodding toward the salad bar where Jen and Annabella are chitchattin'.

"Not yet, but it's gonna be," he says.

"What's the plan?"

"Water Tower Park. Before the bonfire."

Water Tower Park—as if you couldn't figure this out—is a park that they built around Deerfield's largest water tower. It used to be the only water tower, back before Central's enrollment zoomed up over ten thousand. That happened right after they lowered their academic standards. The ultimate result is that every high school senior in the state with a C average, tuition money, and a pulse is accepted there. That's where Deerfield's claim to fame—the most bars per capita in the state—comes from. *Playboy* even listed Central as one of the biggest party schools in the country. Anyway, the university built its own water tower, which meant the city council could get away with paintin'

across the front. You can see it all the way from I-35, since it sits at the top of a hill that overlooks the town. All the nooks and crannies make it a popular place for parking. Every now and then there's a letter in the *Herald* demandin' a curfew from some PO'd mom who stepped on a used rubber while strollin' through the park. No one ever does anything 'bout it, though. Guess our local elected officials found their thrills on Water Tower hill themselves.

"How're you gonna get her up there?" I ask.

"Charm," Trim says. Trim's blond with this diamond-shaped head, and I know this may sound sick . . . like I'm goin' homo, but as he's diggin' through his pocket for somethin', I can't help thinkin' he would be a pretty girl. He finds what he's looking for: From what I can tell, a piece of tinfoil. He holds it up.

"And if charm's not enough—this."

I sit there lookin' dumb. He peels back the foil, revealin' a white tablet. I sorta recall someone in sixth grade sayin' somethin' 'bout how if you put aspirin in a girl's Coke she goes, like, totally nympho, but I filed that with the one about growin' hair on your palms from you know what. Trim looks agged.

"It's X, man!"

"You're gonna do X the day before a game?" I say. The whole senior class is full of Jimis, but Trim knows the team rules: No alcohol, no drugs during the season. If the coaches find out you've been drinkin' they run you three miles a day for five days at six in the morning. They find out 'bout drugs and you're off the team for a year. Trim looks at me like I'm stupid.

"Naw, man. I'm not worried 'bout *me* bein' in the mood. It's for her."

"Does she know 'bout it?"

"I wanna surprise her," he says, and the way he says it, I know for sure that he plans on slippin' it to her.

JENNY

Annabella Guzaldo pours another bucket of ranch dressing on her salad. Already she's spread a handful of cheddar on top and surrounded the lettuce with a ring of olives. I look at my own plate. No dressing. No olives. No cheese. Just some lettuce and cabbage that I plan on spicing up by squeezing a little lemon over the top. Why does everything come so easy for some girls? If I ate her salad I'd have to Slim-Fast for the rest of the week. I want to resent her, but she's too nice. It's not like we're pals, but we're both Rebelettes, so I'm practicing with her all the time. Some of my friends hate her and say she's stuck-up, but I know it's because they're jealous. She's not stuck-up. She's reserved. She keeps to herself mostly. That's why it surprised me that she called us over to sit with them.

A lot more girls would like Madonna if she would get herself a steady boyfriend. Then she wouldn't be so much of a threat. She could sure pick and choose, but she doesn't seem all that interested. In fact, she always seems more worried about grades than anything else. It's funny. In fact, it's *ironic* that the boys call her Madonna because Annabella isn't anything like the singer. She's a Gap girl—just like me. She's the opposite of a boy toy; she's a boy ignorer. That must drive them crazy. Guys like Timm Trimble can't deal with that. Last year she dated Joe March for, like, three minutes and went to the prom with Steve Wacker, but I heard she had a crush on Jennings Crawford, that guy who plays guitar on the cafeteria steps during lunch.

Bonanza has a soft-serve ice cream machine, and I'm not surprised to see Annabella pick up a bowl and head toward it. I can't decide whether to follow.

"Sorry I'm being so much of a pig," she says. "It's just that the more time I spend chewing, the less I'll have to talk to him."

"It's been that bad?"

"Did you know that his family was one of the first to settle in this county?" I shake my head no. "Did you know that his family once owned slaves for real?" Again I shake my head. "Did you know he's got a three-hundred-watt Alpine amplifier in his trunk?" I think Clint has actually told me about this, but I shake my head no anyway.

"At least it sounds like he's doing all the talking."

"But he expects me to say things like, 'Wow, that's great,' after everything he talks about." Annabella makes a perfect little ice cream curlicue on top of her sundae.

"So that's why you called us over to your table?"

"Yeah, I'm sorry. I know it sounds like I'm using you, but you've always been so nice, and you and Clint always seemed, well, you know, happy. He's such a sweet guy."

I have a jealous moment, but it's brief.

"Go ahead and use me," I say. "I don't mind."

"Thanks," she says. "I knew you wouldn't."

SHAWN

1:29 P.M. Lunch, cafeteria

All You Can Eat Chicken-Fried Steak Day at Bonanza, and I'm stuck here on the cafeteria steps, stomach growlin', waitin' with Tubby here for the "big surprise" he's promised. To make matters worse, I'm havin' to listen to some guitar-strummin' guy in a bowling shirt sing these kill-yourself Smashing Pearl Blowfish songs. He's got some kinda haircut club gathered at his feet. Meantime, Keeneboy's displayin' the same weak-ass moves with Tamika Jackson that he uses on the court. She came up thankin' him for stickin' up for her with some teacher, and Keene says—get this— "no sweat." Man, they must be showing *Mod Squad* on Nickelodeon again. Then he asks her if she wants any lunch, hands me some cash, and says to hurry back. Fine. Anything that means gettin' away from Don Juan DeNegro, here.

Don't know what he's all in heat for. You *could* say Tamika's a good-looking woman, but it would be in the same qualified way you'd say Jeff Wetler is a good, slow, white, no-hops center. She got a plain face, fair body. No kinda fashion sense. Sat next to her in a couple classes in junior high. Girl's crazy entertaining, but nothing to pop a chubby over.

The lunch line is long. Too long. Reminds me of my free lunch days during my freshman and sophomore years—before Mr. Braintree hired me to mow his lawn. Fifty bucks a week, every week, whether it needs mowin' or not. Shit, comin' in here used to embarrass me. Gramma tried to give me an allowance, but I knew she couldn't afford it. She'd leave money on the counter for me, but I'd just ignore it. I tell you what. One day that lady is gonna have the nicest house in Deerfield. Nicer than Walter Braintree's. Bet on it.

You wouldn't know from lookin' around the cafeteria that this is a mostly white school. Could be Compton High, 'cept for all the Mexicans and the scattered cowboy clumps. Everyone in their own little section. That's probably how Brotha Keene likes it. Miss Killarney spots me in line and calls me up to the front. I hear some grumblin' from behind me as I push my way through.

"What are you doin' in here?" Miss Killarney says in her Irish accent.

"Slummin'," I say, as she hands me a loaded tray.

Old Killarney cracks me up. She's always sayin' how the Irish people are the blacks of Europe—always getting run over and shoved to the back. Ever since I was a freshman, she's been tellin' me that I'm gonna amount to something someday. And that's why, she says, I get the special service.

"Remember the little people," she says.

When I carry the tray back out to the cafeteria steps, I learn what Keene's next attempt at embarrassing me is gonna be. He's got one of those shoeshine boxes that most guys make for their first project in shop—like anyone still shines their shoes. He's set it up in front of one of the benches out on the cafeteria stoop.

"Time to shine," he says. It's the most hilarious line to ever come outta the boy's mouth, but I don't think he meant it funny.

"You gotsta be kiddin'," I answer.

"I don't *gotsta* be anything."

Once again, I hafta tell myself it's in everyone's best interest if I don't hit him. He pulls a rag from the box and holds it out in front of him, actin' a little too showy in front of the lady, if you ask me. Out in the courtyard behind Keene, I see slaves bringing lunches out to whole circles of people; Perry Willis has got ukelele-strumming Mr. Denhart serenading him and his girlfriend; just then Mr. History comes speed-walking by in an Indian headdress. Slave Day sure does lead to some weird shit.

"Give me that," I say, swiping the rag from his hand.

MR. TWILLEY

1:33 P.M. Lunch, sidewalk outside cafeteria

One would think that after more than twenty years, I would be able to behave like an adult in front of Linda Amenny.

T. S. Eliot hit the nail on the head when he said, "Why do we feel embarrassed, impatient, fretful, ill at ease. Assembled like amateur actors who have not been assigned their parts." I feel like that all the time now. Like I have no role, and I just show up where I'm supposed to with nothing to say. I used to have good roles: respected teacher, loving husband.

Linda Amenny is probably the one person on campus who continues to think of me as anything other than a blustering ogre. I stopped dating her the day Esther began teaching here. Still, Linda never held a grudge. I used to kid myself, imagine she never got married because she couldn't . . .

"Yo, slave!"

I turn. Coming up behind me on the sidewalk is Thomas. He's wearing a ten-gallon hat and chaps. He's carrying an Indian head-dress.

"You forgetting something?"

I *had* forgotten. It's surprising how differently my day with Mr. Parks is turning out. Differently than I expected, that is. He's a handful, no doubt, but I assumed he would spend the day taking out his frustrations on me as payback for his failing grade. Yet, to my surprise, he's seemed as interested in livening up his own day as inventing ways to degrade me. Perhaps more so.

"Sorry," I say.

"Put this on," he says, handing me the headdress. "Here's your gun." He hands me a Colt .45 cap gun. "Here's the deal. Cowboy and Indian all the way back to my fifth-period class. I'll give you a head start. I'll try to track you. If I get a good shot at you, I mean dead to rights, you've got to perform a death scene. I'm talking award-winning. I've seen you act, so don't think you can do some weak-ass, fall-down thing. If you can avoid me until the tardy bell rings, you don't have to herald my arrival in Mrs. Griffith's class. I'll give you a minute head start."

Maybe I spoke too soon. "Thomas, I don't think . . ."

"One Mississippi, two Mississippi . . . ," he begins.

So I'm off. I have no idea how I'm going to avoid him for the next few minutes, but I try to put distance between us. I've got a bright red and yellow mane of feathers on my head. I'm carrying a cap gun in my hand. And as I scuttle past students, they drop their books, turn and stare, either becoming dead silent or shouting nonsensical things at me like "Go, Speed Racer, go!" I can't imagine that tracking me will present much of a challenge.

I enter the cafeteria and duck behind the partition that separates the faculty tables from the students'. A dozen or so of my peers stop eating.

"Don't tell me," Denhart says, snapping his fingers and pointing. "You've done something with your hair?"

The cracks of cap gun shots alert me to Mr. Parks's presence in the cafeteria. I peek around the partition in time to see a number of students gesturing to Thomas, letting him know where I've holed up. Before he looks up to see me, I point my gun and fire. Thomas dives and belly-rolls behind a table. When he stands, he's using a young girl—from all appearances a freshman—as a shield.

"Come out, redskin, or the squaw gets it."

I hear a few of the students boo their peer's lack of chivalry as I break for the faculty rest room. I'm without cover for ten feet or so, but from this distance, I think it's fair to say that the one shot he gets off misses. Maybe it grazes me. No more than a flesh wound.

I lock the door behind me. Thomas starts pounding on it soon after.

"You can't hide in there the rest of the period. That's not fair.

You'll be doing my laundry the rest of the day, Cochise!"

What Parks doesn't know is that I have no intention of staying in here for the few minutes that remain of lunch. The faculty rest room also has a kitchen entrance. I hurry out the other side and almost knock down one of the cooks. She screams, drops the tray she's carrying. Frozen Tater Tots tumble across the floor.

"Hush!" I say, realizing a second after I do so that I'm pointing the pistol at her.

I can still hear Thomas pounding on the door of the rest room behind me as I ease my way out of the kitchen, around the corner, down the hall, and back into the cafeteria. The students who see me are too intrigued to warn their classmate, or perhaps they are still disappointed in his choice to use that poor girl as shield. Regardless, they say nothing as I tiptoe behind Parks. I get one glimpse of the remaining faculty members: Denhart is grinning ear to ear, Mrs. Mills has stopped knitting.

I stick my pistol into the back of Parks's head.

"Game over, paleface."

Parks freezes. "I'll take that," I say as I relieve him of his weapon. I back up a few steps. "Now I want you to raise your arms and turn around very slowly." Parks does as he's told. "Though it troubles me to do so, I'll forget all about Wounded Knee, 1890; the Manhattan Purchase, 1624; the Trail of Tears, 1830 to 1842. I'll put that all behind me."

Parks smirks.

"Like heck I will!" I blast him with both cap guns. Thomas clutches his heart and stumbles forward, his eyes wide in shock. He falls into the condiment table, and when he rolls off it, his hands and arms are covered in blood. Or ketchup, rather. The students at near-by tables applaud his untimely death.

CLINT

1:52 P.M. Lunch, my Jeep

Times like this I'm glad to be alive. Offspring cranked. Top's off. Three chicken-frieds down the hatch. Jen's hair is flyin'. Tomorrow's game day. Kinda from outta nowhere I scream—my weight-lifting power scream. It's gonna be a long night for the Liberty Valley ground game tomorrow. I'm mighty aggêd when Jen commits a serious party foul by turning down the jams.

"What?" I say.

She cranks it back up and pouts. I turn it down and soften up a bit.

"I'm sorry. What'd you wanna say?" When I look at her I can tell she's bothered by somethin'.

"What do you think about Timm?" she shouts over the music.

"Great hands, fair speed, doesn't care much for blockin'."

"No. I mean do you think he's a good person?"

"He's kinda wild," I say, rememberin' his plans for Madonna, "but you girls don't seem to mind."

"Some don't. Most girls see right through him. Annabella isn't interested in him at all. I can promise you that."

"Bet."

"Bet what?"

"I'll bet that after today they're dating, or at least that she wishes they were. It's tough to tie Trim down, ya know."

"We can't bet about something like that," she says.

"That's what I thought," I answer. I reach down to turn the stereo back up.

"Just a sec," Jenny says. She grabs her flailin' hair and pulls it out of her face. "What did you want to bet?"

"Sexual favors?"

"Get serious, Clint."

"Didn't think you'd go for that," I say. "How 'bout if I win, you wear that lipstick two days a week 'stead o' just pep rally days?"

"And if I win?"

"Name it."

"If I win, you hafta make me cookies."

"I can't just buy you some cookies? You want 'em edible, don'cha?"

"Uh-uh. I don't care what they taste like. You hafta bake 'em. You can't have your mom do it, and I want 'em wrapped up in a box with a little note tellin' me to have a great day and how great

I am. Maybe one of those poems you left on my answering machine ought to be included, too."

"I can live with that," I say.

I turn into the parking lot of good ol' Lee High. As a matter of principle, I don't slow down for any o' the speed bumps. Jen knows my routine and she hangs on to the handlebar above the glove box. When I got D. and Alex with me, they unbuckle and try to catch air. Jen just ain't that adventurous.

KEENE

1:54 P.M. Lunch, cafeteria steps

Tamika is sticking around, talking, eating fries. She offers some to Shawn, but I ask her politely not to feed the slaves. She's acting kind of nervous around me—she keeps thanking me for "being so nice"—that *has* to be a good sign. A bunch of students, mostly black—odd, isn't it, that all the white students have cars and can afford to eat off campus?—have gathered around to watch the basketball star shine shoes.

At first, people are getting a pretty good free shine. Shawn's whistling that "bluebird on my shoulder" Uncle Remus song, snapping his towel, calling his customers "boss." The fun winds down when Tyler Rutherford, this notorious redneck who once beat up his own sister for supposedly holding hands with some poor brother in Laurence's grade, sits in front of Humphrey and sticks his boot up on the box. People returning from off-campus lunch are walking by, a lot of them stopping to watch. The crowd is beginning to reflect Lee's standard racial breakdown.

"Glad to see you're learning a trade that'll be useful some-day," Tyler tells Shawn. "Or are you planning on being one of those millionaire basketball stars?" Then he and maybe a couple others start laughing.

Shawn looks over at me, obviously perturbed, but I can't tell if it's at me or Tyler. Half of me wants to tell Shawn he doesn't have to shine Tyler's shoes, but then again, maybe *this* will finally do the trick. Maybe Shawn won't be able to laugh this one off.

"Come on now, don't be lazy," says Tyler.

Shawn's wrapping the rag around his hand, and I think maybe he'll punch Tyler—I'm sort of hoping he does—but instead he takes a deep breath, gets back on his knee, and starts buffing the Nocona calfskins.

"Aren't you gonna whistle me something? Maybe that 'We Shall Overcome' song?" asks Tyler, laughing some more.

About that time these football players stop next to Shawn. Humphrey Brown, Jody Anderson, Ray Cook—all of them looking seriously agitated.

"What's up?" says Humphrey.

Let me explain for a minute how Humphrey says "What's up?" because it's important. There are lots of ways you can say "What's up?" Most of the time you say it, it sounds friendly. Sometimes you're genuinely curious about what's going on. And some guys can say it, add a "Yo, G." and sound seriously down. (I'm not one of those.) But the way Humphrey says it to Shawn right now—it's the first time I've heard it sound scary.

"Humpty Dumpty!" responds Shawn, oblivious to the anger in his homie's voice.

"Well?" says Humphrey.

"Ah, you know, it's a student council *thang.*"

"Man, you gotta cut this shit out," says Humphrey. "You look like some kinda"—he pauses, struggling for a way to finish this off—"fool," he says finally.

Porch monkey, buffoon, Uncle Tom—I could have come up with better ones, but I wasn't asked.

"Ain't nothin' but a *thang,*" says Shawn, sounding as *black* as I've ever heard him. "If you don't make it anything mo'."

"What the hell are you thinking?" says Humphrey.

I'm curious about this as well, and I'm waiting for an answer when I notice that the quarterback of the football team is talking to me.

"What?"

"I don't know what you're trying to prove," says Humphrey,

"but whatever it is, it ain't working."

This turn of events gets me thinking about how W. E. B. Du Bois was ignored by most everyone except his intellectual equals. God, how many times did Mr. History go over that?

"I'm raising consciousness," I say, hoping Tamika notices how I'm holding my ground.

"I don't know 'bout *that*," he says. "Whole thing looks personal to me."

I don't really have a response. Humphrey shakes his head and looks around, first at me, then the football players, then around the circle of people who've gathered. "Shit," he says and walks off.

JENNY

1:59 P.M. Passing period, foreign language hallway

I put Damien out of my mind for most of lunch, but he's waiting for me by the door to Spanish. My first thought is "happy to see him," but almost as fast, I want to turn and head the other way. Since it's obvious he sees me, I press on. Two of my friends appear over Damien's shoulder, and I wonder what they're thinking. Nothing. They can't think a thing. I talk to Damien all the time.

"I had to know, before I go to fifth period, if you told Clint anything," Damien says.

"No," I say, but I catch myself holding my books in front of my chest, rocking back and forth from my heels to my toes. Try to be cool for once in your life, girl.

"Did you get rid of the note?"

Panic. Look at the hallway clock. "Yeah," I lie.

"Great," he says. "It would mean certain death."

Damien takes off his glasses and rubs the bridge of his nose, one of the many habits that Clint and Alex tease him mercilessly for. As he does it, I try to judge his cuteness factor. Like, what would he look like with contacts? Without the goatee? Next to me? He starts pulling something out of his backpack.

"This is for you," he says. "I printed it during lunch."

I take the photo from his hand. It's one that he shot this morning before the assembly. That seems like days ago. I realize that he took this shot before I noticed him, before he started asking me to pose. I'm sure of this because I don't have that stupid fake grin or that fake model outer-space look on my face. The print is out of focus, but not as out of focus as most of Damien's work. It's what they would call soft-focus. It makes me look like I'm in a dream. A sweet dream—I'm smiling a bit. But the photo isn't what impresses me the most. It's the frame. It's not some expensive frame like the ones I always buy myself down at the Paper Bear. It's homemade. The backing is some sort of thin pressboard, but the frame is covered completely with fortunes—you know, from fortune cookies. He's glued the little strips of paper so that they completely blanket the cardboard surrounding the photo. I read a few of them: IT IS WISE TO SAMPLE ALL OF LIFE'S MANY FLAVORS; GREAT THINGS AWAIT THOSE WHO SEIZE OPPORTUNITY; IN MATTERS OF LOVE, IT IS BETTER TO TRUST YOUR HEART THAN YOUR HEAD.

"It's great," I say.

"Have you thought about tonight? About after the bonfire?"

I catch myself rocking again. Stop it! "Damien, I don't know what I'm going to do."

He looks disappointed and relieved at the same time. The tardy bell rings.

"Gotta boogie," Damien says, "Herr Twilley, you know." Then he drags his index finger across his throat and makes a noise like it's being cut. I step into Ms. Cisneros's class. She hasn't made it in from the teachers lounge yet.

CLINT

2:00 P.M. Fifth period, history

The twenty-two people in this school you can count on to get back from lunch on time are the ones sittin' in here right now. You just don't show up late for Twilley's class. Not only does he give you a zero for the day—doesn't matter if he's givin' a major test, pop quiz, or plain daily grade—but he makes you stay after class for just as long as you were late to his class. So you might end up tardy to your next class, too. That sucks, 'cuz other teachers like to tell coaches when they have a football player show up late. Then the coaches run you like a dog.

I've been waitin' for fifth period to talk to Damien. We both have Twilley, but early in the year he caught us talkin' and moved the Beast up to the front o' the room. I still sit in the back. Funny thing is, I think Twilley sorta likes Damien now. D's as close to being a teacher's pet as you get with Twilley. Every time Twilley asks a question and no one knows the answer, he gets this real sour look on his face, then he asks Damien. Bingo. D likes history. Don't ask me why. Once, after Damien got an answer right, Twilley put his hand on D's shoulder. I 'bout busted a gut tryin' to keep from bustin' a gut.

So anyway, the tardy bell rings and no Damien. Spookier still, no Twilley. People start lookin' around, 'cuz this's never happened before. Everyone stays at their desk, though. Twilley counts you tardy if you're not in your seat and quiet when the bell rings. A minute later, Damien slips in, but he doesn't look back at me. By now there's some murmurin' goin' on, but it's not what you'd call loud. Then in comes Twilley. He's wearin' a full Indian headdress, and he's carryin' what looks like a pistol.

"How," he says to the class, ignorin' the fact that some of us were talkin'. He's got this tiny smile fightin' its way across his face and he's raised his palm toward us like he wants to share a peace pipe. No one reacts, though, and his minigrin disappears. It's business as usual.

S H A W N

2:03 P.M. Fifth period, math wing hallway

I catch up to Humphrey before he reaches his math class.

"Hump, what crawled up your butt back there, man? You were making me look bad."

Humphrey slows down, but he doesn't stop. "Didn't you hear

anything I told you this morning?" he says. "Were you payin' attention at all when I told you what Coach said?"

"I heard you, but I don't see what difference that makes now."

"What do you think people, white people especially, think
when they see you out on the cafeteria steps shining shoes? Not all
of them get the joke—I promise you that. Plus, I heard all about you
pickin' cotton this morning."

"Who cares what white folk think?"

"You do," he says. "You care more than any brotha I know."

"Shee-it," I say, laughing, though it bothers me that
Humphrey's still wearing his Iron Man face. "You're startin' to
sound like Keene Davenport."

"Well, he's right 'bout one thing—Slave Day is one fucked-up
event."

"Uh, excuse me, but weren't you bidding on me this morning?
How did something we laughed at for three years turn into this big
racist statement in the space of five hours?" I say. We both ignore
the tardy bell.

"A lot has happened."

"Like what?"

"Like I'm off the football team. So are all the brothas—all the
seniors, at least."

I hear the words, but it's tough for me to believe it.
Humphrey's the best football player to come through this school in
a long time, and he's playing on the best team Deerfield's had in
twenty years. But like I say about Humphrey, one thing you can
count on—he ain't joking.

"What happened?" I ask.

"I told some of the other guys about what I heard Coach say
'bout brothas not being able to take a hit. We went in at lunch and
had a talk with him. I told him that he owed all the black guys on
the team an apology and that we weren't going to play against
Liberty Valley unless we got one. He said he hadn't bowed to players' demands in twenty years of coaching, and he wasn't about to
now. He said that if we were going to sit out tomorrow's game that
we might as well turn in our equipment right then."

"So that's what you did?" I say.

"Well, I woulda wanted to talk about it with the other guys. I'm still gonna get to play in college. For guys like Jody and Ray, turning in that equipment meant they would never play ball again. Didn't get a chance to say anything, though. Jody walked right out of the office, got his shit out of his locker, walked back in with it, and set it on Coach's desk. Wasn't even a decision for him."

"We're gonna get our ass kicked tomorrow night," I say.

"Hope not," says Humphrey. "But I don't think I'm gonna be able to watch it either way."

"Are you sure this won't fuck you up for college? You think Penn State is gonna want a quarterback who calls for team walkouts?"

"Don't matter. I'm calling up Eddie Robinson, the coach at Grambling."

"An all-black school?"

Humphrey looks at me real serious, and I think he's got some important shit to say, but all he says is, "Shawn, I ain't goin' pro. There's hundreds of guys out there with arms like mine. I just want to go somewhere, get a free education, and play for someone I can look in the eye."

"Grambling games are never on TV," I point out. I've been holdin' on to the dream of both of us playin' for UCLA.

"You're always missin' the point," says Humphrey, and for a minute I think he's gonna use one of his patented jukes to get by me and into his classroom. "It ain't 'bout all that."

"Naw, G., I know what you're sayin'. I'm just making sure you do. Tell you what—you don't wanna go to tomorrow's game anyway. Plus, I feel like I ought to do something. I can't let you football players take all the heat. You know the student council is supposed to meet the Liberty Valley student council at halftime on the fifty-yard line in some 'spirit of friendship' bullshit thing. I'll boycott that. Then, tomorrow night we'll have a party at the same time as the game. We'll get every brotha and sista in school to skip the game and come to the party. People from Liberty Valley will look up in our stands and think they're playin' Westlake, the stands'll be so white."

"Won't you get in trouble for skipping halftime?" says Hump.

"Who gives a fuck?" I say.

BRENDAN
2:04 P.M. Fifth period, English

After I walk Tiffany to Spanish, I cross the courtyard to the English wing. Lloyd motions me over to his desk before class gets started.

"State of the world?" he asks. "Or do I have to log on and read it with all your new fans?"

"H-D," I say. That stands for hunky-dory.

"And . . . ," says Lloyd. He crosses his legs and rubs his palms together, hungry for dirt. I notice the flip-flops he wears to school every day, all the way up until Thanksgiving. He says the cold doesn't affect him, but I think it's just a random way of getting attention. What's the point, though? Does he think girls are saying, "Wow, that boy doesn't wear shoes? I wonder what he kisses like?"

Who am I to criticize? I dress to evanesce.

I'm not exactly athrob with desire to share the latest developments of my day. On the way back from Austin I asked Tiffany why she bought me. After all, I told her, there were plenty of other guys before me.

"I was late," she said. "You were all that was left."

That would explain it. I didn't really expect her to say she had been fantasizing about me or anything. I guess I just hoped for something like, "You looked like a nice guy," or "I wanted to meet someone new." Pretty dumb, huh? "Scraps" makes more sense to me now.

You know, I think most people—if they had been put in the same position I put Tiffany in—would have tried to come up with something more diplomatic, or at least they might have said it like they were a bit embarrassed. Guess that's not Tiffany's style, though. She just blurted it out like, "What else could it have been, Speed Bump?"

When Tiffany served me a bowlful of undiluted truth, I heard Kyle Gallon's voice in my head say, "So I guess a blow job is out of the question." Here's a shocker: I said nothing. The girl in the picture in Tiffany's locker doesn't look like she could be so heartless. The way the girl was smiling—she was so absolutely giddious.

Maybe the gift she held in her hands was for her grandfather. One of those clay imprints of her hands that you make in kindergarten. Or maybe it was a gift *from* her grandfather: a music box or a doll. Either way, I doubt Tiffany has smiled like that in years. I'll bet that when everything comes to you so easy, it's hard not to be bored. And when there's nothing you care for, it's probably impossible to be sensitive to other people's feelings. There's nothing I could say or do that would hurt Tiffany's feelings.

Well, maybe it's a good lesson to learn . . . Brian.

I realize Lloyd's still waiting for a reply. "She's a bitch," I tell him.

That jolts Lloyd, because I don't swear much. Then I spill the whole melancholious saga.

He looks briefly flummoxed but recovers quickly. "You wanna get even?"

"How?"

"Meet me in the computer lab after school. I'll show you."

KEENE

2:05 P.M. Fifth period, courtyard

So I run into Laurence on the way to physics, and he wants to know what's up with Mr. Twilley and Tamika. I tell my brother that I was under the impression that he didn't want to be seen talking to me for the rest of the school year.

"You really think Twilley's kicking her out because she's black?" Laurence asks doubtfully. "When you were in his class, you used to talk about what a tough, good teacher he was. You said he taught history straight up, no frosting. Now I'm reading on all the computer bulletin boards about how you're accusing him of nineteenth-century lynchings."

"The man's old enough. Have you checked his alibis?"

Laurence is funny. His computer screen name is THE FALCON, maybe the only black comic book hero. That screen name is the only area I know about in which Laurence acknowledges his race. Sometimes I'll check my E-mail and I'll get these messages asking for a ride home signed THE FALCON. Hell, the Falcon was nothing but Captain America's boy. Ask anyone.

"I'm telling you again, big brother, don't get carried away today. You may end up over your head."

The warning bell rings and Laurence's ears prick up like the Pavlov dog they're turning him into.

"Later," he says as he makes like one of those Olympic walkers heading to class.

It's funny how Shawn just forgot about his slave duties after Humphrey got in his face. I mean he *should* be walking me to class right now. Then again, it kind of momentarily slipped my mind as well. It was like everything just ended back there on the cafeteria steps. I won't be surprised if I don't see him again for the rest of the day.

Right as I'm thinkin' this, Sleepy and a couple out-of-place-looking underclassmen catch up to me. The copper-skinned youngsters are decked out in enormous, glossy Karl Kani boots, calf-length shorts and size XXXXXL T-shirts featuring the Gravediggaz and the Wu-Tang Clan. One of the duo wears a red leather beret and the other, slightly shorter dude has the male symbol carved into his hair with the arrow pointing forward. Sleepy gestures to me and says, "The man." It takes me a second to realize that he's introducing me to them. *The Man*—I like the sound of that.

They turn out to be Rashard and Melvin Jones, brothers who moved down from Chicago last year when their parents decided they were less apt to get into trouble living "in the country." It takes less than sixty seconds of conversation to learn they hate the South. In that span, and without stopping for breath, they manage to curse the humidity, the size of the cockroaches, country music, Mexican food, and our "shuffling, bug-eyed, grinning student-council president." I realize the two of them have been around every time I've had Shawn perform. They were the ones yelling for him to speak up during the Robert E. Lee speech. I seem to recall them urging other students to come over and watch Shawn shine shoes as well.

"Man, that 'I'm Robert E. Lee' speech you made Shawn

read—I thought a couple of those white boys listenin' to it were about to fetch a rope," says Melvin.

"Then havin' him shine shoes on the cafeteria steps—by the end of the day, no one's gonna wanna say they know him," adds Rashard.

"So what's up next?" asks Melvin, the chattier of a chatty pair.

"I don't know if anything's up next," I say. "I don't have any more plans. You saw Humphrey Brown get in his face, didn't you? I think he may have learned a thing or two back there."

This news seems to disturb both Melvin and Rashard.

"Yo, man, we just begun." Melvin says it, but it's the way that Rashard cackles that makes me uneasy. "We can't let up now. We're this close to winning." Melvin holds up his thumb and index finger an inch apart. "Have you heard about the football team?" he asks.

"I heard they're having a good year."

"Not anymore, they're not," says Rashard, cackling again.

Melvin takes back over. "Humphrey Brown overheard one of the coaches calling him 'our franchise nigger.' Humphrey went after him, but some of the assistant coaches held him back. When the other brothers on the team heard, they all up and quit."

The first thing I feel is rage—intense and consuming. How many generations, I wonder, will it take for racists to just die off? But as quickly as that emotion hits me, it's gone, and I'm left wondering how much of what I've just been told is the truth. One of our coaches saying something that obviously racist? It sounds pretty unbelievable. It doesn't mean we can't use it, though.

"For the rest of the day, tell anyone you see that the football players are quitting to protest Slave Day."

Melvin grins at Rashard. "I like the way the man thinks," he says. Then he turns his attention to me. "Don't worry about us doing our part. I promise you, tonight's gonna be a night everyone'll remember."

And I wonder what he means by that.

JENNY

2:22 P.M. Fifth period, Spanish

Thursdays are rehearsal day in *español* for our weekly *Teatro para Dos*. We get paired up with some other student in the class, and we're supposed to come up with a two-minute play that accomplishes something beneficial: getting your car fixed, ordering a meal at a restaurant, asking directions to the local *biblioteca*. This week my partner is Tiffany Delvoe, and I'm scared. Tiffany, I've heard, spends half of her summer in Cancún or Puerto Vallarta. She uses slang that makes Ms. Cisneros blush, and she invents situations a lot wilder than anyone else in the class. Memorable lines from Tiffany's *Teatro para Dos* include . . .

"¡You must sell a lot of cocaine to be able to afford an apartment like this!"

And . . .

"Send over the cabana boy. I need a rubdown."

Ms. C. checks roll, then tells the class to start working on our assignment. I glance over my shoulder to the back corner of the classroom. Tiffany waves me over. I pick up my English/Spanish dictionary and a notebook and head back. As I'm walking I remember the night that Jill and I spent the night at Tina's, and we all took turns trying to imitate Tiffany Delvoe's walk. None of us had much success.

"So, hon," Tiffany says, "did you have anything you were hoping to act out? Bartering for one of those red ceramic bulls, maybe?"

I can't tell if she's making fun of me or the assignment, so I just say no.

"Well, I've got some ideas." This doesn't surprise me. "I was thinking we could be two groupies invited backstage at a Julio Iglesias concert. We know one of us is going to be the lucky lady, so we keep slagging each other. You know, to try to make ourselves look better."

"Please, let's do something that doesn't involve boys," I say. I'm sure I sound a bit bitchy as I say it, but Tiffany doesn't seem to notice or care. I lay my head on the desk.

"Cramps?" Tiffany asks. "You want a Midol?"

"No, it's not that—just boy trouble."

"Valium?"

I shake my head no. Tiffany returns to the subject at hand.

"How about if we pretend that we've been sent to assassinate that Colombian soccer player who . . ." She goes on and on, but I can't stop thinking about what I'm going to do tonight. So many girls would jump at a chance to date Clint. A lot of my friends would, I know. So why am I not happy? Would Clint ever make me a present like Damien just did? Put me first? Even the poems that I gave him so much credit for turned out to be Damien's words and thoughts. But there's something a bit sleazy about the way Damien is coming on to me behind Clint's back and all. Damien was right about one thing—Clint would never do that to one of his friends. But Clint was willing to cheat on me. He . . .

". . . so after I lure him onto the balcony, you'll step out from behind the fountain and . . . Hey! Missy! Anyone home?"

"I'm sorry," I say. "Whatever you want is fine."

Tiffany looks peeved. She narrows her eyes to thin slits, glances at her watch, and takes a deep breath. "Look, let's take care of this boy thing first. Otherwise we might not ever get to the good part of this assignment. Your problem can't be too difficult. Just remember that boys are dogs."

"What, you mean, like, they lie and cheat?"

"No, I've never had a dog lie to me. What I mean is—they're simple like dogs. Easy to please. Easy to keep in line. Throw them a bone once in a while, and they'll be like . . ." Tiffany sticks her tongue out, holds her hands out in front of her like a begging dog, and pants.

"What do you mean, 'throw them a bone'?" I ask.

Tiffany rolls her eyes in a major way. "Not important. Look, why don't you tell me the situation? Write a little 'Dear Tiffany' letter. Advice for the lovelorn—it's my specialty."

I can't believe I'm even thinking of telling Tiffany Delvoe about this. I don't even know her. Then again, I already know what all of my friends, otherwise known as the Clint DeFreisz Fan Club, would tell me. Plus, I'm fairly certain Tiffany doesn't give a flip about high school romances. She hasn't gone out with a boy here since she was a sophomore. Why should she, when half the guys at Central have asked her for her phone number?

"Well . . . ?"

And I tell her. I leave out the names, but she's not stupid. She knows I date Clint, and she probably saw Damien talking to me before class. She interrupts a couple times. When I tell her all of my friends think the world of my boyfriend, she says, "So?" She says "So?" again, when I tell her how attentive Boy Two is, and how he'd do anything for me. Is my story boring her, or is she just unimpressed with these details? When I've finished explaining everything, Tiffany takes over.

"First of all," she says, "you've got completely the wrong attitude about this. Two guys fighting over you—that's a good thing. That's something we can work with. Quit acting like today sucks. This is an opportunity. Do you know how many girls here will go four years without *one* guy liking them?"

I nod along, already starting to feel a bit better.

"Daddy—Ford dealer that he is—says you can tell a sucker the second he walks into the showroom. You can tell just by looking at him, the way he glances around at the salesmen or kicks a tire all shy-like. Daddy says all people can be divided into these two categories: proactive or reactive. Which basically translates to the screwers and the screwed."

Tiffany digs through her purse as she continues.

"Proactive people take charge. They know what car they want, how much they want to spend, the color of the trim. If you've got what they want, they'll buy. If you don't, they're out the door. Reactive people, on the other hand, have no idea what they want. The salesman ends up deciding for them. And believe me, what the reactive person wants is always on the lot."

I'm genuinely confused by what Tiffany's telling me. How does this apply to me, Clint, and Damien?

"Following me?" Tiffany asks as she plucks a Jolly Rancher out of her purse, unwraps it, and sticks it in her mouth.

I nod.

"See, I've tried to take this theory into the real world—I am the consumer, not the consumed. I know what I want, so I do the picking and choosing. I don't allow myself to be picked up, squeezed, tried on for size, or taken through the express line."

"But I know I'm the one doing the choosing," I say. "I explained that already. I'm just not sure who to pick."

"Really?" Tiffany says. "But are you being reactive or proactive? Are you being sold a package deal, or are you picking out exactly what you want? You know, in my store there are these long aisles, there are no clocks on the walls, I've got plenty of cash. And you know what? There are no salespeople. I don't take my friends shopping with me. Or my parents."

"Well, that might work for you, but . . ."

"Look, you know half the boys in this school probably want to win stuffed animals for you at the county fair and take you home to meet their parents, so don't go sounding pitiful on me. It just sounds to me like you're shopping in one of those old communist department stores."

"How's that?"

"They give you a choice, but it's the blue shoes or the red shoes."

CLINT

Twilley puts his headdress back on, picks his pistol off his desk, and instructs us to use our time wisely. "Start reading chapter thirteen," he says.

Sure thing.

Then he heads out the door. Immediately the classroom disintegrates: Books slam shut, headphones materialize from backpacks, desks get scooted across the room, Game Boys are fired up. I'm glad to see Damien get up and start walking back toward me, but he just walks by. Says "Hey," though, as he passes. He sits down at one of the LONS in the back of the classroom. Every time he gets a free minute, he's on one of 'em, always tinkerin' with yearbook stories. Me, I avoid the LONS at all costs. I'm the guy who'd end up on the last page of a major paper when lightning hits the school and fries the system. I always forget how to log on and have to get help, so why bother? I'm a notebook and pencil (#2) man; thanks for askin'. I get up from my seat, walk over, and lean against the wall next to Damien.

"What's the haps?" he says.

"You tell me."

"Huh?"

"What were you thinkin' at the auction this mornin'? What were you doin' biddin' on Jen?"

"Oh, that." He pushes his glasses up but keeps his eyes on the screen. How can he type and talk at the same time? "I was just checkin' out all our pitiful classmates quivering and shaking at the feet of the nasty linebacker."

"So?"

"So, I couldn't let you get off that easy."

"Well, that's kinda what I thought, but then you kept biddin'."

Damien stops typin' for a sec and looks at me. "Did you see how embarrassed Jenny was when it looked like she was gonna be the cheapest slave in school?"

"She didn't look any diff'rent than she always looks."

Damien returns his attention to the screen but keeps talkin'. "Man, you gotta pay better attention to her."

"Since when did you become Dr. Ruth? Look, if you think—"

"You know you're leadin' the league in tackles?"

"What?"

"It's right here. I've logged into the *Austin American-Statesman*'s on-line sports information databank. You're three ahead of that guy from New London."

"Lemme see."

He scoots his chair over and I pull one up to the terminal. Sure 'nuff. There's my name sittin' above a buncha also-rans.

"You can call that up from here?" I ask.

"Absolutely."

Now I'm startin' to see some practical applications for computers. "What else can you call up?"

"All the league stats. Articles they've written. Schedules. I use this all the time when I'm writin' the sports copy for the *Stars & Bars*." Damien calls the info up as he's talkin'. I'm stunned. He shows me how I can get the latest college top-twenty rankings or the *Statesman*'s list of the top fifty recruits in Texas. We find Humphrey's name at number three.

"Tight!"

"Do you ever even log on, check to see if you have any mail?" Damien asks.

"I never learned how."

"We had an assembly. They showed everyone in the school."

"Look, bruh, I don't dig on computers. You know how some people don't trust banks? Well, I don't trust computers. I like everything on paper. Right in front o' me."

"Do you want me to show you how to do it, my brotha? Just in case, you know, you have some urgent correspondence. Maybe you've won the lottery, and you just don't know it."

I nod and Damien closes his own files. Then he takes me back to the log-on screen.

"What's your screen name?"

"My what?"

"Your screen name. Look, if you didn't choose one, then it's automatically your student ID number."

I start pulling my ID out of my wallet. Damien shakes his head likes he's disappointed with me.

"Man, you need to change your screen name. Anyone can get your student number: any of those student aides who pick up the attendance cards, any of those old ladies in the office, anyone you show your ID to when you get student discounts. Hell, any teacher in school can just ask for it."

"So?"

"So? So?" Damien takes off his glasses and cleans 'em with a hanky. It's his way of counting to ten. "Look, anyone who knows your student number could get into your files, read anything you have saved in there."

"That's another good reason for not working on the LONS. It's a good thing I haven't saved anything on here."

"You're missin' the point. If they log with your ID number, they can read anything people might be sending you." Damien types the number off my card into the computer. "And they can also send stuff to other people as if they were you."

"Why would someone think that a message came from me?"

"Because, when you get mail from someone, it automatically tells you the sender's proper name—unless you intentionally block it. The computers figure there's no sense in keeping the sender's name confidential."

I look down at the screen. My name is at the top along with my student ID number, the time of day, and a 2 under the number of times I've logged on this year. Flashing in the top right-hand corner of the screen is the message YOU'VE GOT MAIL. I look at D. He looks at me and shrugs.

"Probably just stuff about class rings and signing up for SATs. All that shit the administration sends out." He double-clicks on a little mailbox. A block o' writin' appears. "This is three days old!" Damien growls, but I'm busy readin' the message.

44,
I LIKE THE WAY YOU LOOK IN PADS
WHEN ON THE FIELD YOU RACE
I WISH I WAS A RUNNING BACK
WRAPPED IN YOUR EMBRACE
MAYBE LEADING CHEERS IS BETTER
SO I CAN WISH YOU LUCK
BUT ONE DAY LET'S FIND A WAY
TO GO BACK HOME AND . . .
GET TO KNOW EACH OTHER
XXXXOOOOO

"Who sent it? Who sent it?" I'm looking all over the screen to find a name.

"Trinni Rea," says D., pointing to the sender name on-screen.

But of course. I remember Trinni flirtin' with me two weeks ago. She asked me for a ride home after I got outta football practice. She was just gettin' done with cheerleadin' at the same time. I remember now what she said. It was weird because it was a Tuesday, and our game was still three days away. She said, "Good luck."

TOMMY

3:07 P.M. Sixth period, drama

"What's the deal with Mr. Twilley?"

I ask Miss Amenny the question as I hand her another cup of coffee (two Sweet'n Low/one Cremora). I sit down across from her, a kidney-shaped coffee table separating our two directors' chairs. This is our prerehearsal routine. I'm her aide during her conference period, and we both like to caffeine up before we begin. I take a slug of my own java (black).

"What's what deal?" she says.

"I looked him up in the old yearbooks, and it looked like the whole school revolved around him. He sponsored all these clubs. He was voted favorite teacher a bunch of times. I even saw a picture where he was the Speller. I about wigged."

"And your point is?" Miss A. says, but I know she's jacking with me.

"My point is—how'd he turn into . . . well, what he is? After the 1978 *Stars & Bars*, he doesn't even appear in the books. Not even in the mug shots."

I can tell that Miss A. has to think about whether or not she wants to answer the question. She leans back in her chair and looks up before she says anything.

"'Seventy-eight was a bad year for Marc—Mr. Twilley, that is. You've got to understand that Mr. Twilley, while he was certainly more popular with students early in his career, has never been an easy teacher. He's always been a stickler. He takes his subject very seriously."

"No shit," I say.

Miss A. shakes her head but continues.

"Early in his career, there was no such thing as 'no pass/no play.' Students who failed a class could still play sports, still go on field trips, still be in the school play. When that changed, most teachers changed with it. We got more flexible, allowed students to make up assignments, or we would bend a grade up a bit if it meant the difference between passing and failing. But not Marc. He didn't change at all."

Miss A. takes a slow sip of her coffee, like she's trying to decide how much to tell me.

"You know that big banner that hangs in the gym?" Miss A. asks.

"Yeah, it says DISTRICT CHAMPS 1978."

"Well then, you've probably noticed that it's the only one we have. Fifty some-odd years of football here at Lee, and all we have is one district championship to show for it. And that banner doesn't tell the whole story. That team was undefeated. In fact, no one even played us close that year. People were talking state championship. You've never seen Deerfield as electric as it was back then."

"Mr. Twilley failed one of the players?" I guess.

"Two of them," she answers, "right before the first round of the play-offs. One with a sixty-eight and one with a sixty-nine. Both star players. At first the coaches begged Marc to change the grades, just 'loan' them a point or two from their next grading period. When he told them no, the principal back then called Marc into his office and demanded he change the grades. Marc wasn't very polite when he refused.

"Well, the next week both players suit up for the play-off game, which Lee wins big. Marc does some checking and discovers that someone in the office has changed the kids' grades, so Marc calls the state athletic offices and turns us in. We're forced to forfeit the game. We're eliminated from the play-offs. Marc's name appears in all the papers, and everyone blames him for the town's collective humiliation. Our principal takes away all of Marcus's honors classes and reassigns him to the remedial sections. The students turn on him. His Quiz Bowl team asks for a new sponsor. His house gets vandalized. The *Herald* is full of letters from parents saying things like, 'That teacher is what's wrong with education.'

"Most people would have just left Deerfield, and maybe Marc would have too, but his wife was pregnant, and he thought the stress of moving would be worse than the stress of staying here."

"But Mr. Twilley doesn't have any kids," I point out.

"The pregnancy wasn't successful, Tommy. I think Marc has stayed here since then just to spite the town. He hasn't done anything other than teach since then. He's still a good teacher. He still pushes students hard, some say too hard, but he hasn't sponsored a club, taken a field trip, participated in any school events like the faculty play.

"So that's what surprises me about today," she adds.

"What about today?"

"Why in the world did he volunteer to be a slave?"

CLINT

Thursdays are light days: helmets and shorts. We do some stretching, jog through the special-teams stuff, maybe half speed through any new plays we've put in for that particular week. We hafta be off the field before the freshman game, so the whole thing doesn't take more 'n an hour. That's why it's strange that the coaches are runnin' so far behind today. Team's been out here on Rebel Field playin' grab-ass for a solid fifteen. Ain't a whistle been heard.

I look around for Humphrey, figurin' that, since he's the captain, he could get the stretchin' started. I wanna have enough time to grab somethin' to eat after school and get back in time for Alex's JV game. Then I notice Humphrey ain't here. Neither's Jody Anderson. I don't see Ray Cook or Marvin Washington either. All of 'em are seniors. All of 'em are black.

I don't like the look of this.

I see the double doors of the field house have been pushed open and all the coaches are walking out with these grim-lookin' faces. Coach Rossy shouts into his bullhorn.

"Let's line it up and get 'em stretched out. DeFreisz, you lead 'em."

Now everyone starts noticin' their missin' teammates. I see guys lookin' at me like I should know what's goin' on, but I don't. Least not for sure, but I do have some ideas. I'm tryin' to lead the team through the stretches, but I can't seem to count out loud, 'cuz I got too much runnin' through my head. Mainly, how're we gonna beat Liberty Valley without Humphrey and the rest o' those guys? Why couldn't Coach've kept his stupid mouth shut? Why did Humphrey hafta take it personal? I know for a fact Coach thinks the world o' H. B. I mean, how many other coaches in the district start a black quarterback?

I call for hurdler's stretch.

Tweeeeeeeeeeeeeet.

Rossy gets in my face. "DeFreisz! Pull yer head out, boy! We already done that!"

"Yessir."

But I'm not the only one with his head up his ass. We practice like girls. Footballs go bouncin' off guys' helmets. Grant Ehlam, our backup quarterback, can't remember the plays; he keeps turnin' the wrong way to hand off. The coaches keep arguin' with each other. When the defense jumps offsides for the third time in a row, Rossy gives up. He blows his whistle and tells us to gather round. This is the time each week that he gives us our big pep talk. He gives a short one right before the game, but this is the speech where he pulls out all the stops: watery eyes, clipboards slammed to the ground, clutchin' his heart 'n' all. Today he pulls a two-foot section of rope outta the pocket of his Rebel Pride windbreaker.

"This, men, is a rope."

I've heard this one already, but it's a classic. He tells us this story 'bout his daddy. Reveals how his old man saved dollars in empty fruit jars to send his boy to college, mentions how when there wasn't enough to eat the old man would just sit 'n' smoke Lucky Strikes on the porch 'til dinner was over. Then he throws in this added detail: The man worked on a farm his whole life despite arthritis, cancer, and a bum leg.

"But you know what, men? If I was hangin' from a cliff, and I had my choice of anyone on this planet to be holdin' on to the other end o' this rope, that eighty-nine-year-old man's who I'd pick."

The team is silent. The new guys who haven't heard this are mesmerized. Us veterans are anticipatin' this next part, 'cuz it's the coolest.

"You see, I know there might be chunks o' flesh comin' outta his hands, blood spurtin' from his eyes, but he wouldn't let go. He might fly off the cliff with me, but he'd still be holdin' on to that rope.

"After him, I'd take any of you boys."

Guys start lookin' at one another. Then Coach starts up again.

"'Cuz we're a team. And when you're part of a team, you put your faith in your teammates. You're there for 'em when the goin' gets tough. Now, you may've noticed we're missin' a few boys today. Well . . . they've decided they don't wanna be part o' this team. That's okay. We'll let 'em go their own way. What's important is that we regroup. Put it behind us."

But I'm not sure I can put it behind me. I'm wonderin'—if I was hanging from a cliff—would I want Coach on the other end of that rope?

Doesn't matter. It ain't some speech that's gonna get me pumped up tomorrow night. Like I'm really thinkin' 'bout ropes when I got some fullback tryin' to remove my kneecaps. Truthfully, there's not much thinkin' involved out there. You may hear people talk about football bein' a thinkin' man's game or some such bull-shit, but it's all instinct and desire. You stop to think and someone's gonna plow your ass. Tomorrow we're gonna get our dicks handed to us, and you know what? I don't even care. I just wanna get out there—hit and get hit. Not thinkin' solves lots of problems.

TIFFANY

3:41 P.M. Sixth period, community service

Talk about bogus classes. While Rainy vents about having to kiss Trailer Parks in *Tom Jones*, I fill in the blanks on birthday cards for the residents of the Golden Years Retirement Village. I thought it would be funny to put a frog on the front and write GLAD YOU HAVEN'T CROAKED on the inside, but apparently I was the only one in the class with a sense of humor, because the cards we ended up with have Raggedy Ann and Andy on them. Do old people really revert to childhood once they're exiled to a home?

To graduate from Lee you either have to take community ser-vice for a semester or volunteer somewhere: a homeless shelter or church or suicide hotline—something like that. Taking the class is easier. Other than penning touching B-day greetings to the *Matlock* set, we also keep Deerfield's first graders off the hard stuff by con-vincing them that Barney hates crackheads. When we're feeling especially ambitious, we empty the recycling bins.

". . . anyway, I tell Miss A. that the guy smells like a giant armpit, and she acts like I'm the one with the problem."

"That's showbiz," I say.

"Thanks for the sympathy," says Rainy. "Hey, by the way, I got interesting news from that freshman who lives with my parents and me."

"Your brother?"

"The blood test hasn't come back. Let's not jump to conclusions."

"What did he have to say? Does IBM have a new catalog out?"

"He said that there's lots of talk about your choice of slaves flying around the information geekway. He read a message your slave posted mapping out the path your tongue took along his body."

"What else did your brother tell you?"

"He said the odds on your slave bagging you went down from a thousand to one to fifty to one after that."

"I wish someone would have told me when it was at a thousand to one; I could have used the cash."

"Bulimia, anyone?" Rainy says, sticking a finger in her mouth.

Just then my pager goes off again. I check the number and recognize it as Delvoe Ford's. Daddy beckons. He can wait.

BRENDAN

3:57 P.M. Computer lab

Tiffany wasn't in her class when I went to pick her up from community service. Her friend Rainy said she had gone to use the phone. I take the opportunity to meet Lloyd in the computer lab. He's already logged on by the time I get there. He faces me. He's wearing this big, evil grin, and he's spinning a floppy around in his fingers.

"Luke, give yourself over to the dark side," he says.

Here's the big difference between Lloyd and me—at least I like to think there's a big difference—Lloyd will hack anywhere and do anything: he'll crash other people's systems; he'll make their credit reports reflect an earlier bankruptcy, he'll add people's names to every single national mailing list. Once he forwarded all of Domino's incoming calls to the local adult bookstore. (Lloyd taped the calls. The funniest one has a woman saying, "I'd like a large pepperoni." "Wouldn't we all," answers the porn dealer.) I try to keep my hacking limited to "victimless" white-collar crime.

"I sense there is goodness in you yet, Father," I say.

"Obi-Wan has taught you well," says Lloyd, then he drops his Darth Vader voice. "But check out what you're missing."

Not for the first time, I'm glad that Lloyd's my friend and not my enemy. He wades through a few commands, and a listing of some of the most popular students in school comes up on-screen. Next to their names are sets of numbers. I make sure Annabella's isn't one of them.

"Are those their passwords?" I ask. Lloyd nods. I continue scanning the list until I find Tiffany's. "You must have had some free time on your hands."

"Not really. I just ran names against a list of student ID numbers I pulled from the office. None of these Greek gods bothered to change their password from the default."

"What are you planning on doing with this list?" I notice the disk he's still spinning in his hand.

"Oh, with most of them, just have some fun. I've been logging in under one pop's name. Then I send out pretty steamy E-mail to another one of the blemish-free. It's kinda my own version of *Love Connection.* They're always trolling the same genetic pool, anyway. They probably won't even notice the difference."

"Hilarious," I say with indifferitude. "What's with the disk?"

Lloyd can barely contain his pride. "This, my paladin friend, is your opportunity to make Tiffany pay for any real or perceived slights. On this disk I have created the mother of all computer viruses. Like a neutron bomb, it takes out exactly what you want it to. It'll reduce a gigabyte's worth of treasured files to electronic confetti in a matter of a few hours. Behold, Expunger!"

"What do you suggest I do with it?"

"Unleash its fury. Vengeance is yours," says Lloyd, more melodramatically than usual. Then he sticks the disk in my book bag. As I stand to leave, he adds, "Destroy all you want. I'll make more."

SHAWN

You know, sometimes, in my darkest moments, I wonder what I
would do if I blew out a knee or had my arms ripped off in a car
wreck and I couldn't play ball. I know what I would be good at—
cruise director. Just like Julie on *The Love Boat*. Making everybody
happy. Figuring out who gets to sit at the captain's table. Getting
the old folks goin' in some shuffleboard tournament. Organizing
the end-of-the-cruise ball. I got a knack for this shit.

Take now, for instance.

I got the idea an hour ago. Already I got us a location. A friend
of mine knows the guy who owns the Knights of Columbus hall. I
got a DJ. No trick to that—I just told Anthony Hill and Jason
Cohen (aka Zebra Posse) that they could rap their asses off if they
took care of the rest of the jams. DeWayne Haynes, who used to
be a hell of a halfback here, is our campus cop. I got him to work
security tomorrow night on the condition that I put in a good word
for him with LaTisha. I must be spendin' too much time with
Keene, 'cuz I told him "no sweat." Getting the word out, now
that's my specialty. Not necessarily 'cuz I talk to *everyone*. More
because I know who to talk to if I really gotta make sure everybody's gonna hear about something.

Presently I'm talking to the last person on my list of key big-
mouths, Derlinda Seals. She'll fill in all the Mission of God
Baptists. I don't mention the political angle to her at all. I mean, it
seems like they're all willing to let themselves be put into "God's
merciful hands." They're not so tight-assed once you get some
Boone's Farm into 'em. Bell rings and I remember one last duty. I
am, after all, still technically a slave. I try to remember where
Notorious B.I.G. told me his next class was. Not necessary,
though, 'cuz I can spot his Congo clothes from a mile off.

"Sorry I'm late, boss," I say to him when I catch up. I make
sure it comes out friendly.

"I didn't think I'd see you again," he says.

"Deal's a deal," I say. He doesn't say anything to that. He

looks like he's far away somewhere in that mixed-up head of his. "Hey, Keene, look, my man, maybe I been wrong 'bout some o' the things I've done today. I just cared more about not getting shown up after that stuff you wrote in the paper than I did about doin' what's right. Slave Day is kinda wack."

Keene looks at me like he's confused. If I woulda known this worked so well, I woulda tried it earlier and not waited till school was about over.

"Maybe I got carried away a bit too," he says.

"Well, all right, then," I say. I offer up a palm for a high handshake, and the Reverend takes it almost immediately.

"As long as we've got things worked out," I say, "let me tell you about a party I got happenin' tomorrow night. We're takin' your idea of a boycott, but we're boycottin' the game instead. No one darker than you is allowed in the stadium tomorrow. Anyone shows, they answer to me. You heard about the football players, didn't you?"

"Yeah, but I wasn't sure it was true."

"It's true, all right. But we're gonna show everyone we're behind 'em. I'm supposed to be there for some student council thing, but hell with that. Lee High is gonna learn what's up, tomorrow night."

"*Cool*," says Keene, just like it's 1980-something.

"Yeah, very *cool*. Anyway, I want to make sure you're comin' to the party. I mean, in a way, you got this whole thing started."

"Sure, yeah, I'll be there."

"That's what I wanted to hear. Hey, it'd be tight if you brought a date, too."

Keene smiles so big, you'd think he was me.

TIFFANY

4:12 P.M. Delvoe Ford

Daddy sounded utterly spooky on the phone. Possibly drunk. Sometimes it's hard to tell with him. He never slurs, but sometimes he'll repeat himself or just go off on some tangent. He did a bunch of that just now.

"Come down to the dealership. I need to get your signature on some forms."

"Can't we do that at home?" I asked.

"Goddamn it! For once will you not argue with me? We need them notarized, and we need it done today, plus we need to get them notarized."

"Should we get them notarized?" I asked.

"Just get your ass down here."

I spotted Brian . . . Brendan . . . whatever . . . in the parking lot after I hung up the phone. He looked like he was trying to scam a ride home from somebody. At first I was hoping I was done with him for the day, but he might come in handy as an excuse to get away from Daddy and his pal Jim Beam. I still had a few hours left on my hundred dollars, so I told him he was coming with me.

I parked the Probe in the washing stall and told my slave I would be giving it the white glove test after I got through unstressing the parental unit. He looked chafed. Sure hope I'll be able to sleep tonight.

As I walk up to the door of Daddy's office, I notice that the miniblinds are drawn. That's not like him. I knock—which isn't like me.

"Who is it? Is that you?" he says.

"Yeah, it's me," I say as I open the door and enter. I notice the whiskey bottle open on his desk next to the family portrait we took last Christmas when both my brothers were home from New Jersey. Remember in *Lady and the Tramp* how, when the two stars had puppies, all the boys ended up terriers, like Tramp, and all the girls ended up cocker spaniels, like Lady? That's sort of how our family worked. The boys have Daddy's same billboard-size forehead, sandy hair, and green eyes. They're a bit on the short side, with these Tasmanian Devils' bodies that look like they've been through a trash compactor. Regrettably, I don't think either of my siblings got Daddy's brains or ambition. In twenty years they're going to be co-managers of the dealership with one eye each on Daddy's will. But just look at the old man. If his liver holds up, he may outlive them both just so he can cheat them out of an inheritance.

"Glad you made it." He pulls a file out of his drawer and removes a stack of forms he has paper-clipped together. The man *is* organized. I've seen him locate a twenty-year-old warranty with enough alcohol in him to power a squadron of F-14 Tomcats. "Here you go," he says, plopping the papers down in front of me. "Sign."

I start reading the first one. It's the title to the Probe. From what I can tell, he's signing it over to me.

"Stop reading. Start signing," barks Martin.

"Who was it that told me to never sign something without reading it?" I point a finger at my brain, knit my brows, purse my lips like I'm trying to remember.

"You're eighteen now. I'm just signing over everything that should be yours."

I thumb through the remaining papers. I notice he's also giving me my brother's car. Daddy can't still be mad about that hazing incident, can he? "Boy, I can't wait to tell Phillip that I own his Bronco," I say.

"Just sign the papers, Tiffany. Let me do the thinking for the family," Daddy says. He pours himself another whiskey and wind.

The next form gives me access to my trust fund, the one Mammy and Pap set up for me. But I wasn't supposed to be able to get anything out of it until I was twenty-one. Now I'm positive something's up.

"You're not still mad about last night, are you? Are you kicking me out? Picking up a few extra bucks renting my room?"

"Sign!" he yells.

But I've got too many of his genes. I set the pen down, lean back in my chair, and play the game. I know I'm playing against the guy who practically wrote the book. After all, Daddy invented the "This is our floor manager's last day here. He's practically giving cars away" scam. He perfected the "How low did you want those payments?" ploy. Car salesmen from across the state make pilgrimages to Delvoe Ford to learn firsthand how to milk an extra seven hundred dollars out of a customer for "rustproofing and undercoating." But this time I've got the absolute best weapon on my side, and it's not that he's been drinking. That just gets Daddy feisty. No, it's that he's desperate, and it shows. "Desperation," the old man always says, "makes suckers of us all."

"What are you doing?" says Daddy when he realizes I've set down the pen.

"Why don't you tell me what's up."

I notice that it's time to regloss my nails. I sigh.

"I don't have time for this, Tiffany."

"Really?" I say. "Why not?"

I set the little knocker balls on Daddy's desk in motion. I yawn. Daddy pushes two fingers into each temple. He's caving.

"Look," Daddy says, "we may be running into some financial difficulty. It's important for these items not to appear as assets. Now, will you just sign these papers?"

"What sort of financial difficulty?" I say. For safety's sake I go ahead and sign the trust fund over to myself. But I stop there. Now it's Daddy's turn to sigh. I've won. He takes one long sip of his drink and tells me the story. Five months ago, he says, a long-time friend, a former wildcatter who'd undergone a postbank-ruptcy conversion to the high-technology faith, approached Daddy with an offer to get a computer chip company off the ground. A half million dollars guaranteed to turn into two million within half a year. The trouble was, Daddy was suffering from poor cash flow, so he sort of "borrowed" the money from the dealership without telling his Yankee partner. Daddy does the books, so hiding the money for six months didn't seem like it would be a big problem. And it wasn't—until two weeks ago. That's when Ford made an unbelievable offer on a hundred Mustangs to Mr. Milligan. When Daddy rejected the offer, his partner grew suspicious. Yesterday he called for an audit. That happens tomorrow, which is why he wants me to sign all these documents today.

"You handle the books. Can't you make it look like the money is out there somewhere?" I ask, suddenly worried about where I'll be sleeping. "Hey, can you sign the lake house over to me?"

"I think that would look a little suspicious," says Daddy. "And no, I can't figure out anywhere to hide the money. All the invoices have been entered into the computer—the computer that's locked in that Yankee sumbitch's office."

Daddy takes another sip. I reach out, and he hands the glass to me. I take my own sip as Daddy continues.

"The thing is, I almost pulled it off. Another sixteen days, and I would have seen my first dividend check, more than enough to pay back the business."

"What we need is a fire to wipe out the building," I say.

"No, what we need is one of those computer experts, a hacker who could get in and destroy all the files."

"That's it?" I say.

"Why?" says Daddy. "You know one?"

"Know one?" I say. "I own one."

MR. TWILLEY
4:45 P.M. Theater

I sit in the tenth row of the auditorium during Thomas's play rehearsal, and aside from being sent to purchase sodas for the entire cast, I'm left alone. I'm surprised by the quality of Thomas's acting. All the frenetic energy that makes him a difficult student to teach becomes a positive onstage. He finds humor in lines where none seemingly exists, though he does have a tendency to swallow entire scenes even when other characters should be the center of attention. Several times Linda directs him to "Leave space, Tommy. Leave space." I wonder if she's ever looked into any small college theater programs that might accept a student with a transcript as spotty as Mr. Parks's.

"Mr. Twilley?" The voice comes from behind me. I turn to find Leonardo Tristan walking down the aisle.

"Yes?"

"Well, there you are. Got a minute?"

I nod and Mr. Tristan takes a seat two down from me.

"Marcus, I wanted to talk to you about Tamika Jackson. You know she's the only black female we've got in NHS?" he asks.

"Someone was telling me that this afternoon," I say. "So?"

"So I wanted to talk to you about this alleged cheating incident."

"It's more than alleged. It happened. I left my room for a moment during a quiz, and when I came back in, she had a boy leaning over her shoulder with her quiz completely uncovered. I don't think she'd deny that."

"Well she does deny cheating or helping the other boy cheat."

"That's hardly surprising."

"Look, Marcus, if you turn in a report on Tamika, I'll have to kick her out of NHS. And it looks bad enough that we only have one black girl in the group as it is . . ."

"But that's not my problem," I say.

"Well, it could be," Tristan says, "because the rumor going around school is that you're busting her because she's black, or more specifically, that you don't believe her because she's black."

BRENDAN

6:56 P.M. Delvoe estate

I'm in Tiffany Delvoe's den playing pool, and I'm not sucking so bad. Pool, after all, is no more than a combination of geometry and physics. If all I had to do was figure out where to hit the ball I'd be Deerfield Slim. It's the actual hitting that's the problem. Still, I'm making more than I'm missing. I've won my second game, and Tiffany seems strangely present in both body and spirit. She keeps saying things like, "Good shot, *Brendan*" and "Wow, you're good."

I bank the cue ball off two rails and tap in a four ball that had been previously left teetering on the rim of the corner pocket. Tiffany claps and says, "This calls for a celebration. You want a Coke?" I say sure, even though I was aiming for the seven. Tiffany slips behind the bar and ducks down. When she reappears she has two glasses. She hands me one of them. It's after I've been chugging a second that I notice that there's more than Coke in the glass.

"Slow down a bit," Tiffany warns. "Captain Morgan can sneak up on you if you're not careful."

The phone rings. Tiffany answers it, and I try to pretend I'm not listening. I chalk the tip of my stick and pour some baby powder on my left knuckles. Tiffany says, "Hi, Troy" in that I'm-so-bored-I-could-murder-you-for-sport voice that I'm starting to get used to. She holds the phone away from her head and rolls her eyes.

"Hey, Troy. Look. I've got a friend . . ." *(friend?)* ". . . over here, and he's got me down to my Calvins in a game of strip eight-ball. Later."

I've got no idea whether Troy is able to get in another word before Tiffany hangs up, but the mention of strip pool has given me a minor woody. I pretend I'm interested in something out on historic Belvin Street as I finish my Coke and make adjustments. Tiffany picks up my glass and pours me another. This time, Captain Morgan has a bit more presence in my drink.

"Best four out of seven?" Tiffany says.

"Sure," I say, disappointed that my voice sounds briefly like it did in seventh grade.

MR. TWILLEY

7:29 P.M. Whataburger

Thomas didn't have the time to return home before going to work. He unrolled a Whataburger uniform that he dug out from behind the seat in his pickup. The garment appeared to have gone several shifts without a laundering. He changed inside his truck cab in the student parking lot and tried to convince me not to come to work with him.

"You've got better things to do than hang out at Whataburger for the next four hours," he said.

I replied that a deal was a deal, and that I wanted to see Slave Day through to its conclusion. The truth, of course, was that I had nothing better to do. Besides, sipping coffee and grading papers at

Whataburger would be as easy as doing so in my empty house.

And while I've been sipping, Mr. Parks has been gulping. In the hour and a half I've been here, I've counted four cups of coffee that he's finished. That can't be good for a teenager. I've tried to do my part here tonight. During the dinner rush I bussed a few tables. I can't stand to see a dirty table, and minimum-wage employees always seem blind to them. A few students from the high school have come in, but none of them have spoken to me. I've seen them whisper and point as if I'm an exhibit at a zoo. After the rush is over, Thomas brings a huge bag of french fries out to the table. He rips the bag open and squirts half a bottle of ketchup on the paper.

"Thanks for the help," he says, offering me a share of the fries with a hand gesture. I take a few out of politeness.

"You put on quite a show back there," I say. Thomas has been juggling condiment bottles in the same manner that bartenders at fancy Dallas bars handle liquor bottles. He was also merciless with the customers who ordered via the drive-through intercom. Tommy would demand forty dollars for a small soda, or, if the customers were girls, he would put a "Mac" in front of every item he read back ("You wanted two MacWhataburgers, two MacWhatafries, two MacCokes and one MacDaddy?"). With some carloads he adopted the persona of a snooty French waiter ("Bonjour, mes amis, ees zer sumsing I can have zee chef prepare pour vous?"). If he tired of dealing with a slow customer, he simply hissed static noises into the microphone.

"Helps pass time," he says.

"How late are you open? Do you have to stay until closing time?"

"We're open twenty-four hours, but I'll get out of here by three."

Now I understand the coffee and why he never studied for my quizzes. I don't understand, however, why his parents would allow him to work such long hours. He's a clever boy. I'm sure in the right situation he could be successful academically. I watch Thomas as he arranges a score of fries into cylindrical formation and shoves them into his mouth. He pushes the rest across the table toward me. "The deep fryer calls," he says as he stands. Then he adds in feigned gravity, "Let us strive on to finish the work we are in—Abraham Lincoln. I learned that in your class."

At first I'm pleased. I *was* able to teach Thomas something. But upon reflection this knowledge saddens me. Is this what students are gleaning from my class these days—dried-up old quotations used in place of original thought?

TIFFANY

7:54 P.M. Delvoe den

"Oh sure, you could do that. Why I've heard of a guy who hacked into . . . Boy, you're making everything," says Brendan.

I line up the eight ball. "Just lucky," I say. "Go on."

"Anyway, this guy hacks into what he thinks is a MUD."

"Mud?"

"Multiuser dungeon. It's a place where people can go and pretend to be other people. There are different kinds: castles with monsters and treasure; Old West MUDs with saloons and gunfights. Anyway, this guy, he thinks he's stumbled into a *Goodfellas*-type MUD, because the other people are all talking about delivering cocaine and who they're gonna take out and all that. So this guy, he figures, What the hey? He joins the group, says his name is Nick Tulane, and offers ten thousand dollars to anyone who'll rub out his psychology professor."

"And . . . ?"

"And a week later, they pull the professor out of Lake Pontchartrain."

I watch young Brendan shudder. I sink the eight ball.

"Sounds like a computer version of an urban myth. Rack 'em."

Brendan starts doing as he's told. "What's an urban myth?" he says.

"It's one of those stories that sound outrageous—but everyone has heard it. Most of the people who tell you the story know the person it happened to. It's never them, but they know the person personally. You know, stories about Richard Gere and his pet gerbils. Whoever tells you the story had a friend who worked on a movie set. The Dallas Cowboy cheerleader who had to have her stomach pumped—this time the friend is the doctor. And let's not forget the classic of the close personal friend who bought a small dog in Mexico, brought it back, and then found out it was a giant rat."

"Yeah, but I really know somebody that happened to."

"Brendan, get with the—"

But then I realize he's fucking with my head. You go, boy.

"Oh, yeah," Brendan says. "There's also the one about *Playboy* naming whatever city you live in as the biggest party town in the country."

"I've heard that one, too," I say.

BRENDAN

8:12 P.M. Tiffany's room

Tiffany told me to wait up here. In her room. Where her bed is. Whoop, Whoop.

I lay down on it—the bed, that is—just for a sec. (My impressions available at alt.sex.fetish on the World Wide Web.) I'm a little glummed there's no mirror on the ceiling above me, but at least the bed spins. Or is that me? How many rum and Cokes have I had?

Sitting up, I make an effort to memorize the details of the room. Like her locker, it's pretty anticlimactic. I don't know what I imagined—medieval torture devices, eunuch quarters—whatever it was, I was way off. On the other hand, the room doesn't look anything like the fluffy quarters of other teen girls. I'll admit that my experience in this area is limited, but from what I've heard they normally come stocked with foo foo wallpaper and pressed flowers. Not Tiffany's. First of all, there's nothing here—no Leonardo DiCaprio posters or telltale Lee High banners—that would give away her age, except maybe the stack of alternative rock CDs still in their shrink-wrapping on her dresser. Postcards in random male scripts and exotic languages are stuck inside the wooden frame of her vanity mirror. (Antonio blah-blah-blahs PER LA MIA. Eduardo, the conquistador of love, blah-blah-blahs CON MUCHO GUSTO.) I can see in her closet and I'm immediately reminded of the touring production of *Evita* the Doctors Young took me to in San Antonio last year. Enter? Don't mind if I do. I wander in thinking maybe I should leave a trail of bread crumbs.

The door to the bedroom slams shut and Tiffany soon joins me in the closet. "See anything you like?"

"This is nice," I say, holding up a black leather miniskirt, proud of myself for delivering such a cool line when I should be embarrassed.

"I don't know if you want to show that much leg, but if you care to try it on . . . ," Tiffany offers. I'm sure I blush. I reach up to hang up the skirt, but the movement makes me dizzy. I start teetering, and I latch on to some clothes to keep my balance. No good. The clothes slide on the bar. As I'm falling I try to grab for whatever I can. I wind up on my back, buried in Tiffany's complete fall collection, a stiletto heel pressed to my throat.

"So are you going to do that movie with that guy?" I ask, still on the floor. (That's good, Brendan. Maybe she won't notice.)

"You think I should?" she asks, surprising me not only by her willingness to play along with my charade but also by her desire for my opinion.

"Director seemed like a real winner," I say. Tiffany cocks her head at me. "Uh, that was sarcasm." (There you go, Bren. Impress her with geekspeak.) I stand and start hanging up rumpled clothes.

"You can leave those there. I'll have Wilhelmina take care of it," Tiffany says. "Why don't you come downstairs with me? Daddy had some questions about his computer. I told him what a computer genius you were. I hope you don't mind."

"I wouldn't say 'genius' exactly." But Tiffany's already grabbed my hand (!) and is leading me downstairs. Who am I to argue with such a perceptive woman?

JENNY

Talk about a horror show. I sat between Clint and Damien at Alex's JV game. Not only were we getting killed, but Clint was so upset about all those guys quitting the team that he hardly said ten words the whole time we were there. I watched him clenching his jaws over and over again. Meanwhile, I kept feeling Damien brushing up next to me. I couldn't tell if I was just imagining it. Seemed weird, though. I volunteered to get popcorn, like, three times, and I took as much time as possible getting back.

When the fourth quarter started, with Lee behind, 27–7, Clint said, "Let's go." I've never known him to want to leave a game early, but I don't think he could've taken much more.

"Where are we going?" I asked him as we left the parking lot.

"I just want to drive around. Clear my head," he said, but it seems to me that he knew exactly where he was heading. He drove straight up here to Water Tower Park, crawled into the back-seat, and sat there waiting for me to join him.

"May I help you?" I asked. I wanted to look nonchalant, so I started thumbing through the cassettes in his console.

"You know you can," Clint said, and he patted his chest, which I guess meant "Come here." I picked up one of the cassettes and discovered it was a dub of the mix cassette "Romantic Songs" that he made for me, except on the label of his version it said IN THE MOOD!

"Put it in," Clint said. I wavered for a second, but then I slid it into the deck. I wanted to be mad, but the first song that came on was Billy Idol's "Eyes Without a Face," so it was tough. I glanced down and saw the top of Damien's note sticking out of my purse, and suddenly I was confused again. Everything that had been milling through my brain came rushing back to me all at once. That's when I climbed into the back with Clint. It was easier than thinking.

So now here I am—underneath him with my uniform half off. His hands are inching up the backs of my thighs and I can feel his fingertips start prying at the elastic of my panties. He's breathing my name over and over, and he's grinding up against me, which kind of hurts, but kind of feels good at the same time. His hands make it inside my panties. We've never gone this far. He lifts my butt up and presses his crotch even harder against me. As he does it, his head backs away from the crook of my neck and I'm conscious of my nakedness. I've still got everything on, but my top and bra have been pulled open. I'm embarrassed. I lift Clint's shirt and pull him back on top of me. Partly so he can't see my body and partly to feel his skin on my skin.

"You're trembling," I say. He makes a sound, but I can't tell if it's supposed to make sense.

With his head pressed back against my neck, I'm able to see the lights of Deerfield spread out beyond the Jeep's missing doors. I can see the high school, the stadium lights where the JV game must be wrapping up. I feel Clint's fingers start to make their way around to the front of me. There's the lighted steeple of the Methodist Church where we have our Fellowship of Christian Athlete meetings. Pastor Aitken says that in times like these we have to be strong for the Lord. Clint's hands reach their destination. I can't see my house, but I can see where the river bends, so I can pretty much guess where it must be. I lose my view of the city as Clint kisses me deep. I feel his finger slip inside of me. It's cold.

Last month Tina MacQuarie handed me this Sidney Sheldon novel with the corners of almost fifty pages bent down, marking all the sex passages. I remember the heroine saying she "lost herself" when making love. I close my eyes and try to lose myself, but when I do, I see my mom and dad, my little brother, scenes from when we went camping at Big Bend. Why?

Clint's mumbling things that sound like "Jen" and "Baby." Then he raises himself back up on his knees, and this time he makes himself clear. "You make me feel so good," he says. Then he starts unbuttoning his jeans.

"Don't," I say as kindly as I can—I don't want to embarrass him.

But he keeps going. Then he pulls it out, and it's right there in front of me. It's pointing straight up. This is probably stupid, but I've always pictured them, when they're like this, pointing out instead of up. Clint takes my hands, and he starts pulling them toward his thing. I resist.

"Clint, I can't."

"You have to. You're my slave. Remember?"

I wonder if he's joking and decide he probably is. But then a funny thing occurs to me—I really haven't thought much about being a slave at all—Slave Day doesn't feel much different from any other.

"Button up your pants, Clint." This time, when I say it, I don't care so much about whether I embarrass him. I start fixing my bra and shirt.

Clint starts doing as he's told, but he's got this mean look on his face.

"Sometimes, I swear, you must think you're the only girl in school," he says.

Before I know what I'm saying, I scream, "Fuck you!"

Clint looks horrified. "God, I'm sorry, Babe. I didn't mean it. I'm so sorry. I don't know why I said that." And he leans in to kiss me, but I push him away. He stares straight into my eyes for a moment, then he jumps out of the back of the Jeep and starts running down the road we drove up, leaving me here by myself.

TIFFANY
8:18 P.M. Mr. Delvoe's study

The old man is working his magic. I love watching the master at work. He started off calling Brendan by name, but it didn't take five minutes for the boy to get promoted to "son." I don't think I would have noticed the shift of nomenclature if I hadn't been listening for it. Daddy's explained to the newest addition to our family all about evil Mr. Milligan's plans to take over Delvoe Ford through phony computer entries followed up by the pretense of an audit. Martin better not screw this up. I've kept my end of the bargain. I've delivered a buzzed lech.

We shouldn't have even had to go through this. I told Daddy years ago that he needed to move into the computer age, take some classes. Mom even got him the loaded PC sitting on his desk. What's he done? He's played the Sim City and PGA-Tour CD-ROM games that came with the computer. That's about it.

"Now, Tiffany tells me that you're legendary around campus. A kind of computer Mr. Know-It-All," says Daddy.

"I've been playing around with them for a long time. I'm not sure if—"

"Super. Then you must know a way we can stop that Yankee son of a gun from driving me out of business. I just need a couple weeks, just long enough for me to get all the paper records organized." Daddy reaches out and cups Brendan's shoulder. "Why don't you come around here and take a seat in my chair. Take a look at what we've got here."

Take a seat in his chair? I don't even get to sit in his chair. Brendan stands unsteadily and makes his way around Daddy's giant oak desk and takes a seat in his ibex-upholstered highback throne.

"It's a nice computer," Brendan says, fingering the keyboard.

"That's what they tell me," answers Daddy. "So how does it look? Think you can dial into the computer down at the office and throw a wrench in the works, scramble the files a bit?"

Brendan starts dragging things around on the computer's desktop. I move around the desk and look on from behind his shoulder. I let my hair fall down in front of his face, then I move my head parallel to his body so that my hair grazes his face, shoulders, all the way down his arms. His fingers stop pecking at the keys momentarily.

"Uh . . . ," he says.

"Oh, sorry, Brendan. I just wanted to see what you were doing."

Brendan inhales before speaking.

"This computer doesn't have a modem hooked up."

"Is that bad?" Daddy says.

"It's not good, but we can get one. Now if the computer down at the dealership doesn't have a modem—and if it isn't currently on—this is going to be impossible."

"It damn well better have a modem," Daddy says. "I paid to have an extra phone line installed just for the damn thing."

"Do you know the password?" Brendan asks.

"Password? I shouldn't need a password! This is a partnership!"

"Most computers require one to log on. Have you ever logged on to your partner's computer?"

Daddy shakes his head no. Brendan shakes his head in what looks like futility. He continues hunting and pecking through Daddy's system folder. When it looks like he's found everything he needs, he lifts his head.

"It's possible," he says reluctantly. "This is what I need you to do . . ."

CLINT

8:19 P.M. Water Tower Park

I just sprint. Sprint to clear my head. My toe catches some big tree root that's stickin' up and I fly. Tear the shit outta both palms when I land, but I get up and keep runnin'.

Sometimes I think I got things figured out, and it's like someone just pulls a rug out from under me, and I realize I don't know shit. It's over with Jen. The way she just looked at me. I coulda been dead and she'da been dancin' on my grave. So what'd I do so wrong? What everyone else is doin'? Nothin' more, that's for sure. How long did she think I was willin' to wait?

I oughtta get back to her, but if I had my way, I'd just run all the way back down to school. I start to turn around, but I hear this sobbin'. I look up where it's comin' from, and I see the front end of Trim's Mustang just behind the guardrail at the highest point of Water Tower Park. I just stand there for a moment, listenin'.

There it is again. Cryin'.

I start climbin' the hill because it's faster than takin' the road all the way up. I'm grabbin' weeds and rocks. My hands are stingin' from where I scraped 'em on the pavement. As I get closer I hear Madonna sayin', "Please stop. Please stop." She's sorta cryin', sorta whisperin' it. It fades in 'n' out. I finally reach the guardrail. I hop it, and I can see the top o' Trim's blond head. I assume Madonna's underneath him. The window's open, so I can hear Trim just fine sayin, "It's all right. Come on. No one'll know. It's all right." Suddenly I'm embarrassed 'bout bein' up here. I start back toward the road. I'm hopin' Trim doesn't lift his head and spot me. Then I hear it again, and it freezes me.

"Stop it."

Somethin' inside me snaps. I turn and head back toward the car. Who does he think he is? This is what we've been hearin' 'bout in the locker room. Druggin' girls and pinnin' 'em against the door of his car. Makin' 'em cry? Man, what bullshit. What lame-ass bullshit.

I reach inside the passenger window, grab Trim round his neck, and pull.

"What the fuck!" he yells, but he can't tell who's got him just yet. I got his head out the window, now his shoulders—he starts flailin' around—out comes his waist. When his feet reach the window, I just let go and watch his head drop to the ground like someone jumped off the other end of a seesaw.

While Trim's tryin' to pick himself up, I stick my head in the window right in time to see Madonna—I mean Annabella—pukin' all over the floor mats.

"Come on. I'll get you out of here," I say, but that's about the same time I get hit in the back—not with a fist . . . with a rock? What a pussy. I turn and see Trim about ten yards away. Blood's runnin' down his face. He yells at me.

"Get the fuck outta here, asshole. What the fuck're you thinkin'?"

I don't say anything. I just start walkin' at him and he backs up, keepin' himself a first down away. I make like I'm gonna chase him, sprint a couple steps forward. He takes off into the trees. I go back to the car and help Annabella out of it.

"You okay?"

She nods, but she looks like shit. Her eyes are all puffy, and she didn't quite miss herself when she heaved. I can't even tell if she knows who I am. It doesn't look like she's focusing.

"I'll give you a ride home."

She nods again, and we start walkin' back down the road toward the Jeep. I can hear Trim scramblin' round in the bushes. 'Bout halfway down the hill, Annabella starts cryin' again, and I think that the last thing in the world she wants is some dumb guy puttin' his arm round her. So I do nothin'. Out o' the blue, Trim goes speedin' by, comin' too damn close to us as he passes. I may hafta kick his ass next time I see him, just on general principle.

KEENE

8:21 P.M. Davenport house

I hear the bass from the car speakers coming up the street long before the honking that signals me to get outside. My family is sitting in front of the TV, and Laurence tells everyone to get on the floor, quick. "It's either one of Keene's new friends or a drive-by." I'm just hoping Mom doesn't notice the gangsta rap, window-rattling references to Glocks, pimps, bitches, and blunts.

Of course Laurence is afraid of everything the other side of Boyz II Men. I tell my mom I'm going to the bonfire. I already told her about buying Shawn and about tomorrow's boycott and the party I'm invited to, so she doesn't make me explain why I'm willing to attend the bonfire.

The car I get in used to be an Escort, but there's not much left of Sleepy's original vehicle. The back panel has been replaced with a giant bass cabinet. The windows are all tinted. It's got a spoiler and these tiny wheels. Rashard and Melvin are in the back telling Mexican jokes. I don't catch much of it, because of how loud Sleepy keeps the music, but I know it involves someone named Pedro, Pedro's sister, and the word *frijole*. Whatever the punch line is, it's got Melvin and Rashard holding on to their intestines.

I have no idea where we're going. "To make a point," is what Sleepy said after school. I wonder what point they've already made—there's a few cans of spray paint on the floor of the car and, on closer inspection, I discover all three of my comrades here have paint on their fingers.

Soon enough we pull into Whataburger. Sleepy drives to the very back of the parking lot. He yells into the backseat.

"Is this the right one?"

"*Si, señor,*" answers Melvin.

Sleepy reaches over to my side of the car and unlatches his glove box. He pulls out a bottle of black shoe polish and a small carton of eggs.

"When words fail," he says, handing the items to me.

"Whose car is it?" I ask.

"Mr. Twilley's."

"What's the point?" I ask.

"Do you want Slave Day ended?"

"How is egging Twilley's car going to do that?" I say. "He can be a butthole, but he's not the one who—"

"I thought you told a class full of students that he was trying to keep our sister out of honor society."

"Yeah, but—

"That makes him, at the very least, a symbol—"

Then Melvin chimes in from the backseat. "I told you he was getting all friendly with Shawn Greeley after school."

"Man, he's just like his little brother—wants to be white," adds Rashard.

Sleepy starts to take the eggs and shoe polish from my hands, but I grip them tighter. I don't want to be white.

BRENDAN
8:41 P.M. Tiffany's Probe

Let's see. What's wrong with this picture? I've had a multiplicity of rum and Cokes. I'm driving a twenty-five-thousand-dollar car. I don't have a license. (The only driving experience I've had has been in the Tempo on farm-to-market roads with Mom next to me instructing, "Stop. Look. Listen . . . Good . . . All right, hand over hand . . . Good.") Add to that that I'm about to destroy all the financial records of one of Deerfield's largest businesses. And—for my trouble—I've also been given the privilege of nabbing a chocolate shake for my owner.

You know, on top of all that, there's plenty that's bothering me about what Mr. Delvoe—Mayor Delvoe—is asking me to do. I mean, if he's got paper records of all the invoices and stuff, what's he worrying for? It might take some time, but he'd be able to prove he was innocent. I guess it could just be politics. Mr. Warren says that the appearance of impropriety is sometimes as bad as impropriety itself. Could be Mr. Delvoe's just trying to save himself some public humilification.

I almost got snagged when I went home to pick up the modem and password-cracker software I needed. As I left the house, my parents cruised right by me. I think the tinted windows saved the day. They'd hyperventilate if they knew what I was doing. For one thing, they've voted against Mr. Delvoe ever since he had the park re-zoned. I've been more careful on my way to Whataburger, taking all the backroads I know. All I need now is to be thrown into jail. I wonder if the mayor would come to my rescue.

When Mom has allowed me to drive the Tempo, my goal has always been just to stay between the lines and get from point A to point B. In letting me drive her car, Tiffany is effectively giving a Purina-for-life dog a slab of prime rib. I only need to *think* the word "fast" and my head is slammed back into the neck rest. I'm certain that if I turn on the radio—which, incidentally, looks too complicated for me to operate—I'll get Mission Control. Coincidentally enough, the route I've chosen takes me by Deena's. I creep down her street until I get right in front of her house. There I give the horn a couple sharp taps and hit the gas. Too hard. I burn rubber (do they still say "burn rubber"?) halfway down the block.

I hear a ringing sound. My first thought is that the police are already on my trail—either that, or it's the first warning sign test pilots get when they're about to pass out from pulling too many G's. On the third or fourth ring, I uncover the source; it's a car phone. I try ignoring it, but it doesn't stop. After fifty or so rings, I pick it up.

"Hello?"

"Get me some fries with that too." It's Tiffany.

"Sure," I say, but then, who knows why, I break into hysterics. I can't help myself. This girl is out of control. Also, I start thinking about the message from Lloyd this morning. I'll have to tell him—fries *do* go with that shake.

"Whatever," Tiffany says, before clicking off.

As I pull into the Whataburger parking lot, somebody flashes me with his headlights. I realize I've been driving with mine off. It's not pitch-black yet, but it's too dark not to have them on. I find the light switch, and as I punch them on, they rotate up and out of the hood and shine directly onto this ugly green car in the back of the parking lot. Four people are gathered around it. I recognize Laurence Davenport's older brother, but not the rest of them. It looks like they're writing stuff on it. That's a practice indigenous to popular people—shoe-polishing GO BIG BLUE! on friends' cars or drawing a circle on a front windshield and scrawling STUD with an arrow pointing at the driver. They hang out in the Whataburger parking lot, talking, drinking beer, chasing one another around. So what's appealing about that? Why should I want to be part of it?

So what if I do?

I'm *not* blind, though. I know it when people are nice to me because they need something—help with their homework, computer advice. But somehow, I always feel like, in those moments, I'm not invisible. That suddenly someone's paying attention to me. Someone needs me. Who cares if Tiffany Delvoe only bought me because she was late this morning? So what if she let me beat her a few games in pool just to get me to help her dad? After I do this, there will always be a part of her that knows I exist. Maybe I'll see her in the hall talking with her friends. I'll walk by her, and she'll nod. For me, maybe that's enough.

TOMMY

"What do you suppose he does for fun?" I ask Miguel, our shift leader.

Miguel glances over the bun toaster. "Looks like he gets off grading papers. He's been doing it since the dinner rush ended. I liked him better when he was cleaning the tables. Why don't you order him to do some more of that?"

I hand a couple shakes out the drive-through window to this kid who's driving Tiffany Delvoe's Probe—the guy she paid a hundred bucks for. "So, my man, hear you been bangin' Tiff all day. These shakes nourishment? Tryin' to work your strength back up? Better super-size 'em for a quarter more!" I wink at him and give him a big thumbs-up.

"Uhh . . . uhh . . . uhh . . . I'm just getting her something to drink."

"A true gentleman. Give her my love, will ya?"

"Uhh, yeah."

"Where you headin'? Some big debutante ball? The Hotel No-Tell?"

"Just the bonfire."

"Right!"

I slide the window shut, but I've got an idea now.

"Hey, Miguel, let me off for thirty minutes. It's slow. You got enough people."

"Punch out," he says.

"Which one?" I say, balling up a fist and glaring at my shift-mates.

Miguel laughs, which is why I like him better than the other shift leaders. I head out into the dining room and plop down next to Twilley. He hasn't touched a fry since I left.

"Ten minutes," I say, "we're heading to the bonfire."

"I should be done grading these quizzes by then."

"That's a huge weight off my shoulders." Like I care whether he's done with his grading. Shit.

I head back to the kitchen to punch out and grab a joe to go, but Miguel tells me I've got to take the trash out before I can leave. I grab the Hefty bags that have been stacked by the door and head out the big steel back door. I see Twilley's car before I make it all the way to the Dumpster. It's not easy to miss. It's covered in egg again, but this time the shoe polish says something different, BY ANY MEANS NECESSARY.

I don't get it.

TIFFANY

8:47 P.M. Delvoe study

So I'm on the hallway phone talking to Troy. I've called back to explain blowing him off earlier. He's not a major flame, but he does own Sundance CDs, and let's just say I get a very good deal.

"Strip pool?" he says, more intrigued than pissed.

"Look, I was just humoring this kid we've got working for us. He's harmless."

As I say it, a Whataburger shake appears in my peripheral vision on the stair next to my head. Brendan slogs by me and enters the study. Little boozehound forgot my fries. Daddy's right; it's tough to get good help these days.

This whole evening is becoming a big pain in the ass. I've had to sit here for the last forty-five minutes with Daddy, carrying out Brendan's bizarre instructions. We've gone through old employee records, the community calendar, and the phone book, making a list of any piece of information that might be part of Mr. Milligan's password. This detective shit is nowhere near as interesting as they make it look on TV. We've put together a list of all his kids' birthdays, his street address, his phone number, Social Security number, mother's maiden name, wife's maiden name, pets' names, driver's license number, ZIP codes he's lived in, license plate number, favorite foods, favorite sports teams. Daddy even listed the phone number of the White Rock Motel, where he says Milligan takes his secretary for private meetings.

Brendan's a blur of wasted motion. The boy is energized.

Rather than asking where the phone line is in the office, he gets down on his hands and knees and surveys the baseboards. Daddy and I are too entertained to ask what he's doing. When he finds the line (about three quarters of the way around his pace lap), he connects it to the modem he's brought back with him. He yanks wires out of the back of Daddy's computer and plugs them back in the same ports. He asks Daddy the number of the computer line at the office, punches it in, and instructs us to cross our fingers. The modem dials, rings, then starts screaming.

"Connectage!" says Brendan. "The computer at the office *is* on. It's asking for a password." Then he inserts a disk and begins keyboarding in all the random numbers and names off the list Daddy has handed him.

"Are you trying all of these as passwords?" I ask, thinking this could take all night.

"Not exactly," says Brendan. "This program will try them all, then try them in different combinations, then try them backward, sideways—you name it. Most people aren't dumb enough to just use their phone number or birthday or student ID number in order, but they might switch around the numbers."

There's something in the way he says "student ID number" that reminds me—I need to change my password at school.

Brendan continues typing while Daddy pours himself a bourbon. Right now, his future's in the hands of a teenage hacker, and I would swear, Daddy's digging the rush. He's pacing the room, cracking his knuckles, muttering little oaths of vengeance under his breath.

The computer, which has been clicking away, becomes silent.

"Well?" says Daddy.

"No go," says Brendan, looking disappointed. He drums his fingers against the desk. Even as I'm envisioning life in a trailer home, I can't help noticing Brendan's hands. They're beautiful. They look like they belong on a concert pianist or a split end or something. I wonder why I didn't notice them before. They're completely out of proportion with the rest of his body. The fingers are long but thin and his nails are perfectly pink and trimmed back to appropriate guy length. The boy's not through growing.

"Is there anything else you can think of?" Brendan asks Daddy. "A lot of people hang up their password on a little Post-it right by the computer. It's not very smart, but they do it."

"The only thing the greedy bastard has hanging up in that office is a scorecard from the one *and only* time he beat me in a round of golf," Daddy says. "He hung that up in there just to get my boxers in a wad."

"What was the score?" Brendan asks.

Daddy launches into an epic with frequent references to the shifting winds, Mr. Milligan's disregard for the rules of the sport, and Daddy's own miserable putting display.

"What was the score, Martin?" I interject. "That's all he wants to know."

"Oh, I'm sorry—eighty-one to eighty-seven. But why do you . . . ," Daddy begins, but Brendan's already plugged the numbers in. The computer sputters and clicks.

"We have a winner!" he says. "We're in."

"The golf score? That sumbitch!" Daddy says, pounding his fist against the desk. "Erase the whole damn computer!"

"I don't think you want to do that, sir," says Brendan. "It'll be obvious. What I was thinking was that I would infect the financial records with a virus that will eat them away bit by bit. They might be able to retrieve chunks, but they could never get an overall picture."

"Fine idea, son," says our father. "Glad someone here's got his head outta his butt."

"I'll need two or three blank disks to do this. Do you have any I could use?"

"What on earth," I begin, "do you need *blank* disks f—"

"Could you get me another one of those Cokes, Tiffany? I'm feeling kind of faint," Brendan says.

What the hell. I'll leave the computer stuff to the expert. I head to the bar.

MR. TWILLEY

When I reach the bottom of the stack of quizzes I'm grading, I find Jackson's and Wilson's already marked with their zeros. I consider what Mr. Tristan said—that students are saying I'm giving Tamika a zero because she's black. It's not the first time I've been accused of racism. Back in '78, both of those players were black. Star athletes who thought they could get away with anything. It seems the rest of the community agreed with them. Of all the spiteful things said of me at that time, none hurt more than the accusations that the grades were racially motivated.

Out of curiosity, I pull Jackson's and Wilson's quizzes from the stack and begin checking them, question by question. As usual, Jackson has done a fine job, scoring a ninety-two. I expect to see a once-in-a-lifetime mark from Wilson as well, but as I begin grading, my assumptions are quashed. Wilson manages only a D. It's the first quiz he's passed this semester, but it's by no means spectacular work. Then I find an anomaly I didn't expect. Number 19, one of the last questions, called for only a year—Trevor has the correct answer. Tamika got it wrong.

Still, they *were* talking during the quiz. And Tamika *wasn't* using her cover sheet. How much easier this would have been had the answers been identical.

It occurs to me that I haven't seen Tommy for nearly twenty minutes and we're closing in on the starting time for the bonfire. I don't see him in the kitchen, so I wonder if he's waiting out in the parking lot for me. I gather my papers and clean off my table. I step out into the darkness. There with his back to me is Thomas. Beneath him is a bucket, in his hand a sponge. He's washing my freshly vandalized car. I can still make out the BY ANY MEA . . ."

I step back inside the building to wait for him.

KEENE

9:10 P.M. Lee High parking lot

I get Sleepy to drop me off at school. The bonfire's about to start, and I've got one thing left to do for the day. The lights are still on over at the football field, which means the JV game must still be going on. I'm not interested in the game itself, but I decide to head in that direction anyway. For the first time that I can remember, I *want* to be seen. People may actually notice me and say something like, "That's the guy who had Shawn doing all that crazy stuff today."

As I'm crossing the parking lot, I'm thinking how glad I am that I didn't stay home today. It's funny how Slave Day may be my greatest day of high school.

"Keene Davenport!"

I turn and see Principal Gant.

"I need to have a word with you."

Damn.

"Follow me to my office," he says.

The campus is dark and the shadows make it look somehow frightening. I don't think I'm ever up here at night except to pick Laurence up from debate meets and science club meetings. Mr. Gant isn't saying a thing, and I can't muster the energy to play stupid. Right before we get to the administration building, he stops in front of the marble sign in front of the office.

"You know anything about this?" he says, gesturing toward the sign.

Below where it says PRESENTED BY THE SENIORS OF 1976, in the spot where it normally says ROBERT E. LEE HIGH SCHOOL, HOME OF THE REBELS, someone has spray-painted STOP SLAVE DAY NOW!

"No," I say, but I'm not a very good liar.

Mr. Gant unlocks the doors into the administration building and points to a chair in his office. I sit down while he disables the alarm. I feel my palms getting soggy. I wipe them on my jeans, but I leave streaks where I do so.

"This has been a very bad day for me, Keene," Mr. Gant says as he enters his office. "Do you know why?"

"No, sir."

"Because of you, Keene—because of an *honor* student." Gant is still standing. I feel defenseless sitting in this chair, having to turn around to face him. "I get a call at six in the morning today from the president of the school board. He reads me your whole letter."

"Really?" I say, not nearly as upset by this news as I'm sure Mr. Gant would like me to be.

"Let me see your hands," he says, shifting gears. I do as I'm told. I'm sure I'm busted. Little beads of sweat are forming on my knuckles as Mr. Gant examines my hands, particularly the index fingers.

"Well, if you had anything to do with the spray-painting, you did a fine job of washing your hands."

"I didn't do it, sir," I say.

"Frankly, I was surprised you showed up here at all today," says Gant, returning to the subject of my letter. "I heard about some of the stunts you pulled with Shawn Greeley this morning. I've just wondered how responsible you are for everything that's happened today."

"What's happened?"

"We're in the middle of some crisis involving a student being kicked out of the honor society. From what I understand, you've been telling people it's a racial issue."

"Well, sir, you know that—"

"Don't try to convince me it's true, son. I had Mr. Twilley for history when I was your age. He's one of the best teachers I've ever had—high school or college. I believe you made an A in his class. That's quite an achievement in itself. Do you suppose he didn't notice you were black?" Gant runs his fingers through his thinning hair. "Bottom line? All he cares about is whether students—*any* students—learn the material he's teaching."

Finally he decides to sit down.

"Then, on top of that, I've heard that none of the black football players plan to play for the rest of the season and that they're protesting Slave Day. I haven't been able to get to the bottom of this one, but I've heard some pretty outrageous stories about what happened. Someone's spreading a lot of misinformation. Could this be part of the master plan, Keene?"

"Master plan?"

"Did you know that every car in the parking lot with a Confederate flag bumper sticker on it has been egged?"

I think immediately of Melvin and Rashard. "No, sir."

Gant studies me for a moment. "Well maybe you don't, but you sure haven't helped matters here on campus today. You know Slave Day is supposed to be fun for students. It's been a favorite event since I went here, but real frankly, it's not worth the aggravation. How would you like the rest of the students here thinking that you ruined one of the best-loved traditions on campus?" I try to keep a forlorn look on my face while Gant pulls what looks like a cough syrup bottle along with a teaspoon out of one of his top drawers, pours himself a spoonful, and gulps it. As he does so, the phone on his desk rings.

"Gant," he says when he answers it. Then I hear him say something like, "Yes, Mrs. Guzaldo." It's tough to decide what they're talking about, but it sure seems to upset Mr. Gant, who proceeds to pull an aspirin bottle out of his medicine drawer. He mentions Timm Trimble several times. And then he says, "No, Mrs. Guzaldo, it's not our intention to sponsor activities that put our girls in compromising positions."

Laurence has talked about the Guzaldo girl before, says she's the smartest girl in the sophomore class. Laurence, of course, believes he's the smartest boy, which he probably is. And I didn't want to be compared to Laurence. You know, when he's up on stage in a couple years, giving that valedictory speech, he'll do more for blacks in Deerfield than Sleepy or Melvin or Rashard ever will. As long as I'm being honest . . . more than I ever will either.

Gant looks up. The surprised look on his face makes me think the telephone call has made him forget that I'm still here. He pushes one hand into his temple and waves me out of his office with the other. The last thing I hear as I'm leaving is Gant saying, "Mrs. Guzaldo, I can assure you nothing like this will happen here again."

CLINT

9:20 P.M. Bonfire

It's official. I'm a single man.

I knew it was comin', so when Jen broke into that, "You know, Clint, I don't think we . . ." line, I just cut her short.

"Yeah, I know what you mean," I said.

"I hope we can still be friends," she said.

"Uh-huh," I answered.

She pulled the trigger as I drove us both back to the high school after we dropped Annabella off at her home. Annabella was lookin' healthier by the time we got there. Jen sat with her in the backseat on the way. They were whisperin' stuff that I couldn't hear. Probably better I couldn't. When I pulled into the school, I blazed over the speed bumps, and I was surprised when Jen caught a good foot and a half of air—on purpose.

She hugged me when she got out of the Jeep. She told me that I owed her a box of cookies. Then she headed up to the old baseball field where the senior class builds the bonfire. I spotted Alex comin' outta the field house, so I jogged over to tell him what I thought of the JV's piss-poor effort against Liberty Valley, but as it turned out, the JV scored three fourth-quarter touchdowns to win the game. Figures I missed it. And for what?

As we walk over to the bonfire, Damien joins us, and I tell 'em 'bout me 'n' Jen splittin' and 'bout havin' to pull Trim offa Madonna.

"What a dick!" Alex says.

"Yeah," I say.

The Future Farmer guys start dousin' the railroad ties and cedars at the bottom of the bonfire with gasoline. Pretty soon the whole thing's ablaze. Everyone has to take a few steps back. The band starts playin' "Dixie." I turn to see if Damien's singin' these dirty lyrics he made up for the song, but he's disappeared. The cheerleaders begin their first routine right in front of where Alex and I are standin'.

I check out Trinni Rea, and I swear she's lookin' straight at me. Everyone says she looks just like that *SI* swimsuit model, the Norwegian one. I'm diggin' the way she dances, all sexy, and the way she looks away when I catch her checkin' me out. They end the cheer with some line 'bout how "We're *Red Hot!*"

"Yes, they are," Alex says in my ear.

High fiveage.

TIFFANY

9:25 P.M. Bonfire

After Brendan assures Daddy that everything has been taken care of, I drive him up to school to see if we can catch any part of the bonfire, and he asks me how old I was when some picture in my locker was taken.

"What picture?" I ask.

"You know, that one with you and your grandfather—well, I guess it's your grandfather. Anyway, you're holding a present in your hands." Brendan demonstrates the pose.

"Oh, that," I say. "That was in my locker when I got it. It's not me."

"Yeah, I guess it wouldn't be," he mutters. Then he starts whistling. The boy is a case.

Once we reach the school, I park the Probe all the way out in the faculty parking lot and hike up toward the festivities. Eventually I find Rainy and Suzi. They're standing at the edge of the ring of fire—the spot farthest from the Rebel band. The scuffling of Keds lets me know that the ubiquitous Brendan is still tailing me. Suzi hands me her forty-four-ounce Road Warrior mug as I join the conversation. Instant Bacardi party.

"Kill me now," whimpers Rainy as she takes the vessel from my hand and slugs down a lungful. Her eyes roll back in her head.

"Pardon the girl. It's that special time of the month," Suzi says.

"She hides it well," I say. "At least the Central basketball team can sleep a bit easier tonight."

"Feels like . . . someone . . . stuck knife . . . in stomach . . .

twisting . . . ," Rainy's voice quivers with each syllable. Her pain is convincing. She ought to try the method approach in all her work.

"Are you there, God? It's me, Rainy," I add.

"Die, bitch," she hisses in response.

"There, there, hon," says Suz. "This is just nature's way of celebrating your womanhood."

The cursed one grunts in agony.

"Can I get you something? Some aspirin, maybe?"

I glance behind me and see it's a concerned Brendan who's spoken. My friends stop talking and stare at my slave like he's just asked them if they're interested in a three-way.

"A shotgun," is Rainy's suggestion. It's pretty clear she doesn't want it for herself.

"Uh, yeah, okay, um, I'm sorry," says Brendan.

TOMMY

9:26 P.M. Bonfire

The chant starts almost as soon as we get there. I was counting on that. I let it build. Then when it seems like everyone at the bonfire is screaming for the Speller, I turn to Twilley.

"You're on, slave," I say.

Twilley's eyes grow into cue balls.

"Tommy, you can't mean . . ."

"You're the man," I shout. By now it's the only way he'll hear me. "It'll be just like old times." The way he gawks at me—he knows that I know. "Come on. I want to see the master at work."

For a split second, I see something there. A gleam, like he's far away or somewhere back in time. And I think he might do it. But then it's gone, and I'm positive that nothing I could say or do would make him get up in front of Lee High and perform.

By now students around me are pushing me toward the fire, away from Mr. Twilley. I quit fighting them. I've got a duty. I jog to an open spot and students scream. I arc my body, and the school whispers *R*. I keep going, letter by letter, but my heart isn't really in it.

SHAWN

I convinced Keene that it would be better for everyone if we just went our separate ways after school. I had a lot of work left organizing the party. He seemed more than happy to split up.

First thing I did was I had this office aide sneak into the teachers lounge and make us a couple hundred flyers. They're tight. At the top they say LEE HIGH'S FOOTBALL GAME FRIDAY NIGHT WILL BE BLACKED OUT LOCALLY. I'm always amazed how much shit you can get by white people. There's probably not a black student here who doesn't know about the party, and I'll bet you only three white people in school even have a clue, one of 'em being Jason Cohen—half of the Zebra Posse—and he don't know he's white. Priscilla has no clue. I'm sure she'd advise me against doin' what I'm doin', but she'll get a secret thrill about "acting in my stead" at tomorrow night's game.

The ag boys have already fired up the bonfire when the band breaks into our fight song, "Dixie." You know what? I can listen to that whole song, and all I think about is draining three-pointers. I don't think for a minute about Colonel Sanders–lookin' dudes whippin' my ancestors and makin' 'em change their name to Willie. Dumb me.

The band finishes, and it's time for me to free the slaves. It took Lincoln a war and an amendment to the Constitution. I do it with the sound of my voice. "We'd like to thank all the slaves and owners for making Slave Day such a success. I know I had a cotton-pickin' good time." Laughter. Much laughter. "But all good things must pass—that's what my gramma always tells me—so let it be known that, as of this minute, all slaves are free!" The drum corps bangs out an appropriate racket, and my duties for the day are complete.

Humphrey and the rest of the football players didn't show up for the bonfire. Now don't get me wrong—I love the boy. It's just that he always had more pride than savvy. He's gonna spend the next four years in some backwoods town playing in front of nobody. Ain't no scouts gonna see him. Ain't gonna be nothin' to do on weekends. He's gonna be tellin' all the other nobodies there that that's his friend on TV, the one with the ball, the one takin' it strong to the hoop, the one gettin' interviewed after the game. Ain't nobody gonna believe him.

I spot Keene across the way from me. He's lookin' all confused. And the poor boy doesn't even know what he's gotten himself into yet.

Tomorrow night's party'll be hype. I'll ditch my date early. There's a couple sophomores I've had my eye on. Plus, we can't forget amazon Denise. I'll call up Mr. Denhart sometime tomorrow mornin'. Tell him I got stomach cramps or the flu or something, really play it up for him. Then, when this whole thing settles down, I'll be right back where I started—without a care in the world.

Yeah, tell *me* 'bout politics.

JENNY

9:33 P.M. Bonfire

I tell our dance team sponsor, Miss Taylor, that Annabella's sick and won't be able to make it to the bonfire.

"She was healthy enough to make it to school today," says Miss Taylor as she jots down Annabella's name on the demerit list. Then the former Texas Junior Miss examines me critically. "Check your buttons, dear."

I look down and discover my blouse is buttoned up wrong. I've got an extra buttonhole by my neck.

"And where's your lipstick, *young lady?*"

Miss Taylor says the last two words totally sarcastically. She's got her painted eyebrows raised up to her wigline.

"I think Heidi Fleiss still has it," I say, and before Miss Taylor thinks of anything else to say, I sink into the line of other Rebelettes.

All the girls are talking about tomorrow night's homecoming dance. Everyone wants to know what everyone else is wearing and where they're going to eat afterward—and, in the case of girls without boyfriends, who they're going with. Sandy and Sherri are mouthing off because their boyfriends rented a limo for the dance. Sherri takes a break from telling us about the TV in the backseat to ask me what Clint and I are going to do.

"Nothing," I say. "We broke up."

And all of a sudden it's like a funeral. Everyone is trying to console me. Tell me everything will be okay. I know that some of the girls putting their arms around me now will be the same ones who "just bump into" Clint after the bonfire. No matter how many times I say, "I'm all right," someone else comes up and says, "But no, really, how are you feeling?" Everyone is using baby talk with me. It's driving me crazy.

Out of the corner of my eye I see a flash. Damien's taking pictures of the bonfire for the yearbook. He's a sweet guy. A girl couldn't ask for a better boyfriend—sensitive, funny, smart, cute in his own way. I smile, thinking about the note he wrote me this morning, and I wonder how long he'll wait for me in the yearbook room. He'll be a real prince of a boyfriend.

But for someone else, not me.

I'm nobody's girl. And I'm fine.

TOMMY

9:35 P.M. Bonfire

Once I'm done spelling, I kinda want to stick around and tell Twilley I'm sorry for putting him on the spot like that, but I can't push my luck timewise. Probably every Whataburger fryboy is already whining to Miguel about me getting "special privileges." Besides, Twilley's likely halfway home already, wonderin' why in the hell he put himself through Slave Day and cursin' the fact he ended up with me and not some egghead.

I'm cuttin' through the crowd tryin' to avoid any one of my "bad crowd" friends who'll lure me into stayin' longer. That's when I feel a hand on my shoulder. I turn and see it's Twilley. He's shoutin' somethin' at me, but that band has kicked in again, and I can't hear a word of it. Maybe this is where I get bitched out. He leads me outside the circle, where it's not so loud.

"I've got something for you," Twilley says. His hand reaches inside his coat pocket, and it makes me think of the scene in *Reservoir Dogs* where Chris Penn pulls out a .44 and executes that cop. Twilley doesn't murder me, though. He takes a small pad from his pocket and scribbles something on it and hands it to me. "This is the number of an admissions officer up at Central. He used to be a student of mine."

I've got no idea where he's going with this, but I take the slip from him and stuff it in my pocket.

"Tell him I suggested you call. They have a lot of work-study programs available to students who can't afford college. They might let you in on probation."

"Yeah, thanks," I say. "Hey, I wanted to tell you—I wasn't tryin' to embarrass you back there. I just thought it might be fun. I mean, for you, even."

"That's what I thought," he says, glancing back up toward the fire, before looking at me again. "Stop by my room sometime and let me know what you find out when you call."

"All right," I say. "Why'd you do it, anyway?"

At first I think I'm going to need to explain the question, tell him I'm talking about why he volunteered for Slave Day, but he just answers.

"You know, Thomas, I couldn't tell you."

That'll have to do. We shake hands, and I walk back out to my truck. When I get there I pull the number out of my pocket. At first I'm having trouble imagining a student of his ever wanting to do him a favor. But when I think about Twilley bellowing Partridge's lines or hunting me down in the cafeteria or bussing tables at Whataburger, I decide it could happen.

I open the door of the pickup and pull my uniform back over my T-shirt. Sliding into the cab, I open my ashtray and cram the slip of paper in. It's time to go back to work.

TIFFANY
9:41 P.M. Bonfire

One of the Booster Moms, dolled up in a red and gray puff-
painted sweatshirt swaddling a well-larded body, wanders up to
the three of us and asks if we're interested in buying a spirit button. ("Yes, and can I get an Epilady and a brain tumor with that?")
I stick my hand in my pocket, since Daddy always tells me to buy
whatever trinkets the local citizenry are peddling, but I make the
snappy realization that I never got my shake change from B-boy.
I look around, but he's nowhere to be found. It must be his bed-
time. I explain to Madre Spiritus that she'll have to catch me
next time.

"Yell loud at the game tomorrow night anyway," she says
cheerfully. "The boys are going to need all your help with those
niggers quitting."

Nice.

I turn away and watch the fire. After the Speller performs,
these things go downhill fast. It's the only part of the entire spirit fest that isn't staged and artificial. Why do I feel like I have to
make some kind of appearance? It reminds me of seventh grade
when I tried out for cheerleader. I spent the week before the
election trying to be perky and involved. Somehow getting picked
seemed important at the time, but when you're young, every little bullshit thing somehow does.

On the way back out to our cars, I invite Suzi over to lounge
around in the hot tub.

"Rainy, you're welcome too," I say. "Just stay out of the
water."

As expected, they decline, claiming social obligations. I suspect, however, curfews and homework are the true cause. A van
that's been blocking my view of the Probe backs out, revealing
my erstwhile slave lounging across my hood. Doesn't that boy
know that when the bonfire starts, our time together is through?

Seeing him there reminds me—I've got to remember to take
down that picture of me and Pap from my locker.

MR. TWILLEY
9:45 P.M. Bonfire

I suppose I had hoped for Tommy to be more excited about the phone number I gave him, but maybe forcing that number on him was silly of me—expecting him to be thrilled by my notion of success. It's possible, maybe probable, that Tommy doesn't need a degree. Maybe he should join a comedy troupe, audition for equity productions, hone a stand-up comedy routine. Do anything to get out of Deerfield.

Perhaps I should as well.

As I walk toward my car, I spy Tamika Jackson and one of my better former students, Keene Davenport. As I walk toward her, their conversation dies.

"Tamika, may I have a word with you?" I ask.

She appears nervous. She fidgets and pulls on a strand of hair. "Umm, yeah," she says. From Tamika, this almost seems like defiance. She's always been a "yes, sir/no, sir" girl.

"I wanted to let you know that I graded your test and Trevor's, and I found no evidence of collusion."

"So what does that mean?" Tamika says, softening a bit.

"It means that I won't turn in a report, so you'll be able to stay in the National Honor Society. It also means that you can keep your grade on the quiz."

"I told you I didn't cheat."

"Well, the proof's in the . . . You know what? I should've listened. Just remember to keep your paper covered from now on."

"I will," she says. I detect a small smile forming.

"Drive safely," I say as I resume the trip out to my car.

As I'm walking, Esther enters my mind. I wonder what she would say about my day. Something about faith in mankind. Something about giving of yourself. And yet, it would still be over between us. Too many things said. Too many things never said. No, I don't think I did this for Esther.

I think I did it to remind me.

I notice that there's still a light on in the theater. I head toward it. I'm in the mood for coffee. Maybe Linda Amenny wouldn't mind joining me.

BRENDAN
9:50 P.M. Parking lot

As I'm waiting for Tiffany, I'm thinking about the outlines of the bodies we saw painted on the sidewalks in Austin. Tiffany just stood right on them. Didn't even notice them or care why they were there. I guess that's just her, never paying attention to who she's stepping on and over.

I was retarded this morning to think those girls were willing to say all that stuff in front of me because they thought I was semicool; the only reason they say anything in front of me is because my existence simply doesn't matter to them.

So now I know what I've got to do.

My days of letting Blimp Stimmons copy my homework are over. The next time someone in a pep squad uniform asks me to format her disk, I'll just act like she's speaking Zulu. And while I'm at it, I think I'll tell Mr. Zarsky he can find someone else to take up space at the student council meetings. I don't want a nod in the hall from Tiffany Delvoe if all that's going through her mind is, "There's the dope I played like a puppet."

Because, you know what? Existing—just being—it isn't enough.

The van that's been parked next to me backs out, and I see Tiffany walking that stupid prostitute walk up to the car. I reach into the pocket of my backpack and find what I'm looking for.

"Watch the paint, dude, I just had that thing washed," Tiffany says. The ways she says it is charming, and I can't help noticing, again, how beautiful she is. *Come on, Brendan. Go through with this . . .*

"I need a ride home," I say.

I make sure there's no question mark at the end of that. I'm not asking. Tiffany notices.

"I'm sorry. Is there a sign on my car there that says 'Delvoe

Taxi'?" She wanders around the car, pretending to look for one. "Nope. I don't see anything here that says 'Free Rides for Sophomores.'"

I pull my hand out of my backpack and fan out the three floppy disks in front of Tiffany. She looks at me, and I look right back at her.

"Let's see, here," I say. "The complete financial records of Delvoe Ford. Three copies: one for Mr. Milligan, one for the *Deerfield Herald*, and one that I may just upload onto the Net for anyone else who's interested."

She stares at the disks. This is my big play. If she immediately says, "Do what you want with them, our family is in the clear," I don't know what I'll do. But she doesn't. Instead she's in shockdom, and I know my hunch was right. At first I don't think she's going to speak at all, but then she says the strangest thing. "Brendan," she says. "You've got really beautiful hands."

I don't even try to understand the strategy behind that. I slide down off the hood and move toward her.

"Throw me the keys, Tammy," I say. "I'm driving."

"Tiffany," she says.

"Whatever."

KEENE

9:54 P.M. Parking lot

I was nervous, at first, that Tamika wasn't going to show up at the bonfire. I had to look all over before I found her, but she broke away from a couple of her friends and walked right over here when she noticed me. It was too loud, really, to try to say anything to her there. But when it was over, I asked her if she wouldn't mind giving me a ride home. She said no problem. As we walked out to the parking lot, Tamika told me about all the people who had come up to her during the day and told her they were on her side. She thanked me again, and I could swear she was glowing. The same girl I saw crying this morning was practically dancing out to her car.

That's when Mr. Twilley called to her.

I didn't want to be there when the two of them spoke, but the way things worked out, I was. And Mr. Twilley was nice. He said he'd made a mistake, and he told Tamika that he wouldn't turn in a discipline report.

I watch him as he walks away, and there are a million things going through my head that I know I'm going to have to sort through later. I can't dwell on it now. Like I said, there's one thing left to do.

Tamika gets in her VW bug and unlocks my door. I climb inside. I've been rehearsing this moment, so before she turns on the ignition, I speak up.

"Uh, Tamika, uh, I'm sure you've probably heard about the party tomorrow night."

"Yeah, I've heard about it," she says, smiling so nice.

"Well, uh, I was, uh, you know, wondering if you would go with me?"

She reaches over and pats my hand, which seems friendly enough, but then she says, "I'm sorry, Keene, but after school today, Shawn Greeley asked me if I wanted to go with him."

When she says that name, it's like my brain has been a spinning TV picture and someone's instantly fixed the vertical hold. Everything locks in place, and I remember who I am. And *that* someone is a very different person from the one I've tried so hard to be today.

By any means necessary.

I wasn't the only one living by that motto today. Shawn Greeley sure was. So were Sleepy and Melvin and Rashard. In our own ways, each one of us got exactly what he wanted.

As I hear the car's engine turn over, I take comfort in the one thing I am sure of: At Robert E. Lee High School, home of the Rebels, there will never be another Slave Day.